THE TRUTH BETWEEN US

ROBIN CUTLER

MICHAEL ANDERLE

DON'T MISS OUR NEW RELEASES

Join the Florid Romance email list to be notified of new releases and special promotions (which happen often) by following this link:

https://floridromance.lmbpn.com/about/sign-up-for-our-newsletter/

Published by Florid Romance
an imprint of LMBPN Publishing
2375 E. Tropicana Avenue, Suite 8-305
Las Vegas, Nevada 89119 USA

Version 1.01, August 2025
eBook ISBN: 979-8-89354-928-7
Print ISBN: 979-8-89354-929-4

CHAPTER
ONE
EMERY

Travel Note: Mount Pleasant taught me that quiet places do not always mean peace. I have been to remote villages in Iceland and bustling squares in Morocco—and sometimes it is the silence that unsettles you most.

—EW

Emery Westbrook stood inside Charleston International Airport, trying to remember how to breathe. Her flight had arrived only minutes ago, yet the wave of heat rushing through the automatic doors made her feel as though she had stepped into a memory. The air was thicker than she remembered, laced with salt and honeysuckle that clung to her skin. Dull fluorescent lights overhead caused her reflection to glint in the polished floor tiles. She looked tired or maybe simply unprepared. Her jeans were already too warm. Her boots, so practical in Chicago's windy spring, were now a poor match for the muggy Lowcountry.

Two nights earlier, a nurse from Mount Pleasant Hospital had called to say her father was in critical condition after a heart attack. The news reached Emery in Chicago, not from her sister Laura who still refused to speak to her but from a someone from the hospital dialing numbers from David Westbrook's phone. Emery booked the first flight home and prayed she would see him again.

Dark-gold curls framed her face in loose, travel-rumpled layers now, and the humidity coaxed them into soft waves. Beneath them, hazel eyes surveyed the terminal with guarded intensity while the lean set of her shoulders hinted at a lifetime spent on the move.

Her suitcase rumbled behind her, a sound she once associated with easy departures. This time it offered no comfort. Her phone remained silent with no call from Laura, leaving her to face Charleston alone.

At the rental car counter, she forced a polite smile while handing over her license. The last time she left Charleston was after her mother's funeral and a vicious argument with Laura. They hadn't spoken since, and the silence had become its own form of punishment. As the clerk returned her ID with the keys, Emery wondered if she was the same woman who had left. Maybe traveling the world all those years abroad had changed her enough to face what waited outside the airport.

She trudged outside to find a row of compact sedans, metal so hot to the touch that she flinched. The chirp of the key fob led her to a small silver car with tinted windows. She tossed her suitcase into the trunk and slid into the driver's seat. Warm leather pressed against her as she started the engine and adjusted the air conditioning to full blast. Sweat dotted her forehead almost immediately. Charleston was not in the mood to let her ease in gently.

The drive began with a stretch of highway that gave her no real challenge. It lulled her momentarily, allowing glimpses of offices and suburban sprawl on either side. As she navigated toward the heart of downtown, there was no skyline of glimmering skyscrapers. Charleston, she recalled, did not do that sort of thing. Its buildings were low, curated by strict preservation codes. She soon reached the older streets, flanked by pastel-painted facades and numerous church steeples towering above. The place was hauntingly familiar in its refusal to change.

Emery had won awards for her writing over the last seven years. *Time Magazine, Smithsonian, National Geographic,* and other outlets praised her observational prose and her ability to capture a city's soul in just a few paragraphs. The irony never escaped her. She had chronicled corners of the globe, from Morocco's markets to Iceland's remote fjords, but never once committed Charleston to paper. She told herself it was because she preferred distance, which writing demanded new spaces and unknown vistas. Yet the real reason pulsed beneath her ribs. She had never been ready to unpack the memories knotted here.

Driving deeper into downtown, she noticed how Rainbow Row still glowed in pastel perfection. Tourists strolled the sidewalks with sun hats and cameras, no different from how they always had. She passed by a historic church, St. Phillips, her parents had been married there. The sight of the stone doorway, wreathed in climbing vines, stirred something she quickly suppressed. Then the Ravenel Bridge loomed in the near distance, an unmistakable landmark spanning the Cooper River. The pointed cables seemed to reach for the sky, daring travelers to cross into Mount Pleasant. Her hand tensed around the steering wheel. One tilt of the turn signal, and the bridge would lead her back to the neighborhood where she grew up. But she wasn't ready. She ignored that exit, the taste of salt sudden on her tongue, and steered toward another route that led to James Island. Blame it on her bruised pride or the memories of the day she left, but she could not face that road. Not yet.

The thoughts came unbidden, the letter she never sent, that voicemail from her sister she once kept but had since deleted. And the funeral, right after her mother's death. Seven years had not dulled that pain. She tried to remind herself she was only here for her father, David. His health had taken a drastic turn after suffering a near fatal heart attack, and duty demanded her return. Still, beneath the sense of obligation was a knot of resigned anger. She had spent so long pushing Charleston away. It felt like the city had a thousand hands stretched toward her, ready to drag her into everything she fought to forget.

Finally, she reached James Island. The neighborhoods unwound in a mix of old, cozy bungalows and newer ranch homes. Live oaks canopied the narrow roads, Spanish moss drifting like ghosts from the branches. As she pulled into her cousin Callie Sumner's driveway, she tried to steel herself for the onslaught of warmth and questions. But she only had space in her chest for quiet exhaustion.

Callie's bungalow was as bright and lived in as Emery remembered from the last video call. She got out of her car and saw the porch light still on, though the afternoon sun had not yet set. The wide front porch displayed a few rocking chairs with two that were child sized, and an abandoned plastic dinosaur. Callie had two toddlers, a girl and a boy, 18 months apart, both fond of running around with sticky fingers and no shoes.

Before Emery could knock, the door swung open to reveal a flurry of activity. One small cousin, Jack Jr, darted by, hollering something she only half understood, while the new baby, Sadie, rocked peacefully in a baby swing. Callie emerged, auburn hair tied in a messy bun, a grin lighting up her face.

"You're here," Callie's voice brimmed with relief and a trace of gentle reproach. She closed the gap between them and wrapped Emery in a tight hug. "Welcome to Carnival Sumner," Callie laughed after releasing Emery and simultaneously wrangling her children. Emery felt wooden at first. It was not that she disliked affection, but after all these years of building walls, letting someone in so quickly felt foreign. The air inside smelled of melted butter and mild chaos. Plastic dinosaurs littered the floor, and a faint trail of flour suggested a failed baking experiment. It was comforting, in a way, to see such unpolished life thriving here.

Callie took Emery's suitcase and ushered her cousin to the guestroom down a seafoam green painted hallway.

"Why don't you freshen up after your journey and then come back out to the sunroom and we'll sit and have some tea. I made some fresh." Callie put the suitcase down on a lovely quilt covered bed overflowing with pillows.

Emery noticed a desk covered with papers under the window. "You're still working?" she asked as she nodded toward the desk.

"I love having my own money as much as these two adorable brats. So, I burn the candle at both ends during tax season, and they hold my place at the accounting firm whenever these two hooligans are ready for preschool. It was too good of a deal to pass up. And it helps that I'm married to Jack. At some point he would be so happy to give up lawyering and become a full-time house husband," Callie volunteered as she finished straightening the desk. "Bathroom is next door and I managed to find some fresh towels, so make yourself at home," she laughed as she left the room.

Emery opened her suitcase and found a cotton t-shirt and shorts and changed into something more suitable to the clinging humidity. She went into the bathroom, brushed her teeth and splashed some cold water on her face. When she came out, she saw Callie out on the porch setting a tray on the table. In moments, they each had a tall glass of tea, ice cubes clinking with every movement. Emery drank slowly, letting the sweetness almost sting her tongue. It tasted like home, more than she cared to admit.

They made small talk at first. Callie peppered Emery with questions about her travels. Did she really visit the souks of Marrakesh? How about the hot springs in Iceland? Emery answered in short bursts, at ease talking about anywhere but Charleston. Finally, Callie said she had to put the kids down for their naps and told Emery to relax and make herself at home.

About ten minutes later, Callie came back. "Let's enjoy this bit of solitude, shall we?" Callie picked up her glass and poured in some more tea. Her gaze locked onto Emery's. "I guess you should know something that's going on over at the estate."

Emery's fingers tightened around her glass. "Yes?"

"Your dad hired someone for the restoration." She paused, as if measuring Emery's expression. "It's Xander Langley."

Emery's entire body went cold, despite the humid evening. She could not force a casual tone, so she asked point-blank, "Could you repeat that?"

Callie's voice softened. "He's been working on the house for six months. He's got his own preservation firm now. He's doing a wonderful job."

Silence stretched uncomfortably. Emery's mind tumbled through old scenes: Xander as a teenager, paint-splattered jeans, that crooked smile. Then later, Xander with her sister, whispering after the funeral. She had spent so many hours forging reasons to hate them both. The memories tore through her chest as she faced this new revelation.

"You couldn't give me a heads-up before I flew in?" she demanded.

Callie shrugged, appearing entirely untroubled by

Emery's anger. "If I had warned you, you might not have come."

Emery wanted to argue, but the words would not form. Instead, she took a gulp of her tea, wishing it were something much stronger. She stared at the condensation on the glass, trying not to betray that her heart was racing.

They lingered in the quiet a bit longer until Callie mentioned David. "He's not doing well. The nurses say he has good days, but he's weak." Hurt flickered in Callie's eyes. "He wants to see you."

Emery nodded curtly. She had known her father was ill but hearing it from Callie pricked at her defenses. She was not ready to discuss him or how complicated their family had become after her mother's death. The evening wore on until the sky deepened into a bruise of purple. The heaviness of Charleston's humidity settled over them, coaxing droplets of sweat along Emery's temples despite the whirring porch fan. After supper, the cousins parted company. Emery went to the cream-colored guest room to catch up on emails and to try to stave off the headache that was building. Callie was still ensconced in the hall bathroom with mounds of bubbles and floating toys. She heard Callie's voice reading until the children were finally asleep, quiet at last.

But Emery could not rest. She paced inside the guest room, the overhead light too bright, the air conditioning ineffective. Her mind cycled through unwanted thoughts, her father's waning health, Xander's steady hands on the estate's woodwork, the vision of her mother's casket. She picked up her phone, hunting reflexively for that old, unsent text to her mother, a text she knew by heart.

> Hey Mom. I am sorry I left. Wish you were here to tell me if I should come back. Let me know somehow. Please.

That text had never been delivered. She had typed it in the middle of the night two years after the funeral, consumed by longing and guilt. Now she read it for the hundredth time, her finger hovering over the delete key before she tucked the phone away again. She left it unsent, just as she always had.

The weight of the night pressed in, so she wandered outside one more time. The porch felt different without Callie's presence, emptier. The fan creaked overhead, struggling against the thick air. Cicadas droned in a chorus that would not relent. She noticed a flash of lightning in the far distance, heat lightning, too far away to bring any real relief. It illuminated the clouds in ghostly silhouettes.

"I'm not staying long," she whispered. The words sank into the darkness, met only by the chirping of nighttime insects. Yet it was impossible to ignore the shift in the atmosphere, as if the old city beyond the porch had heard her and held its breath. A dog barked somewhere down the street, its tone oddly plaintive. Emery let out a breath, feeling a cool trickle of sweat at the base of her neck. She could tell herself she would leave soon, that she was only here for her father. But Charleston's pull was already at work, coaxing her with an undercurrent of what once was and what might still be.

CHAPTER

TWO

XANDER

Travel Note: In Kyoto, a woman once served me tea and said every room keeps its memories. This sunroom does too, dust motes drifting like conversations left unsaid. Houses hold us even when we swear, we have left.

—EW

Xander ran the palm of his hand across a stubborn patch of paint, feeling the sunroom's old window trim heat beneath his touch. Late afternoon sunshine poured through the wide windows, outlining the dust he had yet to wipe away. Outside, cicadas chirped in slow rhythms, as though reminding him time was slipping on. He set his sanding block on the drop cloth and studied his progress.

The trim needed more work than he had thought. Layers of cracked paint peeled away to reveal the original wood, a warm pine that smelled faintly of turpentine and

11

history. A low, bluesy guitar riff trickled from a battered speaker near the drywall, a small comfort against the June heat. Drenched in sweat, he wiped his brow with the side of his forearm and left a chalky smudge at his hairline.

Dark hair clung to his temples, and the sinew of his arms hinted at years of meticulous labor. Sharp green eyes surveyed the sunroom with a craftsman's focus, missing little despite the oppressive heat.

Working on this house usually kept him steady. He needed the routine, the slip of sandpaper across wood, the measured breath that followed each stroke. It reminded him why he had stayed in Charleston for so long. His life was built on tasks like this, day by day, board by board.

Even before Emery, this house had been a refuge. He remembered his own quiet, cramped childhood home, the constant abuse by his father. Coming here to work for David at twelve wasn't just a job, it was an escape into a world of sprawling rooms, solid foundations, and the scent of history instead of anxiety. He learned the language of its architecture, the groan of the third-floor joists, the specific slant of light through the foyer windows at dusk. It was the first place he'd ever felt truly steady.

He found solace in resurrecting what everyone else had given up on. If he could save old houses, maybe it meant broken things could be made whole again.

He glanced at his phone, which lay on a nearby windowsill. No missed calls. No texts. The summer light had begun to soften, painting the floor with streaks of gold. He stood and let the sweep of jazz chords lull him into a calmer state. Then he heard footsteps in the foyer.

At first, the sound barely registered. He was used to contractors checking on him unannounced. But these footsteps clicked against the tile in a sure, measured way, different from the usual. He paused, sander in hand, as the steps grew closer. When a slender silhouette flickered in the sunroom entrance, his entire body tensed.

Emery Westbrook stood in the doorway, aviators perched on her head, hair slightly disheveled from the humidity. She wore a loose shirt, frayed jeans, and that guarded expression he recognized all too well. It felt like someone had pulled the air from the room. He had not seen her in seven years, but it might as well have been yesterday.

"Xander."

The sound of her voice saying his name sent his pulse skittering. She did not speak it as a question, nor was it an outright greeting. It was a challenge. He turned down the speaker's volume and straightened his shoulders, dragging in a breath that did little to steady him. She was every bit as striking as the last time he had seen her, although now a brittle energy rolled off her.

He managed to nod in acknowledgment. "Emery." He forced himself to sound casual, though his heart hammered in his throat.

Emery crossed her arms over her chest, her gaze moving across the half-sanded windows. "What are you doing here?" The question cut through the warm air with old resentment.

He cleared his throat. "Working on the estate. Your

father hired me to restore it." The explanation felt inadequate, but it was the truth.

"How long?" Her voice held a sharper edge, as though she already suspected the answer might unsettle her.

"Six months," he said, wiping grit from his hands. "He called me out of the blue. Said the house needed to be brought back to its original state. I took the job."

She inhaled so quickly that her shoulders jerked. She looked from the sanded window trim to the fold-up ladder, then to the drop cloth covered in dusty footprints. "He never mentioned it," she muttered. "Or maybe he tried, and I just wasn't listening."

He watched her struggle with that realization. Something flickered in her eyes, confusion, maybe anger, definitely something else. Then her gaze settled on him again. She opened her mouth as though to speak, but no words came out.

He rubbed his neck. "I didn't think you'd be back in Charleston." His voice emerged low, as if he were afraid any volume might set her off.

"Clearly." There was no warmth in her reply. For a moment, she let the silence thicken, leaving only the quiet push of the fan overhead. Then she stepped forward, arms still crossed and planted her gaze on him. "Guess it's good work, living on-site, sealing cracks, scraping away mold."

A sour heat pooled in his gut, as if he were scraping her memories raw. He lifted the sander as though it might shield him. "Your father wanted the place made liveable again. I wasn't expecting this."

A faint tremor rocked her voice. "Me?"

He nodded slowly, meeting her stare. "Yes, you."

For a moment, they stood at an impasse. That old tension crackled between them. The last time they had spoken was at her mother's funeral, a conversation that ended with her storming out, tears on her cheeks, while he stood by, too uncertain to chase after her. He had replayed that scene in his head a thousand times, each replay more a punishment than a memory. And now, here she was, in the flesh, looking as if she wished she had never walked through that door.

"Whatever," she said finally, voice tight. "Pretty sure you'll be hearing from me again soon." Then she turned and strode back into the foyer, each footstep as unforgiving as her tone.

He stared after her, too stunned to move. Even her departure felt like a silent rebuke. The moment stretched long enough for the jazz track on his speaker to change tempo. The next song began, but he did not listen. He set down his sander on a window ledge and walked to the door that opened into the hallway, half expecting her to come back.

She did not. The echo of her exit drifted away, replaced by the quiet of the house. He stood in the threshold, trying to make sense of the turmoil ripping through his mind. The sunroom felt too warm, too small. Taking a shaky breath, he headed toward the back of the house.

Silas, his golden retriever, lay near the back porch steps. The old dog lifted his head at the sight of him, ears perked. Xander gave him a gentle rub between the ears. "Hey, buddy," he murmured. Silas's tail thumped twice, a calm reminder that not all was lost. Some things in this place were constant. Yet Xander could not shake the tremor in his own hands.

He ambled around the side yard for a while, letting the light shift from gold to soft copper. Memories hovered, unbidden. Emery at eighteen, perched on the porch swing with her sketchbook, laughing at his clumsy jokes. The funeral, a week of gray clouds, the heaviness of her mother's coffin. And then the final day, when he found her suitcase by the door. He never forgot the way she had looked at him, like he was part of some betrayal that had shattered her.

Now she was inside that house again. He wondered if everything he had done these past months, every plank replaced, every wall refinished, might turn into a battleground. Perhaps he deserved that. He had told himself for years that if she ever came back, he would find the right words to explain the secrets that strangled them both after Margot's death. But seeing Emery in the doorway had drained him of courage. He asked the sky for answers but only got the silent shimmer of a coming twilight.

With a final pat to Silas's head, Xander got in his truck. He had an evening meeting with a subcontractor who had been pestering him all week about a potential job on Daniel Island. Work was work, and he was committed to finishing what he started at the Westbrook estate, no matter how complicated, but he needed the paycheck from smaller side projects to keep his business afloat. He tried to focus on the practicality of that, not dwell on the woman he had just seen.

Driving over narrow streets, he felt his pulse calm. He cranked the windows open, letting warm air roll in. Charleston's old roads and shadowy corners used to be comforting. Now, they felt haunted, brimming with the tension he could not leave behind. By the time he reached the contractor's site, the sun had nearly sunk behind a stand of pines. He parked, got out, and forced himself to nod politely as he shook hands with the crew.

They talked schedules and budgets. He walked through a half-framed house, noting the layer of sawdust under fluorescent temporary lights. He checked his watch often, impatient for the meeting to end. Emery's face refused to leave his mind. Eventually, he caught himself rubbing his palm over his heart, as though to press down the ache that had surged earlier. He needed to get back. Or at least he needed to know if she was back at the estate, ready to toss out more accusations or go quiet with anger.

When the meeting concluded, he said curt goodbyes, then drove back across the bridge to Mount Pleasant. Darkness settled in, and side streets glowed with street-lamps. He kept the radio off, preferring the company of his own thoughts. At a red light, he wondered where Emery had gone after storming out of the sunroom. Part of him hoped she would stay away. Another part pleaded for her to return, no matter how much they circled each other with hurt.

He arrived back at the caretaker's cottage just after nine, the sky a velvety purple. He grabbed leftovers from the fridge, cold chicken and a wilted salad. He ate standing at the narrow countertop, eyes drifting toward the window. One lamp glowed on the second floor of the main house. A silhouette crossed the window, lean and unmistakably feminine.

His stomach twisted. Had she truly decided to move in tonight? He dropped the fork in the sink. Of course she would not give him a heads-up, not after how she left the sunroom. She probably hated the thought of sharing a single property line with him.

He left his plate unwashed, stepping outside onto the cottage's small porch. A humid stillness pressed against his skin. Night creatures called to one another from the marsh. He looked at the massive silhouette of the West-brook main house, the columns faintly visible in the moonlight. He saw her light upstairs again, blinking off, then on, as though she was unsure what she wanted.

He walked slowly across the yard, each step a measured attempt to calm his pulse. Reaching the porch, he climbed the short steps to the old swing that he had recently repaired. The boards creaked gently beneath him. The faint smell of rosemary drifted from the flowerbed, mixing with the heavier sweetness of magnolia. It reminded him of childhood dinners in that very dining room, Margot Westbrook hosting with a bright smile that hid her worries too well.

He leaned forward and grazed his fingers beneath the swing seat. Three letters were carved there, an E plus an X, with a small heart. They had been young and foolish when they did it, breathless with the idea of forever. He had never worked up the courage to sand it away. Even when he repainted the swing, he left that patch alone.

He remembered how Emery always insisted it was silly to carve initials at all. "We'll just keep them in our heads," she had once joked. But she had let him do it anyway, covering his hands with hers as they pressed the blade into the wood. He had not thought about that moment in a long while, but it hit him now, raw and insistent.

Pulling his hand back, he closed his eyes. He pictured Emery's face in the sunroom hours earlier, set in a blend of fury and something heartbreakingly fragile. He should have told her more, but the words had knotted in his throat. Perhaps he was destined to always speak too late.

As a single lightning bolt lit up the summer sky, he let out a trembling breath and murmured, "Welcome home, Em." The words spilled from him like a secret he never intended to share. Of course, she could not hear him. She was somewhere upstairs, unpacking or pacing, angry at the entire situation.

He stayed on the swing for a long time, lulled by the gentle sway and the memory of their carved initials beneath his fingers. He told himself it was not his place to say anything more, that she had to decide on her own how this would go. But deep in his chest, he felt a flicker of hope that perhaps, despite everything, they could find a way to mend what they had lost.

When he finally rose to return to the cottage, he glanced over his shoulder at the house. The upstairs light remained on, though the silhouette was gone from the window. The faint hum of cicadas echoed in the warm air. The porch swing drifted, still bearing the imprint of his presence, and he left it that way, unmoored to the night. He walked away, heart unsteady, already longing for the moment when the two of them might stand in the same space without so many ghosts between them.

CHAPTER
THREE

EMERY

Travel Note: The peeling facades of Havana taught me this: what looks abandoned may still be sacred. Charleston's old bones are no different. Some stories cling to paint like they're afraid of being erased.

—EW

Emery Westbrook woke long before dawn, the echo of a dream slipping away the moment she opened her eyes. Her bedroom lay in half light, shadows drifting across faded wallpaper. She stared at the ceiling fan overhead. Its blades wobbled with a slight rattle, a tired old rhythm that persisted no matter how many times she willed it to be quiet. In that predawn hour, the house felt like a living thing around her, as if it exhaled centuries of memories through the worn floorboards.

Pulling the sheet closer, she inhaled slowly. The scent of lemon oil and dust hung in the air, underscored by something that reminded her of old novels stacked in a forgotten library corner. She once thought Charleston's humidity would oversaturate every memory she left here, but the dryness in her throat now felt more suffocating than any foreign climate she had traveled to. In Morocco's busy squares, she could disappear in the swirl of people. In Havana, she could stand beside peeling pastel walls and envision entire stories hidden beneath the paint. Here, she felt every secret trembling just beneath the surface.

She let her gaze roam the room. The wallpaper, soft cream florals chipped along the edges, remained the same pattern she fell asleep to as a child. She remembered nights spent scribbling impossible dreams into the margins of her notebooks, longing for a future far from these walls. The squeak of the floor near her closet used to wake her mother whenever Emery tried to sneak out. She tested that memory now by getting up and walking to that spot, half expecting a ghostly creak to confirm she was still fourteen. But the house refused to indulge her fully. The only sound was the fan's stuttering click. She got back into bed.

Her thoughts drifted to her confrontation with Xander the previous day. It still clung to her mind like a damp coat, heavy with the tension she couldn't shed. He had looked too much like the boy who used to offer her quiet smiles on the front porch swing while seeming older, more guarded. Part of her hated that nothing about him felt truly different, yet his presence in the estate unsettled her. She pressed her fingertips against her temples. That memory of Xander leaning in a sunlit doorway scraped at her, reminding her of what she thought she had buried for good.

Emery exhaled and let herself sink deeper into the thin pillows, attempting to reclaim sleep. Darkness wrapped around her, lulling her eyes shut. In the moments before she drifted off again, she imagined her mother. Margot's face appeared at the edge of her dream, whispering something she couldn't decipher. Emery saw her mother's fingers brushing tangles from her hair the way she used to when Emery was little. She tried to speak, but every word died in her throat. She reached out in that hazy dreamscape and felt the weight of Margot's hand, then woke with a start, heart pounding.

For a moment, she lay motionless, struggling to separate dream from reality. The oppressive feeling in her chest lingered, and she rubbed her eyes, willing the memory to fade. It was still too early for sunlight. She decided that lying there, tangled in old sheets, would not bring answers. She stood, grabbed clothes from her open suitcase, then disappeared into the adjoining bathroom. The estate's plumbing groaned in protest. The shower sputtered, finally sending a spray of lukewarm water that smelled faintly of metal. She braced a hand against the tile, letting the water run over her face. This was what she came back for, or at least it was part of it.

An hour later, a morning glow seeped through the thin curtains. Emery dressed in jeans and a loose gray tee, then tied her hair into a simple knot at the base of her neck. She made her way downstairs, footsteps slow on each step as she listened for any sign of Xander. Silence pressed in. The front hall stood empty, the only movement a shifting square of light across the floor. The smell of coffee did not greet her. No subtle hints that anyone was awake. She felt relief and an odd pang of disappointment. Running into him might have forced them to talk. Or perhaps they would have simply stared each other down.

Without pause, she snatched her keys from a small bowl near the door and stepped outside. The morning air kissed her skin, warm and humid already. Live oaks stretched overhead, swaying heavy branches draped with Spanish moss that seemed to whisper among themselves. For a moment, she gazed at the estate's white-columned porch and noticed a movement near the side yard. Xander. He carried a stack of lumber on his shoulder, face turned away. Emery's gut twisted, an urge to retreat warring with a strange need to watch him. But she did not linger. She strode to her car, slid in, and revved the engine.

As she drove, memories kept edging in. She pressed them back, focusing on the curve of the oak-lined drive. Charleston's roads beckoned just beyond the estate, offering an escape she could not quite name. She left without breakfast, though a dull ache gnawed at her stomach. Possibly guilt, possibly hunger. She refused to consider that it might be something else, like regret for not trying to speak with him.

Downtown reminded her why she used to call Charleston a place that refused to modernize too freely. The historic silhouettes of buildings rose modestly against the sky, pastel exteriors capturing morning sunlight. Tourists in hats strolled along sidewalks, cameras in hand, drawn by these carefully preserved streets. She felt a flash of envy for their casual wonder. To her, the city was not a box to be ticked off a travel list. It was a part of her DNA.

She parked near a small independent bookstore on a quiet street. The bell above the door jingled softly when she walked in, the smell of paper and dust greeting her with gentle insistence. A single overhead fan circled lazily, reminiscent of the one in her bedroom. She let her fingers skim the spines of travel guides on a display table. Portugal glistened in bold letters on one cover. Nepal's Himalayas called out from another. There were entire worlds in these pages, places she had been, places she might go. Yet not a single glossy photograph generated the spark she yearned for.

She lifted an Amsterdam guide, flipping through pictures of bright canals and bicycles. It reminded her of a prior assignment, one that earned her praise from an editor who once said she had a gift for capturing intangible atmospheres. She let the book fall shut and moved on to the next table, but her restlessness flared. Everywhere she looked, she saw echoes of journeys she had already taken. None of them felt like an escape anymore.

The bookstore clerk offered her a polite nod, but Emery mumbled a quiet greeting and made her way to the exit. Outside, traffic had begun to thicken. She glanced at her phone, nearing midday. Her empty stomach growled, but she ignored it. She was not sure what she was looking for downtown, only that she needed to keep moving. Instead, she ended up back on a familiar route, crossing streets that led to James Island.

Callie's bungalow stood bright against the midday sun. Its small front lawn boasted plastic dinosaurs and tricycles strewn about, silent evidence of her cousin's busy household. Emery parked in the driveway and let out a breath. She wished she could walk inside that house and find exactly what she needed, a sense of belonging wrapped in laughter and toddler chaos. But the moment she entered, she felt the warm embrace of family life converge with her own unsettled heart.

Callie appeared, wiping flour from her hands, a tired but welcoming grin on her face. They exchanged brief pleasantries, but Emery felt pinned by her own thoughts. She accepted a leftover sandwich without argument, biting into it mechanically. The children were napping, so the bungalow was calm. Yet Emery could not settle. She looked through her phone, scanning a text message she had deliberately ignored, a reminder from David's nurse detailing his next treatment appointment. Emery's throat tightened. She started drafting a response and then erased it. She was not ready, not for pitying looks from the hospital staff, not for more guilt about her absence. Eventually, she pressed her phone to her chest and closed her eyes, letting the worry build.

She stayed at Callie's until the late afternoon sun stretched the shadows along the yard. Restlessness crackled in her nerves, making her want to run even though she had no plan, no flight to catch. She stood, mumbled an excuse about needing space, and left her cousin adjusting a toddler's blanket in the living room. Outside, the sky flirted with the idea of dusk, orange and pink hints at the horizon. It was the kind of Charleston evening that normally lulled her, but tonight it felt like a warning.

When she reached the estate, she shut off the engine and did not move. She stared at the front porch where the very swing she once carved her initials into remained, personally restored by Xander's steady hands. The house windows glowed with interior lights. It made the place look welcoming, yet she knew how the emptiness inside could echo. She gripped the steering wheel, breathing in and out. It took a full minute before she resolved to step back inside.

The door opened with a gentler creak than she remembered. The hall lamp cast a warm glow onto the polished floor, and footsteps, soft, deliberate footsteps, rounded the corner. Her heart lurched for an instant, but it was only Silas, the golden retriever. His gray-whiskered muzzle twitched when he saw her, one tail wag stirring the air. He padded over and nudged her thigh, as if to say he had been waiting all this time. Emery crouched, running her fingers through his thick fur.

"Good boy," she whispered. Something in her chest clenched at how simple it was for him to welcome her. Just like that, the dog accepted her return with no questions asked.

She patted Silas one last time and made her way upstairs, passing the closed door to what had once been her mother's room. She felt the old urge to open it just to prove that she could face what waited inside, but her resolve faltered. Another time, she mouthed silently.

Reaching her room, she flipped the light switch. A soft glow illuminated walls filled with remnants of a life she barely recognized. Her gaze fell on a framed photo atop the dresser. In it, she saw the reflection of a happier past: she was thirteen, Laura was eleven, and their mother stood between them, all three smiling without restraint. Emery felt a sour tightness curl in her gut. She hadn't realized the picture was still there. She set her bag on the bed, then turned away, heart squeezing from the weight of that memory.

Her old sketchbooks lined a shelf near the window. She pulled one free and skimmed a pencil drawing she had made at seventeen—her attempt to capture the porch view at sunset. The lines wavered in places, as if she lacked confidence even then. Experiencing that swirl of nostalgia felt like stumbling into a riptide. She pushed the sketchbook back. Enough.

She rummaged in her bag until she found the journal she now used. A cool wave of relief washed over her at the familiar pages waiting to be filled. She grabbed a pen and propped herself against the pillows on her bed. The overhead light cast pale rings on the walls, and Silas, having followed her, curled up near the door as though he meant to defend her from ghosts of her own making.

She pressed pen to paper. At first, she could think of nothing to say. Finally, in a neat scrawl, she wrote:

There's no such thing as going home. Only going back.

She contemplated that sentence. It felt truer than any essay she had published about foreign places, truer than the admiration she once wrote about faraway alleyways and bazaars. Here in Charleston, she confronted a deeper honesty she'd never let herself face.

Closing the journal, she set it on the nightstand. Her muscles felt weighed down by the day's emotional tug-of-war, and she let her head sink into the pillows. From the floor, Silas let out a low content huff, as if granting permission for her to rest. She watched the silhouette of her bedroom door for a moment, listening. A distant creak broke the stillness. It might have been Xander working. Or it might have been the old house moving the way it always did, refusing to let anyone sleep without its presence being felt.

Emery got out of bed and went into the bathroom to change into pajamas. She returned and pulled the blanket over her body. The soft cotton tugged gently at her shoulders, grounding her. She was home, and simultaneously, she felt as though she were in uncharted territory. Tomorrow, she would see what space the house left for her, and how many of its secrets still demanded an answer. But tonight, she could only whisper what she hoped was a promise:

"Just one week."

CHAPTER

FOUR

XANDER

Travel Note: Sunrise over the Himalayas is humbling, but so is the quiet of Shem Creek, where the water laps against the banks as if it is trying to remember your name. There is something spiritual about this kind of quiet. It makes you feel both infinitesimal and strangely held.

—EW

Xander woke before the first hint of daylight broke across the sky. The estate's half-finished kitchen greeted him in the murky gray, a silent witness to his routine. He switched on the single overhead bulb, which cast a faint glow over the counters cluttered with brushes, stray sheets of sandpaper, and boxes labeled Margot's linens and Laura – attic. He frowned at the state of things. He had every intention of organizing it, but each day brought new tasks more urgent than tidying up. He inhaled deeply, catching the scent of sawdust and leftover paint that clinging to the walls.

He could not quite shake the feeling that the house itself breathed in time with him. It settled differently at night, and floorboards groaned as he listened close. He found some odd comfort in that intangible presence. He paused a moment beside the refrigerator and let his gaze roam, as though the walls could speak and soothe that persistent coil of tension in his chest.

He filled the kettle with water, though half of him thought about rummaging for the coffee maker. The estate's original coffee maker had died a slow death weeks ago, so he used a replacement bought on sale. Its plastic edges were cheap, but it did the job. He set it up, brewed coffee, and wondered how the day would unfold.

Silas, his golden retriever, wandered in then, nails scraping lightly against the half-installed kitchen tile. The dog padded over, front paws splayed out, then flopped beside Xander's ankles. Xander stroked Silas's ears. "Mornin', buddy," he murmured, voice soft in the empty space. The dog's tail swept across the dusty floor and raised a small cloud.

While the machine sputtered with slow determination, Xander surveyed the labeled boxes again. Some belonged to Laura, stuffed with items for the attic that he had never gotten around to delivering upstairs. Others once belonged to Margot, her stored linens and personal keepsakes. The top flap of one box gaped open, revealing a neat stack of embroideries and an old, folded tablecloth. Memory tugged at him, but he set his jaw and turned away. Certain things were Emery's to rediscover, or perhaps her father's. Not his.

When the coffee finished trickling into the carafe, Xander pulled two mugs from the overhead cabinet. It was habit. For so many weeks, he had grown used to the notion of someone else being there if only in his mind. But he paused, thinking of the quiet that usually defined his mornings. It was only him and Silas. With a sigh, he set one mug back on the shelf. He poured a single serving and took his first sip, bitter, hot, and strong enough to pry him fully awake.

"I guess it's just us," he muttered to Silas. The dog responded by thumping his tail once.

He walked to the back porch and pushed open the door that squeaked at the hinge. The screen rattled, letting a soft breeze brush his face. Outside, the marsh spread out behind the estate, a rippling silver mass in the early light. Through sparse branches draped in Spanish moss, he spotted Shem Creek shining like a ribbon along the horizon. He let out a long breath and let the damp warmth settle against him. Charleston mornings always had a distinct texture, a blend of salt and dew that reminded him of possibilities. It also reminded him of everything he had lost or thought he had lost.

He took a sip of coffee, then mentally reeled off what needed doing: repaint the west parlor trim, which had begun to peel where moisture seeped in at the corners. Patch the hairline crack by the dining room's crown molding before he forgot again. And if he had any sense, avoid Emery as much as he could. But that last item on the list felt both difficult and unnatural. She inhabited the same house, choosing a bedroom upstairs while he stayed below in his caretaker's routine. Encountering her had become inevitable. Yet every time he saw her, something in him pitched sideways, as though his heart wanted to respond, and his mind demanded it stay silent.

The morning birds stirred in the branches overhead. He smelled the timber stacked behind the carriage house, still damp from last night's humidity. He eased onto one of the porch steps and cradled his mug in both hands. Silas followed, settling at Xander's feet with a weighted sigh.

Xander tried to center his thoughts on simpler things: the shape of the yard, the new wood boards that needed sanding, the ragged edges of an exterior shutter that required a final coat of paint. But his mind slid toward Emery. She had returned to Charleston in a dark mood of tension and quiet rage. The moment he first saw her, leaning in the sunroom doorway, he could not deny how it jolted him. Part of him longed to fix it all, piece by piece. Part of him knew that old wounds did not mend so quickly. She had come back with her own secrets, and he was not entirely sure if he still featured in her life or if he was merely part of the house she intended to reclaim for a short while.

He lifted the mug to his lips, letting the steam warm his face. For a few minutes, the only sounds were the cicadas and the soft rustle of moss-laden branches. Then the back door creaked.

His entire body tensed. He did not need to look over his shoulder to know it was Emery. He heard her footsteps, light, cautious. She must have found the coffee in the pot. Her presence shifted the air, pulling him out of his half-dream state. He braced himself for their usual clipped exchange.

She came up behind him and joined him in gazing at the marsh. She wore an old Tulane sweatshirt, threadbare at the cuffs, and her hair was pulled into a loose knot at the nape of her neck. He heard her sip from her mug before she spoke.

"Still up before sunrise, huh," she said, her voice raw from sleep.

He stared at a cluster of reeds swaying near the water. "I like having the day to myself before the chaos starts."

Emery shifted from one foot to the other. She stepped closer, where the porch railing curved outward and offered a clearer view of the yard. Her stance was hesitant, as though she weighed each motion. "You always did," she said quietly. "I hated that about you, by the way."

He sipped his coffee with forced calm. "You told me many times about how you preferred to sleep in. I never took offense."

She huffed out something that might have been a wry laugh. "I hated a lot of things about you back then."

Silas scrambled to his feet and trotted over, dropping a small stick at Xander's boots. Emery's mouth quirked in a half-smile, the kind that was gone almost before it formed. She scratched Silas behind the ears. The dog's tail beat against both Xander's leg and the porch post.

Xander set his mug beside the step. "He's spoiling for a game."

"You should indulge him," Emery said. Her gaze moved toward his face, then slid away across the marsh again. The morning silence between them felt thick with unspoken truths.

He leaned down, picked up the stick, and tested its strength in his hand. It threatened to snap if he threw it too hard. Gently, he set it down again and decided to hold off until Silas found something sturdier. If he was lucky, it would break the tension coiled in the porch planks.

Emery blew over the top of her mug and took a deliberate sip. He watched the line of her jaw and saw the way her eyebrows drew together in concentration. She cleared her throat. "I might go see Dad today."

Xander nodded. "He'll be glad for that." His tone came out more subdued than he intended. Her father's illness was one thing that overshadowed everything else. It had spurred her return, forced them together, and made them dance around the fact that old resentments still flared.

Another heartbeat of silence passed. Then she glanced at the half-sanded porch railing. "You've done a lot of work here." She gestured to the yard, the scratched paint, the tools stacked in one corner. "I didn't realize how extensive it was until I walked through each room yesterday."

He rubbed a hand across the back of his neck. "I've tried to keep the bones intact. Your father wanted it as close to original as possible."

Emery's gaze followed a swirl of dust near his boots. "You always did love old bones. Guess you respect the past more than you trust the future."

He could not deny how she spoke the truth, he had

always found solace in the steady comfort of history. "I guess so."

She offered a tiny, almost shy smile, though her guard did not fully drop. "Anyway, it looks good. My dad's going to be impressed." Her eyes shone with a softer light. Then she drew away. "I should get ready." The screen door squeaked as she stepped inside. She did not rush, but she did not linger.

The door banged shut with a mild rattle. He sat there, listening to her footsteps fade into the house. A part of him wanted to call after her, to ask her if she remembered the times they used to wake early for different reasons: him to work on small restoration tasks in their youth, her to scribble notes in her journals when insomnia struck. Another part of him knew that conversation would only dredge up more fragments of a past they had not fully addressed.

He picked up his coffee mug and finished the last few lukewarm sips. Then he turned to Silas, who gazed at him with the patient look only a longtime companion could muster. "Well," Xander said, his voice a near-whisper, "she's going to see her dad." He paused, as if the dog might reply. Silas merely wagged his tail.

The morning had shifted. If Emery was awake and moving, the house would soon stir with complicated energy. Xander rose and left the porch step behind. He walked down into the yard, coffee in one hand, the flimsy stick in the other. Moisture clung to the grass. His boots left small impressions in the wet soil. He approached the garden near the side of the house, where a cluster of rosemary and hardy plants had survived the last few seasons of neglect.

He studied the plants for a moment, remembering how Margot had once tried to cultivate herbs for her kitchen. The memory pulled a sting of regret through him. This entire place pulsed with recollections that refused to settle. Some were good ones, others carried the weight of heartbreak. He set his empty mug on a ledge and shook off the feeling as best he could. The tasks of the day were waiting. He would repaint the parlor trim, patch that crack, and try not to think about Emery stepping through the foyer with a million things she was not telling him.

"Focus," he told himself. "One board, one brushstroke at a time." That had always been his method. Restoration was like solving a puzzle. You confronted the damage, decided on the right materials, and put in enough painstaking labor to see it through. And if you did it correctly, the result stood strong for decades.

He crouched, inhaling the scent of damp earth. Someone had left an old trowel there. He picked it up and knocked the excess dirt off the edge. His mind wandered back to Emery's face a few minutes ago. She had looked so composed, as if summoning a wall between them. Yet there had been a fleeting moment when Silas trotted over with his tail brushing her legs that she almost smiled. He saw something in her eyes that reminded him of the girl he once knew, the one whose laughter lit up entire afternoons. The memory left him both hopeful and uneasy.

He stood again, exhaled and walked across the grass until he neared the back corner of the porch. The boards there needed minor reinforcement. He nudged one with the toe of his boot. It creaked, not dangerously but enough to justify attention soon. He made a mental note to add it to his list.

At the far edge, beyond a slight slope of land, the marsh opened wide. The water glimmered under the emerging sun, turning from silver to pale gold. Shem Creek glided beyond with a new day. The quiet had once been his respite, the silent acceptance that let him work without the noise of heartbreak. Then Emery came back, and every quiet moment crackled with tension.

Behind him, he heard the creak of the screen door again. For a moment, he thought Emery had returned, maybe to pick another fight or to say something else. But the door closed with a gentle click, and footsteps moved away inside. She must be heading upstairs. Perhaps she was already gathering her things to leave for David's hospital room. He forced himself not to follow that sound. Instead, he stared at the horizon for a few more breaths, letting the breeze brush his hair against his forehead.

Finally, he made his way back to where Silas had been waiting, stick at his feet. The dog wagged his tail slowly, ears perked in anticipation. Xander sighed and set his coffee mug on the porch. He reached down and grabbed the slim piece of wood. It had a slight bend, as if it had been lying out in the yard too long.

He straightened and threw it. The stick sailed through the air, arching across a patch of sunlight before landing in the grass a fair distance away. Silas bounded after it, tongue lolling, eager to retrieve. Xander watched him go.

A ray of warmth touched his face as the sun climbed higher. He wiped the back of his neck and released a breath he had not realized he was holding. The day had barely started, and already he felt the weight of everything she made him remember. He wanted to believe it could end well. Yet each passing hour told him she was only here because of circumstance, not desire. She had never planned on coming back unless forced.

He stuffed his hands in his pockets. Silence settled around him again, broken only by Silas rummaging in the grass. In the distance, the faint hum of a car engine passed on the main road. Maybe Emery would stay long enough to see how much he had poured himself into this house. Maybe she would slip away as soon as her father's condition changed. He tried not to dwell on which scenario would hurt more.

When Silas trotted back, the dog's jaws clenched around the stick, tail wagging in frantic bursts. With a grunt, Xander patted Silas's side. "Good boy," he said. He took the drool-slick piece of wood, looked at it a moment and sent it skyward again. This time, it spun slightly off course, landing closer to the low shrubs.

He exhaled and ran a hand through his hair, letting the tension slip from his shoulders. It was only early morning, but it felt as if he had lived half a day already. He pictured Emery stepping out in that worn sweatshirt, her coffee mug in hand, eyes scanning the water. It was a sight both comforting and jarring. He told himself not to read too much into it.

He stooped and picked up the coffee mug he had set

aside. He weighed it in his grip. A residual warmth lingered against his palm. Turning toward the sun, he murmured, "She's not staying."

Yet the words were hollow. A traitorous part of him longed for the day she might decide otherwise. Deep in his chest, he felt the trembling hope he had buried for seven years, stirring like it might refuse to be ignored. So, he closed his eyes, listened to Silas's distant panting, and spoke softly:

"But part of me... God help me... hopes I'm wrong."

CHAPTER

FIVE

EMERY

Travel Note: On King Street, ghosts do not hide. Their faces lurk in old windows, appearing in the corner of your eye if you dare to look too long. I have seen similar spirits in the souks of Marrakesh and the cathedrals of Prague, as though history refuses to rest no matter how often we blink.

—EW

Emery sat behind the steering wheel for a full minute before guiding the car out of the driveway. The late morning sunlight stung her eyes, or perhaps it was the remnants of a restless night weighing on her. She glanced at the estate's porch as she pulled away. The swing hung motionless in what felt like a silent vigil. Her stomach turned with an odd mix of apprehension and guilt, yet she drove on, determined not to think too hard about why she felt so tense.

Traffic along the older roads into downtown

Charleston moved slower than she recalled, clogged with sightseeing carriages and midweek construction vehicles. She navigated around them, passing a clothing boutique she vaguely remembered. It had changed names at least twice. Sighing, she rubbed at the tightness in her neck.

Her father was at Roper Hospital, a place she once thought of as a fixture of Charleston's skyline. Now, as Emery neared the downtown district, she spotted the skeletal form of a high rise under construction. It rose like an unwanted addition to the city's subdued silhouette. She frowned at the concrete pillars and the crane perched overhead. Charleston was not meant to look like a modern metropolis, she thought. It reminded her of someone tacking new frames onto a centuries old tapestry. She told herself she did not care what changed while she was gone, but the anger that flared in her chest proved otherwise.

She pulled into the hospital parking area, fighting the urge to drive away and blame traffic for missing the visit. The building's sliding doors ushered her into a blast of air conditioning that prickled her skin. A faint tang of anti-septic swirled in the hallways. She took the elevator up to the floor where her father's room was, and the climb felt agonizing.

At the end of a long corridor, she knocked briefly on the partly open door, then eased inside. David Westbrook rested against a stack of pillows, reading a battered biog-raphy about historic architecture, his horn-rimmed glasses perched low on his nose. His sandy brown hair was now streaked with gray, and the lean lines of his frame looked almost fragile against the sterile bedding. Despite the tired droop of his shoulders, he lifted his gaze with a half-smile when she entered.

"You always did show up when I stopped expecting you," he said. His voice held a gentle rasp that made Emery swallow hard.

She shut the door behind her. "I suppose I like proving people wrong." She tried to smile, but it felt wobbly. She stepped closer to the bed and noted the thinning skin on his hands. She caught sight of the IV line in the crease of his elbow.

"So, you do," David said with a tight exhale. He pulled off his glasses and studied her. "Where have you been wandering this morning?"

She glanced at the book in his lap. "Just finding my way. Charleston is busier than ever, apparently. More traffic. More buildings. I spotted a new tower downtown." She sank into the chair beside his bed, crossing her arms loosely. "I guess it was bound to happen."

David nodded. "Things change, no matter how much we try to slow them down."

Emery kept her gaze on him. She wanted to say that she never meant to stay away for so long, that each day turned into a year before she could figure out how to come home. Instead, she settled for a deflection. "How are you feeling? Do you actually like it here?" She gestured at the hospital room, its sterile walls softened only by pale drapes.

"I prefer my own sheets, but the staff is kind. They

keep me feeling upright most days." He replaced his glasses with a faint smile. "I hear you have been spending more time at the estate."

She ignored the pang in her chest. "Yes. I got in yesterday, and I have been looking around. It feels like a museum of my childhood. One that never quite left the past."

"It is your past," David said, tapping the edge of his book. "Just like it was your mother's, and your sister's."

She heard that slight edge in his voice when he mentioned Laura. She decided she might as well bring it up. "Speaking of Laura, I am trying to reach her. I have her address on Seabrook Island, but I am guessing that might be out of date. Do you know if she is still there?"

He shifted, the corners of his mouth pulling in. "She might be. We are not exactly on daily speaking terms." His tone closed the subject before it began. "If you do catch up with her, that would be something good to do."

Emery felt disappointment lodge under her ribs. She wanted some direction, some clue on how to fix things with her sister. Instead, David had neatly sealed that conversation away. The old pattern set in, the Westbrooks did not push too far, not even with each other. At least, that was how it used to be.

She cleared her throat and stood. "Well, keep me posted if you hear anything."

He reached for her hand with surprising swiftness. His grip felt thin, bones more prominent than she remembered. "Em," he said softly. "It is good to have you home."

She managed a nod, afraid her voice would crack if she

replied. She squeezed his hand, then sat on the bed and told him about her travels from the past year. In about ten minutes he had drifted off to the sound of her voice. She bent over and kissed him on his forehead before leaving the room.

Outside, she escaped into the blistering midday heat and let it press around her. She had no interest in returning straight to the estate, so she drove in a loose circle through the downtown's narrow streets. Buildings she had once known still stood, but some had new signs or fresh coats of pastel paint. She slowed near King Street, watching the tourists who snapped photos under wrought iron balconies. A memory tugged, and she found herself parking in a spot near an old wine bar, a place that used to serve gelato when she was younger.

She walked aimlessly for several minutes and turned onto a quieter street that led into the French Quarter. Faint recollections of meandering with Xander in the late afternoon floated to the surface of her mind. She remembered the corner bookstore they often visited. Her heart skipped when she saw the store still had the same name. She did not go in, only stopped to peer through the glass. The interior looked exactly as before. Shelves lined with hardbacks, a chalkboard sign advertising events. She inhaled, feeling off balance, then continued until she found herself outside The Harbinger Café.

Inside, the warm air smelled of freshly ground coffee and something sweet. She placed a quick order, a black coffee and a cinnamon scone, and chose a booth at the back. Sliding into the seat, she pulled her journal from her bag. The page from last night remained blank except for one scribbled line she had meant to expand upon. She wrote:

My father's dying. My sister is a ghost. Xander is sanding our memories into shape.

Her pen hovered, and then she crossed out the words in sharp strokes. She let out a breath. Truth felt heavy on her tongue, and she could not force it into tidy sentences. Instead, she flipped to a fresh page and jotted notes about the city outside, the clash of modern scaffolding against centuries-old brick, the hum of life inside a café that used to be an antique shop.

She finished her coffee in silence and ignored the subtle glances of the barista who had served her. Emery guessed the woman recognized her from old times. Maybe the Westbrook name was an echo in everyone's mind. Maybe the weight of that echo was what drove Emery to leave in the first place.

When she tossed her empty cup, she realized the sun sat lower in the sky than she had anticipated. Feeling the press of the day's heat behind her eyes, she got into her car and rolled the windows down before turning on the ignition. She needed the sticky warmth on her skin more than stale air conditioning. The short drive back to the estate felt like crossing an invisible border between old regrets and uncertainty.

The house loomed in the glow of a setting sun. She parked in the gravel driveway. The magnolia tree in the front yard whispered with the faint evening breeze. Emery went inside, slipped off her shoes, and climbed the stairs.

She paused at the top, gazing down the hallway toward her parents' former bedroom. The door was closed. A memory struck her, a morning with her mother humming an old lullaby. The recollection came so fast that it stole her breath. She forced herself to keep walking, to keep from knocking on a door that no one would open except her own ghosts.

Hours seemed to pass without her noticing. At some point, she found herself in the library with no recollection of walking there. Her nerves had grown too jumpy to rest, so she decided to roam the house quietly. Then she noticed how hungry she was and went into the kitchen. She opened the refrigerator and found it fairly stocked with milk, juices and what looked to be leftovers. She found a plate, opened the container and realized it was probably Xander's leftover dinner of beef stew. She scooped out some onto a plate and warmed it for a minute in the microwave before eating every delicious bite. She wondered if he had made it himself. Maybe the floors would speak to her, answer questions she could not voice. She wandered past the study, her fingertips grazing the edge of the doorframe. She shuffled through the darkened dining room, noticing how the moonlight gleamed off the large table's polished surface.

Eventually she stepped outside onto the porch. The nighttime air clung to her skin in a damp film. She looked at the newly reinforced ropes attached to the swing. The seat was smooth now, the slats replaced in places where rot had set in. Yet the faint carvings of their initials still marred one part of the wood. She brushed her thumb over them, remembering how she and Xander once sank into an awkward silence on that swing after a sudden summer rain. That memory felt lifetimes away, yet the evidence of it remained in these letters carved by teenage hands.

She sank onto the swing, the boards creaking under her weight. Her phone rested on her lap. The screen glowed as she opened an old text draft. She had typed it three years ago but never hit send:

You said I never let you tell your side. What would you have said?

Emery stared at the words for a long time, her heart thudding in her chest. She had typed them in a lonely hotel room on the other side of the world, imagining what Xander might say if she gave him the chance. With a quick motion, she swiped the entire sentence and hit delete, watching it vanish. An odd hollowness coiled in her stomach.

The porch light flickered behind her, casting faint shadows across the steps. She heard movement, soft footfalls on the floorboards above and a distant creak of an opening door. Her pulse quickened. For one brief moment, she thought it was her mother's footsteps. That was impossible, yet her mind still fluttered with the possibility. Then she realized it had to be Xander, likely checking something in one of the upstairs rooms or searching for a tool he had misplaced.

Emery looked up at the second story windows and spotted no silhouette. She rubbed her arms and felt a chill that was not from the temperature. Her lips parted in a whisper that fell into the humid air:

"I still hate that I want to hear your side."

She closed her eyes, letting the soft sway of the porch swing calm her pounding heart. Above, a single light went dark. The old house groaned, as if in answer. Or maybe it was only the echo of memories that refused to rest.

CHAPTER
SIX

XANDER

Xander stood in the sunroom of the Westbrook estate at daybreak. The windows there offered a hazy light that made dust motes shimmer around him. He leaned his head back to roll out a hitch in his neck, then refocused on the freshly cut piece of molding balanced atop two sawhorses. He had started sanding the edges before sunrise, drawn by the calm of a quiet house. Silas, his faithful golden retriever, rested in a corner of the sunroom, paws tucked under his body. The dog's eyes moved toward the door now and then, as if waiting for someone else to appear.

When Xander ran the sandpaper along the curve of the molding, the rasping sound filled his head and softened his thoughts. Her presence in the house unsettled him. She had been back only a short while, yet it felt like both an instant and an entire season. He could not forget the shape of her face, the way her eyes refused to meet his, or the tension that charged the space whenever they stood in the same room.

He turned the molding over, inspecting the grain, then tested the fit against a nearby corner to ensure the angles matched. Outside, the sun climbed past the hanging moss that draped the oak trees, casting a shifting pattern of light and shadow against the window. Xander paused to stretch his arms. His palms felt raw, and a faint dusting of sawdust clung to his forearms. He did not mind. The ache of physical labor offered a solid truth in a house that still held too many uncertainties.

He heard footsteps. The sunroom door creaked open, and Emery stepped inside. She wore the same jeans from yesterday, along with a simple white T-shirt. Her hair was pushed back into a hasty knot that had begun to unravel at her neck. She paused near the threshold but did not move closer. The morning light highlighted the faint circles under her eyes, proof that she was probably sleeping no better than he was.

Their eyes met, and Xander felt a dull squeeze in his chest. He shifted his weight. "Morning."

She nodded, a gesture so quick he almost missed it.

Her posture radiated confinement, as if the house's unspoken memories weighed on her, though she would surely never admit it. He set the sandpaper on the sawhorse. When the silence stretched, he spoke again.

"Coffee is fresh in the kitchen." He tried to keep the invitation casual, though awkwardness rumbled in his voice.

She shifted her weight. The worn plank beneath her foot squeaked. "I already had some," she said. Her tone was measured, but then he saw the corner of her mouth quirk, almost a smile. "Besides, yours is too bitter."

That response, small as it was, sounded like a tentative joke. He huffed an exhale, letting a wry grin cross his lips. "Yeah, guess I have not changed the brand in a while."

Neither of them said more. Emery took a step back, glancing around the sunroom at the stacked boards, the half-finished window trim, and the can of primer. It seemed she was looking for something else to comment on, or maybe she just wanted to keep her distance.

He broke the silence first. "There is a lot left to do in here. Once the trim is finished, I will repaint the frame around the windows."

She nodded and stuffed her hands into her back pockets. "Well, I will be around," she muttered. She turned and left. The door drifted closed behind her, leaving Xander alone again.

For a moment, he let himself think about her face. She had claimed to have coffee already, but he guessed she had just woken up not long ago. The faint flush in her cheeks suggested she had hurried down to find him or perhaps to avoid him. He had no way of knowing.

He tried to shake off the tension and refocused on the molding. A sigh left him. He reminded himself that it was still early and they had a long day ahead. He inspected the corners once more, then decided it was good enough to attach to the wall. With a nail gun and a light hammer, he began installing the piece, step by methodical step. The click and hiss of the tool reduced the lingering sense of unease.

An hour later, the sun was fully up, and the humidity crept in through the screens. Xander wiped his brow with the back of his hand. Silas trotted out of the sunroom and followed an invisible scent into the hallway. Xander knew the dog would find Emery soon. The golden retriever had a knack for calming the air between disagreeing humans.

Xander moved on to the west parlor to address a portion of the baseboard he had prepared the day before. He found Emery there, settled on the sofa near the parlor's open double doors. She scrolled through her phone, shoulders stiff, but she glanced up when he entered. He offered a polite nod of greeting, then crouched by the wall to work. Neither spoke. Silas, finished with his explorations, curled up between them, as if content to split his loyalty.

They stayed like that for another stretch of time. Xander hammered nails and smoothed the edges of wood putty. Emery occasionally tapped at her phone, scanned something, or sighed under her breath. Outside, cicadas buzzed in the slow-building heat. It felt like a fragile peace, a momentary arrangement that might dissolve if either of them probed too deeply into the past.

Mid-morning arrived with a jarring noise. The front doorbell chimed. Xander froze, brow furrowed. He had a scheduled delivery for antique wall sconces, but he had not expected them this early. He got to his feet, dusted off his jeans, and walked into the foyer. Emery followed him, hands by her sides, looking uncertain as if she might volunteer to answer the door but decided against it.

The door opened to reveal a delivery man in a baseball cap, clipboard in hand. "Hey, Mr. Langley," he said, bright and cheery as he shifted the weight of a box from one hip to the other. "Got those sconces you ordered from White-bridge Antiques. Where do you want them?"

"Perfect timing. You can bring them in this way." Xander motioned for him to step inside. "Thanks for calling ahead."

"Sure thing." The man stepped over the threshold and noticed Emery standing behind Xander. "Oh, sorry. Didn't know your wife was here too." He winked in that overly friendly way some people did, as if encouraging banter that Xander had no intention of pursuing.

Emery's breath snagged, her eyes flaring as her shoulders locked. Xander mumbled, "She's not," in a quiet, curt tone. He saw the confusion on the delivery guy's face, followed by an embarrassed chuckle.

"Sorry, no offense intended," the man said, though the uncomfortable flush in his cheeks suggested he was ready to leave.

"It's fine," Emery replied, but she stood a bit straighter, arms crossing over her chest.

Xander gestured toward the hallway. "You can set the box against the wall in the parlor. I appreciate it."

The man nodded, hauled the package inside, then scribbled something on his clipboard. After a last awkward glance at Emery and Xander, he left with a rushed goodbye and let the front door close. The moment hung like a humidity laden curtain. Emery stared at the closed door, then at Xander. Her expression was unreadable, but her cheeks looked warmer than a moment ago.

He rubbed the back of his neck. "They sometimes assume. Has happened before."

"I see," she said stiffly, as though she was not sure what else to say. The tension scalded the space between them. Silas padded closer, tail swinging in a slow wag, oblivious to the discomfort.

Xander rolled his shoulders back. "I'll take a look at these sconces, then get back to finishing the parlor trim."

Emery nodded once, then turned away without another word. She left the foyer with a brisk pace, vanishing down the corridor. Xander watched her go, heat flushing through him. Even small misunderstandings felt charged when it came to her. He let out a breath, feeling the need to escape before the house pressed too many questions into him.

He carried the box to the parlor, set it beside the wall, and sliced the tape to peek at the sconces. They were as promised, a pair of ornate bronze fixtures from the late nineteenth century, perfect for the older architectural style of the house. He ran a thumb over the metal's patina, satisfied with the authenticity. Then he closed the box, noticing how he had begun to sweat under his collar.

Needing fresh air, he left the main house and headed out back toward the carriage house that served as his workshop. The air outside was no cooler, but at least it held a faint breeze that carried the marsh's salty tang. He kept a measured stride, resisting the urge to break into a frustrated run. The workshop door squeaked as he stepped inside. Paint cans and woodworking tools lined the shelves, and a spread of sandpaper sheets cluttered the worktable. It smelled like varnish and old timber.

He walked over to the drawer where he kept some personal files. He tugged it open, revealing the battered folder labeled "Westbrook – Personal." He lifted it and set it on the workbench. It felt heavier than before, or maybe his frame of mind added weight to the contents. He flipped it open and scanned the documents, the estate's original blueprints, a few black and white photos found in the attic, and finally Margot Westbrook's handwritten list of changes. Margot's penmanship was faint, the ink smudged in places, but he could still read the words. She had written a handful of instructions, potential remodeling ideas, and near the bottom, a single line: "Don't touch the porch swing. Let them decide."

A prickle of emotion crawled up the back of his neck. He remembered the day he stumbled upon that note while rummaging through old papers. He had found it peculiar. Margot had left instructions for nearly every other fixture, but for the swing she was stubbornly vague. Something deep in him wondered if she had known Emery might return and that the swing would be a piece only Emery could truly claim. He considered taking this note to her right now, but that seemed too intimate and too raw. He closed the folder with a gentle sigh.

He pressed his palms against the table's rough edge. The entire morning had thrown him off balance. Emery's tension, the delivery man's remark, the memory of her face. He closed his eyes and let the swirl of sawdust and memories settle. Outside, he heard a muffled hum, someone walking near the garden. He set the folder aside, deciding he would return it to the drawer. Then he moved toward the small window overlooking the estate's back lot.

Through the smudged workshop glass, he saw Emery by the herb garden, strolling barefoot across the grass. Her eyes were half-closed, and her hand grazed the tops of the rosemary and other herb plants. She plucked a twig of rosemary and brought it to her nose. He could not see her expression clearly, but he imagined her breathing in the sharp, earthy scent. Her hair swayed in the faint breeze. She was humming softly, though he could not decipher the tune. Something about that vulnerable snapshot twisted his chest.

A drop of sweat trickled down his temple. He pressed his fingers against the window frame, then forced himself to step away. He did not deserve to spy on her unguarded moments. It only made everything more complicated, reminding him of how deeply he still cared. He replaced the folder in the drawer, slid it shut, and let out a slow breath. He checked his watch. Afternoon loomed, and he had plenty of tasks waiting. Maybe if he stayed busy, his mind would not drift to her every five minutes.

Hours passed in a blur of scraping paint and installing the sconces with careful precision. Xander managed to keep a steady focus on the tasks at hand, but he felt Emery's presence in the house, an unspoken gravity that pulled on him. Once or twice, he thought he heard her footsteps in the adjoining room, but she never came in. He did not seek her out either. It was easier to hide behind work.

By evening, clouds thickened in the sky. The air turned stifling in that way Charleston evenings did before a storm. Xander went to check the windows he had left cracked open for ventilation, then returned to the foyer. A distant rumble of thunder rolled through the sultry dusk. Lamps flickered, and the overhead light in the hallway blinked.

He closed the front door, dropping the latch, and quietly acknowledged that a storm off the coast was about to hit. Another low rumble sounded, closer this time. The house lights went out, plunging everything into sudden darkness.

He stood in the blackness with a short curse climbing his throat. He patted his pockets, found his phone, and switched on its flashlight. The soft beam illuminated a pile of dust on the floor. Silas padded up to him, tail wagging anxiously. He patted the dog's head. "It's okay, buddy."

He moved toward the hallway where he kept extra candles. Lightning flashed, illuminating the windows, followed by a sharp crack of thunder. In the split-second glow, he spotted a figure in the kitchen. He stepped that way with cautious strides. Emery stood at the counter, holding a lit candle. Warm shadows slipped across her face, accentuating her cheekbones and the tension in her jaw.

She looked at him, eyes reflecting gold from the candlelight. "Breaker is still outside in the back, right?"

He nodded. "I'll get it." He grabbed a flashlight from a side table. As he walked past her, their arms brushed, and he caught the scent of citrus on her skin. It triggered the memory of the nights they used to sit on the porch swing, the space between them that felt safe, not strained.

He found his voice after a beat. "I'll be back in a minute." His voice was tight, though he hoped she did not notice. She just nodded, her candle trembling slightly in her grip.

The back door opened to the storm's gust. Rain splattered across the porch steps, and the sky lit up again with a jagged streak of lightning. Xander hustled to the fuse box under the stairs shining his flashlight so he would not slip. He found the breakers and reset them in the proper sequence. The overhead light in the workshop flickered on through the window, so he guessed the circuit was stable.

By the time he returned, water dripped from his jacket collar. He stepped into the kitchen, breathing heavily. Emery stood there holding an unlit candle now that the lights were back on. She had set the candle on the counter and leaned against the edge, looking exhausted.

"Are you okay?" he asked softly.

Her gaze flicked to him. For a moment, he thought she might brush the question aside. Then her carefully held defenses cracked. "No," she said. Her voice was almost a whisper. "But I'm here."

A wave of conflicting emotions washed over him. He wanted to ask her more, to press about which part was hurting her—the house, her father's illness, the secrets she and he were dancing around. But something in her face told him she could not bear more questions right now. So, he pressed his fist to the counter, letting the chill marble hold him back.

He gave a single nod, a subtle gesture of acknowledgment. "All right," he said quietly. He reached for a match to light a second candle. Shadows spread across the counters, flickering in the dark. Thunder rumbled overhead.

She held his gaze for a moment, raw vulnerability in her eyes. He felt an ache in his chest. He wanted to tell her she was not alone. Instead, he stepped back. "I hope the power stays on through the rest of the storm," he said. The words felt hollow.

Her chin dipped in a silent reply. He left her there, with just the faint light of the candle illuminating her presence. He walked out into the corridor, Silas close behind, the rest of the house bathed in wavering darkness. His footsteps echoed off the old hardwood floors, matching the steady drum of rain against the windows.

CHAPTER

SEVEN

EMERY

Travel Note: I once wandered the alleys of Rome at midnight, searching for something I could not name. The stone walls held shadows where lantern light failed to reach, and every step felt like a question. Charleston's side streets give me that same question now, familiar and unknowable, as though each cobblestone guards a secret.

—EW

Emery lay awake, staring at the soft glow of her phone clock. The storm outside pulsed with low rumbles that made the glass panes in her bedroom tremble. Curtains shifted in an uneven dance, and she caught glimpses of the porch swing rocking in the wind. Drops tapped the roof in staggered rhythms, each reminder of sleeplessness more insistent than the last. She wrapped her arms around her torso, trying to steady her breath as she remembered the lightning-slashed sky from another night so many years ago.

61

A flicker of silver by her bedside caught her eye, her journal, the worn cover half-concealed by rumpled blankets. She reached for it without thinking and flipped through the most recent pages. Her handwriting slanted across scattered thoughts about her father's health, lingering frustration with Laura, and the constant ache that shadowed Xander's presence. Nothing in these hurried notes gave her relief. She kept turning pages until she reached a line scribbled two years after her mother's funeral.

I should have stayed. I should have listened.

She traced a fingertip along the words, each sentence an echo of guilt. That was the day she had camped in a remote part of Peru, isolating herself from every piece of Charleston, hoping distance might silence regret. She remembered holding her phone in a cheap hostel bed, drafting messages she never sent. Her mother's face swam into focus now, each memory shaped by a thousand questions Emery never bothered to ask when there was still time.

Thunder shook the heavens again, rattling the glass. It felt like the house itself was clearing its throat, reminding her she was not alone in this old place. She turned on the small bedside lamp, then shut it off again, unsettled by the brightness. When her breath refused to even out, she swung her legs onto the floor, grabbed a thin blanket, and padded out of the bedroom.

Her bare feet sank into the plush runner in the hallway, muffling her steps. The overhead lights flickered now and then from the storm's whim. She was not sure if the house was losing electricity or if the bulbs merely blinked in protest. She heard the quiet rattle of the old windows, as if the estate sighed with her. Everything suddenly fell into darkness again.

Silas's paws clicked on the lower level, soft and measured. The rhythm offered a brief moment of calm. She held the banister, pausing at the top of the stairs. Wind pressed against the old walls, drawing out soft moans from the wood. She shut her eyes and tried to steady her heart. In her memory, she could almost see her mother at the bottom, calling her name. That memory belonged to a simpler time, when Margot greeted her with a grin for no reason other than love. Before the secrets caught up to them.

She sank onto the landing, blanket wrapped around her shoulders. Rain splattered against the tall windows on the main floor, diamond beads chasing each other down the glass. Emery tried to recall the last conversation she had with Margot that did not spiral into argument. Bits of her mother's voice drifted in her mind: We're a family. Don't shut us out. Then the thunder drowned everything else.

Anger, hot and uncontainable, had sparked inside Emery that final week she spent here. She pictured the slam of doors, the raised voices. Each fight had seemed too big to fix. She remembered Laura at the end of the hall-way, arms folded as though bracing for impact, and Xander nearby, his face pinched with worry. That had been enough to ignite Emery's suspicions. She never asked them to explain. She never paused to listen. She just left after the funeral. The storm that night raged almost as fiercely as this one. She had listened to the downpour beat against her windshield and refused to look back.

A fresh crack of thunder made her jump. She rubbed her arms, then stood and headed downstairs. Familiar rooms filled her vision in spectral outlines. The parlor to her left was dark and silent, the library to her right had its door partly ajar. She was not ready to face those quiet corners where leftover memories lurked, so she pushed forward into the dining room instead.

Lightning illuminated the polished table, revealing the old chairs arranged precisely as though awaiting a celebration that would never start. She trailed her fingertips along the table's edge. She could almost see her family seated around it, her mother laughing, her father leaning back with humble pride, Laura gesturing with her fork as she teased Emery. A flash in her mind: an image of them one holiday, laughter and clinking glasses. Now the only sound was rain and her own unsteady sigh.

The lights now flickered back on, and her gaze caught on the china hutch. The door was slightly ajar, as if beckoning her closer. She slipped around a chair and eased the door open with care, half expecting to find only dust. Instead, she discovered a small sewing basket. Its wicker handle felt brittle when she lifted it. She whispered an apology to no one as she cracked the lid.

Inside, spools of thread lay tangled with a few stray needles and scraps of faded cloth. Her mother's nimble hands had once used these tools to fix a loose button or stitch a hem. Beneath the thread, Emery spotted a necklace with a broken clasp. The chain glinted in the intermittent lightning. She unfolded a small piece of paper as well, a grocery list in Margot's handwriting.

Eggs. Flour. Lemons.

Emery's throat constricted. Nothing more than an ordinary list, yet it pinned her chest with fresh grief. She had missed so many small details of her mother's life while chasing distant horizons.

Then the thunder cracked overhead, and the lights went off again.

Tucking the necklace in her palm, she closed the sewing basket and slid it back behind the hutch, uncertain if she could bear to look at it any longer. She needed water, needed something to calm the ache that pressed against her ribs. The hallway leading to the kitchen was dark, lit at intervals by lightning flashes. She felt her way along the wallpaper until she reached the open archway. Dim rust-orange light glowed inside. At first, she thought it might be a candle left burning by accident.

She realized soon enough that Xander stood there, his broad shoulders turned away from her, a single tall candle on the counter casting shadows across his face. He leaned against the sink, arms folded, gaze set on the window over the farmhouse-style basin. His loose T-shirt clung to him in places from the evening's humidity. Even in the gloom, she saw the tension in the line of his jaw. When he sensed her presence, he turned slightly, not startled but more resigned, as if he had expected her.

"Couldn't sleep either?" he asked quietly. His voice matched the muffled sounds of rain outside.

She shook her head and moved farther into the kitchen. She still gripped the broken necklace, feeling the slender chain twist against her palm. "Not for years," she admitted, crossing to the sink. She set the necklace on the edge of the counter, then grabbed a clean glass. She filled it halfway with water, lifted it to her lips, and drank in slow sips. The candlelight revealed the faint circles beneath Xander's eyes.

He nodded at the necklace. "Where did you find that?"

"In my mother's sewing basket," she said. Her tone quivered, and she hated how emotion leaked through so easily. "It feels like I'm stumbling on echoes of her everywhere I look."

Xander rested a hand on the counter, close to the necklace but not touching it. "That's how this house is," he said. "It keeps everything."

She waited for him to continue, but he did not. She sensed how complicated his own thoughts were, the pieces of memory he carried in silence. The tension between them felt like a current, quietly thrumming beneath each word. She set her empty glass aside and faced him.

"Why did you stay?" she asked. Her voice sounded too direct, even to herself. "You could have left Charleston, you could have—" She stopped, uncertain if she had the right to criticize or question. After all, she was the one who ran.

He exhaled slowly. The glow of the candle cast uneven

shadows over his cheekbones, highlighting the worry edged into his features. "Not everything that breaks has to be abandoned," he said. "Sometimes it needs time or better care. But it can be salvaged."

A wave of feeling pressed against her lungs. She nearly lost her grip on the fragile calm she had maintained all night. If she looked at him too long, she would shatter. He was here, in this kitchen, expressing the patience she had never quite learned to keep. He was talking about the house, or he was talking about them. The weight of that truth cut through her with a pang of regret.

Her lashes felt damp, but she forced herself not to cry. "I used to envy that about you," she murmured. "How you always believed in fixing what's broken. I thought you were too attached to the past. I guess I was wrong."

He stepped closer, though he did not reach for her. "I'm not always right," he said. "I could not bear to see the house torn down. Or to lose everything else in the process."

Lightning flashed, revealing dust particles in the air like tiny sparks. Silence stretched so taut Emery wondered if the storm itself would tear the night open. She nodded, swallowing hard. Words clogged her throat, so she reached for her glass, filling it again but not drinking this time. Across the kitchen island, Xander's eyes stayed on her, reflecting both concern and a caution that hurt more than any anger might have.

Her pulse hammered. She had countless questions about why he and Laura stood together that night, what secrets they had kept, but she could not push further. She was afraid of bursting into tears, or worse, wanting him to hold her. So, she placed the glass in the sink with a hollow clink of glass against porcelain.

"I'm going back up," she said softly. "I don't think my mind will let me sleep, but I can at least try."

His nod was almost imperceptible. The candlelight bent around him, painting his face in gold and shadow. He opened his mouth to speak, then seemed to think better of it. She felt his gaze on her until she disappeared from the kitchen, the feeling of missed possibilities pulsing like a second heartbeat in her ears.

The hallway darkened behind her as she made her way up the stairs, each step punctuated by the old wood creaking beneath her weight. The storm continued its relentless rumble outside, but she no longer cared if the night split wide open. All that mattered was the uneasy memories that refused to settle.

When she entered her bedroom, she clicked on the small lamp by the dresser. A faint glow spread across the faded wallpaper. She thought of opening the journal again, writing down everything Xander had told her. But the thought of spelling out her confusion on paper made her chest tighten. She could not handle documenting one more heartbreak.

She set the blanket aside and slipped underneath the covers. Her skin felt clammy from the humidity and her eyes burned from exhaustion. Still, her mind filled with images of her mother's broken necklace, the short grocery list, every regret etched into her recollection. She let her head sink into the pillow. Rain clattered against the roof in chaotic patterns. A low rumble of thunder reminded her of a distant voice, urging her to speak a truth she was not ready to face.

She closed her eyes and pulled the sheets over her head. Warm darkness enveloped her, though she doubted sleep would come easily. She breathed in the comforting scent of linen and tried not to imagine Xander downstairs with candlelight dancing across his face.

In a trembling whisper, she let the question slip out: "Tell me I got it wrong."

CHAPTER

EIGHT

XANDER

Travel Note: In the Scottish Highlands, I watched a storm swallow the horizon. Sometimes the storm is inside a house, not the sky. You do not outrun it; you wait for the calm that follows.

—EW

Xander stood in front of the large mahogany desk in the study, a scattering of architectural drawings spread out before him. The morning light filtering through the tall windows cast a warm glow on the paper, highlighting crisp pencil marks and half-finished notes on sash windows and casement hardware. Every few minutes, his attention drifted toward the open doorway, the corridor beyond silent. He listened for the sound of Emery's footsteps, but the house kept its secrets.

He exhaled slowly and refocused on the drawing in front of him, a sketched plan of the estate's front windows with notations about the refurbished frames he had ordered. A supplier down in Savannah was supposed to call by now. He checked his phone, saw no missed calls, and sighed. He had always prided himself on thoroughness, making sure every piece of wood matched the architecture's original heart pine. Everything had to fit the soul of this house. He believed that once the small details aligned, the rest might begin to heal too.

He lifted the worn folder labeled Westbrook – Personal, flipping past a copy of the estate's original blueprint until he reached the smaller packet of photos. Most were black-and-white images of the estate taken decades ago, but near the bottom was a thin envelope. Years ago, Margot had asked him to bring a few family photographs down from the attic. He had tucked them into this envelope and never opened it again, hoping to preserve some boundary between past and present.

He set the envelope on the desk and peeled back the flap. The pictures inside showed Emery at various ages. In one, she was about fifteen, perched on the porch swing with a sketchpad balanced on her knees. She was laughing at someone just out of frame. He felt something in his chest twist at the memory of her younger self, vibrant, restless, and full of dreams about leaving Charleston. Another photo showed her and Laura wearing matching sun hats, each holding an iced tea and pretending to toast. Tension coiled in his belly as he thought of how complicated things had become between those sisters. He flipped to the next: Emery kissing him under the bleachers at a high school football game, her hand lost in his dark hair. So much affection was captured in that one snapshot, enough to make his pulse quicken with old longing.

He should have destroyed these, he thought. He had told himself once that burning them might erase the ache. Yet the idea of discarding them felt like turning his back on everything he had shared with her, everything he wanted to protect. He returned the photos to the envelope, slid them back into the folder, and closed it with a careful press of his palms.

The morning wore on. Minutes turned into hours, and still no sign of Emery beyond the occasional subdued clink from the kitchen or the hallway. He focused again on his drawings and picked up a mechanical pencil to refine the measurements for a stubborn window that never seemed to sit quite right in its frame. He double-checked the angles and made a few more notations about potential reinforcement near the sill. Despite his concentration, his mind kept wandering toward her. The house felt oddly balanced when she was awake and moving around. When she was too quiet, every plank and timber seemed to hold its breath.

Late in the morning, the soft creak of the stairwell finally broke the silence. He set his pencil down and listened. Her footsteps were light against the wood, followed by the faint rustle of fabric as she crossed the foyer. Standing, he walked out of the study in time to glimpse her heading into the kitchen, barefoot, hair damp from a shower. She wore a loose T-shirt that fell to her hips and faded jeans that had seen better days. He noticed that her cheeks were flushed, though whether from the heat or a lingering tension, he could not say.

She stopped at the counter and ran a hand through her damp hair. He hovered near the doorway, uncertain how to greet her. The memory of their last pointed exchange in this house still stung. Finally, he gave a short cough.

Emery turned slightly, meeting his gaze without smiling. Her eyes moved from his face down to the dusty spot on his forearm where he had brushed up against an old beam. She spoke first. "I forgot how loud this place is. All step squeaks or groans. I could barely stand it last night."

He nodded and stepped into the room. "She talks," he said, echoing a sentiment he had once shared with her years ago. "You just have to be willing to listen."

Emery scoffed softly, though the sound was not quite harsh. She glanced at the coffee pot on the far counter. By habit, he crossed to it, filled a clean mug, and offered it to her. She hesitated, then took it, her fingers brushing against his. She brought the mug to her lips, inhaling deeply before taking a small sip.

Seconds passed in weighted stillness. Then she turned and walked out to the porch as if she could no longer stay locked in the same space with him. He remained in the kitchen, ignoring the sting of her abrupt exit, and poured his own coffee.

They spent the next few hours in a careful dance. She read on the front porch, turning pages that occasionally fluttered in the breeze, while he tackled a cracked molding in the parlor. The dryness of the old wood demanded patience. He sanded methodically, the rasping sound filling the void. Silas trotted back and forth between them, head tilting as if trying to discern why his humans could not relax in the same room.

Around midday, a rumble of an engine sounded outside, followed by the crunch of tires on gravel. Xander glanced out the parlor window to see a delivery truck pulling in. This had to be the reclaimed wood siding he had ordered, a load meant for the estate's outer façade. He set his tools aside and made his way to the front door.

The truck driver hopped down from the cab, calling Xander by name. Two workers started unloading wide planks from the back. Emery lingered in the threshold, arms folded, observing with wary eyes. One of the workers, young, with a face half-hidden by a baseball cap, noticed her standing there. He grinned and nodded to the planks. "Your wife's got a good eye," he said to Xander. "Should keep her around the rest of the reno."

The comment twisted something in Xander's chest. He nearly opened his mouth to correct the man, but the tension in Emery's stance stopped him. She pressed her lips together, likely fighting back some retort of her own. Instead, she said nothing, just watched as the workers carried the load around the side of the house. When they had finished and driven away, the quiet that fell was more awkward than before. Emery left the doorway and headed inside without a word.

The afternoon hours stretched on. He found her again in the kitchen, perched in the small nook with a glass of water in hand. She stared at the worn table surface, her features pulled tight in some private debate. He slid into the seat across from her. She did not look up. Silas lay down at their feet, tail thumping once, hopeful for some sign of warmth between them.

Finally, Xander broke the silence. "What are you going to do when your dad's health takes the next turn?" He had tried to phrase it gently, but the words still felt abrupt.

Emery's eyes snapped up, fiery. "Don't." She lifted her hand in a warding gesture. "I am not discussing that with you."

He inhaled through his nose. "You should prepare yourself."

Her anger flared. "Oh, real advice from the man who spent years burying everything in wood shavings and paint cans, including me." Her breath trembled midway through that accusation. She set her glass down with a sharp click.

Xander felt the sting of guilt. His own voice faltered for a beat, but he refused to look away. "I did not bury you," he said in a low voice. "You left."

He saw the hurt flicker across her face. Emery's expression crumpled for an instant, all those defenses cracking. She pushed her chair back and stood, the wooden legs scraping across the floor. Without another word, she walked out, her bare feet shuffling down the hall. He listened to her footsteps fade. She did not slam the door behind her, but the quiet that followed felt louder than any bang could have been.

He stayed at the table, hands resting on his thighs, heartbeat thrumming. He had not intended to lash out. He wanted to approach the subject of her father carefully, bracing her for what was coming. The knowledge that she felt betrayed cut deeper than the old wounds he carried. At times, he wondered if he had done the right thing by letting her believe certain half-truths to spare her pain. Maybe he had only guaranteed that she would feel it alone.

After a long stretch of stillness, he rose. He needed space. Emery had the porch. He would take the workshop and lose himself in labor. He patted Silas distractedly as he stood and left, crossing through the foyer and out the side entrance to the carriage house. Once inside, the familiar scents of sawdust and varnish wrapped around him like a threadbare comforter. The atmosphere was calmer here, a slow pulse of solitude.

He moved to the far corner, where a locked drawer sat at the bottom of a rickety set of shelves. From his pocket, he withdrew a small key, slipped it into the lock, and opened the drawer to reveal a folded piece of paper addressed in scribbled ink:

Emery Westbrook.

He pinched the letter between two fingers, gently freeing it from the drawer. The edges were frayed from being handled too many times in moments of indecision. The date scrawled on the back was from two weeks after she had first driven out of this city, never looking back.

He started to read the opening line quietly, though hearing his own voice in the solemn space made him feel strange.

You think I betrayed you, but what you saw was me trying to protect you from the truth.

The memory of that day churned up a tightness in his chest. He remembered writing those words in the caretaker's cottage, fury battling heartbreak as he poured everything onto paper. At the time, he had almost mailed it. Almost. But he never did, and it had sat here since, aging alongside his regrets. He pressed his palm to the letter, the gentle brush of paper against his skin reminding him that words never sent could still carry a terrible weight.

He folded it again, smoothing down the creases. For a moment, he considered giving it to her now, letting Emery see what he had tried so hard to say back then. Yet something froze him. The house still felt caught in a web of half-finished confessions, and he was not entirely certain she was ready to hear what he had scrawled in desperation. If he handed her this letter, would it heal a piece of the rift or rip it wider?

Sighing, he slipped the note back into the drawer and closed it. He rubbed the back of his neck, tension throbbing in his muscles. Outside, the afternoon sun was slowly descending, sending angled beams of light through the workshop window. He could hear distant noises from the estate, the faint croak of frogs in the marsh, a door shutting in the main house. Emery might be in her room or out on the porch, or maybe she had gone off again to think.

NINE

EMERY

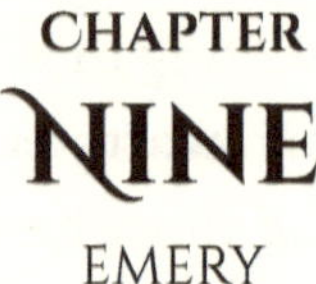

Travel Note: In Istanbul, I met a man who told me the heart never forgets its own ruins. Houses do the same. This one still carries us in its walls, even when we try not to be held.
—EW

Emery gripped the steering wheel with tense fingers, her breath ragged as she pulled away from the Westbrook estate. She did not blast music or roll down the windows. Instead, she drove through the late afternoon, nursing a fresh ache in her chest. The argument with Xander lingered in her mind, replaying in snatches of harsh words and half-silences. She had walked out because she needed distance, needed to remember that she still had a choice to stay or leave. That choice felt thinner by the day.

She ended up on Calhoun Street without planning to go there. She only realized her location when Marion Square came into view, the open green flanked by busy roads and the stirring of weekend foot traffic. Tourists ambled about with shopping bags from local boutiques. A few locals dozed on blankets on the lawn, children darting around in a game of chase. The normalcy of the scene clashed with the hollow feeling in her ribs. She found a narrow parking spot, slid in skillfully, then killed the engine.

"You left," Xander had told her. Just two clipped words that sank like stones in her heart. She hated how they convicted her. She hated how the truth in them left no room for her anger. Because she had left, and she had not looked back until her father's failing health dragged her home. Now, each step she took in Charleston reminded her she was behind on every conversation, every secret, every corner of her own life.

She walked onto the sidewalks bordering Marion Square, letting the humid breeze brush her cheeks. Merchants were packing up a small farmers' market along one side. She caught the smell of kettle corn drifting through the air. The smell sickened her, and she pressed her knuckles to her lips. She needed quiet, so she turned down King Street, weaving past clusters of shoppers. Vibrant window displays lured passersby, but she felt no pull to browse.

Her mind tugged her back to Xander's final look before she had stormed out. He had not chased her. She could not decide if she was grateful or more furious. She told herself she wanted to be alone, but she also felt a pang of disappointment. Maybe she had hoped he would follow, prove something, anything.

Glancing up, she noticed a sign for Buxton Books, a newer bookstore that had replaced an older one she once frequented years back with Xander. Chapter Two Bookshop had been their hideaway from the Charleston heat, a place where they read poetry to each other, sometimes stealing kisses in dusty aisles. The memory tightened her throat, but she still pushed open the door.

Inside, the cool air smelled of paper and ink. Shelves stretched overhead in neat rows, with carefully arranged displays of local authors near the entrance. A tall, wiry man behind the counter greeted her, his eyes crinkling in recognition of a potential customer, but not in recognition of her as a person. Emery paused, uncertain if she should say anything.

He turned his gaze to the computer screen, then back at her, polite but disinterested. His nametag read Elroy Muckinfuss. She remembered him from the old Chapter Two Bookshop. The lines around his mouth were deeper now, and his hair had gone almost completely white. Once, he had teased teenage Emery and Xander about hogging the best reading nook in the back corner. He had known their names. Today, he did not even blink as she wandered by. She considered reintroducing herself, but the words never rose to her lips.

She drifted toward a poetry section near the back. Soft music played overhead, a soothing acoustic guitar piece that felt at odds with the knot in her chest. Her hand grazed the spines of assorted collections until she landed on a volume of Mary Oliver. She pulled it free, turning to a random page. A poem about letting go filled her vision.

Phrases about release and acceptance leaped at her, so poignant they made her eyes sting.

She closed the book, hugging it to her chest for a moment. No. She was not ready to face those words, not in a place where she felt so raw. She placed it back on the shelf, ignoring the pang of regret that followed. Here she was, unable to commit even to a poem.

She turned, then left the store without a glance at Elroy. It hurt more than she expected that he had not recognized her. It was as though her old life had been overwritten by newer memories, and only she remained stuck, trying to piece it all back together.

She stepped onto King Street, feeling restless. She headed south, drawn by an old habit: when in doubt, walk to The Battery. It was several blocks away, but the trek cleared her mind. She passed centuries-old churches, small art galleries with evening lights just coming on, and the occasional carriage horse clomping by. The echo of hooves on cobblestone grounded her. The city felt eternal, as if it never cared who left and returned. That indifference comforted and hurt her at the same time.

Finally, she reached The Battery. Stately mansions lined the waterfront, their pastel colors muted by the dusk. Emery made her way to a long bench facing the harbor, where she had spent countless afternoons scribbling in her teenage journals. The water rolled gently against the stone barrier, lapping in a steady rhythm that used to soothe her. She sat on the bench and leaned forward with her elbows on her knees, her nose filled with the brine of the harbor.

A young couple stood a few feet away, locked in an argument that Emery could distantly overhear. Their words rose and fell, tinged with exasperation. Yet their hands still clung together, knuckles white. A memory stirred in Emery's chest. How many times had she and Xander argued but then still ended up pressed heart to heart, determined not to lose each other? She winced and looked away, missing that urgency. Missing him, even though she had spent years pretending otherwise.

The sky had turned a deep violet by the time she rose from the bench. She walked back to her car and felt a dull ache behind her eyes. Instead of lengthy introspection, she let her body move on autopilot and guided the car back across the peninsula toward the estate. The sun had fully set by the time she arrived, headlights sweeping across the yard. Her nerves bristled as she parked, unsure if Xander was still inside or out in the workshop.

She stepped through the front door into darkness and turned on the nearest lamp. The house greeted her with a warm hello. Yet something felt off. The air in the parlor carried an odd tension, as if someone had only just left. Her gaze swept the room until she noticed a framed photograph had been moved, tilted at an awkward angle against the wall.

Curious, she stepped closer and smoothed her hand across the top of the antique side table. She reached for the frame and adjusted it carefully but then glimpsed an envelope's corner sticking out from the drawer. Her heart pounded as she tugged it free and held it in the lamplight.

Her breath caught in her throat when she saw her name on the front.

Emery Westbrook.

She recognized Xander's handwriting immediately, those firm, slanted letters. Her heartbeat quickened. The envelope was opened. Dread tangled with curiosity, and she almost tore it open on the spot. But something in her recoiled. Not here, not standing in the parlor with shaky hands and a swirl of confusion. She slid the letter into her pocket and pressed her palm over it, as though that simple weight might keep her grounded.

The rest of the night passed in slow motion. She managed a shower, changed into loose pants and a worn T-shirt, but her mind would not quiet. Finally, she wandered downstairs again, drawn by the quiet of the house. Barefoot, she let her fingers trail along the banister, the wood's grain warmed by countless family hands over the years. She imagined how many times her mother and father might have snuck down these steps at night and remembered how she and Laura used to race up and down, skipping two steps at a time until Margot's reprimand stopped them.

She stepped into the dining room. The overhead fixture was off, leaving only the faint glow of a small lamp near the hutch. She pulled a bottle of wine from the cabinet and ignored the way her hand trembled as she poured a glass. The first sip tasted too sour, but she drank anyway.

At the table, she opened her journal. Her pen hovered above the page. The weight of Xander's envelope in her pocket tugged at her thoughts, but she needed to articulate her anger before she read anything else he had to say. Words came out stumbling at first, then cascaded into a quiet avalanche as she wrote.

I don't know if I'm mad at him for not fighting for me, or mad at myself for making it so easy to walk away.

She set the pen aside, rubbed her eyes, and let out a shaky breath. After a long moment, she reached into her pocket. She held the envelope, the paper crisp and cool against her palm, the edges faintly frayed. Slowly, she slid her finger beneath the seal and tore it open, releasing a quiet rasp that made her heart pound harder.

A folded letter fell into her lap, pages of Xander's handwriting. The ink looked old, the paper worn. She read the date at the top. It was two weeks after Margot's funeral. The lines revealed themselves, messy and rushed.

Em,

I do not know if you will ever read this. I wanted to mail it, but I am terrified of what telling you will do. Still, I cannot let you believe a lie.

Your mother did not die of cancer. She was unraveling for months, drinking, taking pills, losing herself. Laura and I wanted to protect you in those last days. You had already fought with

Margot, and we feared how you would blame your-self if you knew.

I see now we might have done more harm by hiding it. She overdosed the night after your argument. She had been so fragile for so long, but she tried to spare you from seeing her at her worst.

We never meant to betray you, only to keep you from believing you caused her death. Please try to understand, she loved you. We all did.

She skimmed the rest of the letter, learning how Margot had overdosed after months of despair and how Xander and Laura hid the truth so she wouldn't shoulder the blame. He ended with a plea for forgiveness, insisting he had never betrayed her:

I do not expect forgiveness. I only want you to know that you were not the reason she fell apart. Whatever you think you saw when you left, me with Laura, was never about a betrayal of you. It was about how to keep you from carrying a burden you did not deserve. I wish I could tell you this face to face. I wish you would come back. Take care of yourself. Xander

Her tears fell faster, soaking the letter's edges. Her hand trembled around the paper as she pressed it to her chest. A sob tore from her throat, and she pressed her free hand over her mouth, unwilling to let the sound echo in the large, silent room. This was the truth. This was worse than she ever imagined. If Margot had overdosed, what might Emery have done differently if she had known? Her pulse pounded in her ears, and words jumbled in her head, cruelty, kindness, betrayal, love. She felt them all at once, each a splash of color on a canvas she never chose to paint.

Finally, she pushed the journal and wine aside, rising from the table. The letter remained clutched in her hand. She padded upstairs, every step echoing on the hardwood floors. In her bedroom, she turned on the small lamp, then paused in front of the mirror. Her tear-streaked reflection stared back, eyes dark and anguished. The letter in her grip felt like the anchor to a new reality she had refused to see. She set it on the nightstand only long enough to slip beneath the blankets.

She took it back into her hands, letting the duvet drape over her, the edges drawn up to shield half her face. The clock ticked softly on the dresser. She doubted she would sleep, not with her heart pounding. Yet she breathed in the scent of fresh linen and tried to remember she was alive, that she was here. This was different from the ghosts that had trailed her for so long in distant cities. Now she had tangible proof that everything she believed might have been an illusion, and that truth could be both horrifying and redemptive.

She curled onto her side, letter pressed to her heart. Tears leaked onto the pillow, but she did not wipe them away. The darkness began to wrap the room, slow and indifferent. Emery let her eyes drift shut, though her mind refused to quiet. She understood something in that moment, she had come home, and this time, she could not just leave. The estate's walls, her mother's memory, Xander's confession, they demanded her presence.

She would not run tonight. She could not.

Tomorrow would bring a thousand questions she was not prepared to answer, but for now, she only had one certainty, she was not back in Charleston out of mere obligation or fleeting guilt. She was here, fully, heartbreak and all. And maybe that was a start.

TEN

XANDER

Travel Note: In New Zealand, I learned to climb mountains by taking one step at a time. Forgiveness is like that too. One word. One breath. One truth after another.
    —EW

Xander Langley rose before dawn. Pale light edged the horizon, and he could barely see through the low fog hovering around the marsh. He had spent most of the night chasing sleep, failing whenever the memory of Emery's expression cut through his attempts at rest. She had come back looking haunted, almost hollow. And then he had found his old letter crumpled on the sideboard, next to her half-empty wine glass. It had taken him a good thirty seconds to admit she had actually read it. She knew. After years of her not knowing, she finally knew.

He moved quietly through the house's ground floor, flipping on the single lamp in the foyer. The estate's quiet reminded him of a theater before a show, all that tension in the air. Silas padded over and nosed at him. Xander gave the dog a small pat on the head, offering the only comfort he felt capable of giving this morning.

He noticed the wine glass. A faint ring of dried red left an oval shape on the wood. The letter was no longer there. She must have taken it to her room. He imagined her reading it in the dim light, breath catching at all the words he had never found the courage to tell her in person. A pang of regret pulled at him. Perhaps he should have told her everything sooner, but he had convinced himself that staying silent would be a kindness.

He stepped outside onto the veranda. Fog curled across the yard, giving the porch pillars a spectral feel. He breathed in the damp air and traced the shape of the porch swing with his gaze. It swayed slightly, rope creaking in the half-dark. It conjured a vision of Emery from when they were both far younger. Her legs tucked up beneath her, sketchpad balanced precariously, calling out to him whenever she needed to show him something she had drawn. He closed his eyes against the sting of that memory.

Instead of wallowing, he walked the perimeter of the property to check for storm damage. The last storm's wind and drizzle had battered the old oak branches. One particularly large limb had snapped near the caretaker's cottage. Xander broke it up into manageable pieces, ignoring the way splinters bit at his palms. At last, the sun began to rise, staining the sky with a fragile pink, and he turned back toward the main house. He thought he should check the old electrical wiring. The last thing he needed was Emery dealing with flickering lights after that letter.

He forced himself to eat a simple breakfast, though the eggs tasted like cardboard and the coffee was too bitter. Then he gathered his tools and headed to the west hallway to continue sanding down the baseboards. The estate was in perpetual need of careful attention, especially in these older hallways where paint had cracked to the point of flaking onto the floors. The day's tasks felt like his only anchor. Measure, sand, repair. It kept him from spinning off into the thoughts that threatened to consume him.

He yanked on the sandpaper with more force than needed. Each scrape became an outlet for the tension in his chest. Ridiculous as it was, he found himself replaying the moment he had written that old letter to Emery. The scribbled lines about Margot's true cause of death, his reasons for not telling her right away, his fear that the knowledge might crush her. He felt anger at himself, at the house, at time itself for not giving him a chance to set things right back then.

He jammed the sandpaper into a rough spot. His grip slipped and a hidden nail snagged the flesh of his palm. He hissed, drawing his hand back. Blood welled instantly, rolling down his wrist. He muttered a curse and grabbed a rag from the nearby toolbox, pressing it against the wound to stanch the flow. But it kept seeping through.

"You are bleeding," a voice said from behind him. He startled, turning to see Emery leaning in the doorway, her dark hair pulled away from her face with a plain elastic tie. Her expression was guarded, but her eyes reflected concern. Without waiting for his reply, she ducked into the adjacent powder room and returned with a wet towel. "Let me see."

He opened his mouth to protest, but she closed the distance between them. Her fingers slid around his hand, and the gentle pressure of her touch sent a confusing rush through him, part warmth, part pain. She dabbed the towel along the cut, making small, precise movements that stung even as they soothed.

Her closeness made him aware of every breath. He could smell the faint trace of her shampoo. He watched the way her lashes moved down when she focused on the cut. He wanted to apologize for the letter or for his silence or for everything that had happened. But he could not settle on the right words.

"You could have told me," she said softly, eyes still on his hand. "Back then. When things first fell apart. You should have told me the truth about my mother."

Her accusation hung between them. He drew in a ragged breath. His voice sounded rough when he finally managed to speak. "I was trying to make it easier for you. I thought if you believed it was just cancer, you would move on. But I made the assumption that I had the right to shape your grief. After reading your face yesterday, I realize how much harm that caused."

She dabbed away the last of the blood, then returned to the powder room to rinse the towel. He braced his good hand on the edge of the baseboard, dizzy with the weight of years compressed into this moment.

Setting the towel aside, she retrieved gauze and an Ace bandage from her pocket. She must have brought supplies just in case. She wrapped it around his hand, each pass of the gauze a clear sign of how intimate it felt to be cared for by the person he once believed might never forgive him. When she finished, she pressed her palm gently over the bandage and met his eyes. "Yes. It did mess things up."

He inhaled slowly, his chest tight as though bracing for a blow. "I know," he said. "If I could roll back time, I would do it differently. But the day your mother died, everything was chaos. You had driven off. Laura was crying. Your father begged me to keep the details quiet so no one would blame Margot. Then he told me to let you have your space, he assumed you would come back on your own terms." He paused, the memory of David's pained, urgent face flashing in his mind. "I should have gone after you anyway. I wanted to."

Emery's gaze flickered, a storm of emotion crossing her expression. She pressed a hand to her collarbone before answering. "It is not all on you, anyway. The day before her death, I said horrible things to her about my supposed father, and that maybe she was too promiscuous to even know who he was. I lost my temper, hammered her with accusations that I barely understood. I did not realize how fragile she was. And then I walked out." Her voice broke. "She was gone before I could say sorry."

He let out a shaky breath. He had not realized the full

scope of the cruelty she had hurled at Margot. "You did not know how bad things were for her. None of us did. If you had been given the entire truth, maybe you would have handled it differently. But we hid so much to protect you. We were wrong."

Her eyes looked down to his bandaged hand. "I have been wondering what I would have done if I had not left. If you or Laura had told me she was overdosing on pills. If my father had told me she was living on a tightrope of medication and depression. I might have fought for her. Instead, I believed it was something unstoppable like cancer. I did not see the nightly drinks, the prescription bottles. And you let me walk away thinking you had betrayed me with Laura."

"I let you think I hurt you because the truth was worse," he said quietly. "It was easier for me to be the villain than for you to face the guilt that your mother's final day was shaped by that argument. I hated seeing how you already blamed yourself for so many things."

His words hovered in the silence. She stared at him, her lips parted in an unspoken reply. Outside, the floorboards creaked under Silas's paws. The dog trotted over and lay down, placing his muzzle on Xander's ankle. The gesture of comfort from Silas felt like an echo of what neither human could articulate.

Emery's voice trembled as she asked, "Then why not send me that letter? The one I found?"

He looked away, every inch of him raw. "I wrote it in a frenzy of guilt after you had left the funeral. I tried to explain everything, your mother's fragility, how Laura and

I were trying to keep you from another layer of sorrow. But I never mailed it because I realized it could break you all over again. And I was not sure I had the right to do that from such a distance."

She exhaled, wiping at an escaped tear before it could slide down her cheek. Then she sank to the floor, leaning her back against the wall. He moved over beside her, careful to keep a small space between them. They sat there, the sound in the hallway broken only by the faint hum of the old air conditioner as it started. Sunlight glinted through a high window, illuminating dust motes spinning in the air. For a moment, Xander wondered if this single shard of morning peace could be their first step toward bridging seven years of heartbreak.

Emery turned her head, regarding him with a solemn gaze. "I thought you had broken me," she said softly. "I convinced myself that whatever I saw after the funeral, whatever you and Laura whispered about, proved I could never trust anyone again."

He closed his eyes against the memory. "There was a time I wanted to chase you down that day and beg you to see reason. But your father told me to let you go. He said you needed time. Then everything spiraled, and I convinced myself that leaving you with a simpler story, one of anger or betrayal, would be kinder than the messy truth."

She nodded slowly, not looking away. "It has not felt very kind."

His voice caught. "I see that now. I am sorry. More than I know how to say."

They stayed there in silence for a span of heartbeats, neither of them moving. Her presence felt like a storm about to break. He noticed her lower lip trembling, but she held it together, turning her face toward the far side of the hallway so he would not see more tears.

Eventually, she braced a hand on the floor and pushed herself up. He followed suit, though more stiffly because his knees felt locked from sitting so tensely. She searched his face. "I am going walking, somewhere I can breathe." There was a quiver in her voice, but also a quiet resolve.

He wished he could ask her to stay, to keep talking until everything was sorted out. But Emery needed space. He recognized that in the set of her shoulders. So, he leaned back and said, "All right."

She left, paused at the threshold, and then glanced over her shoulder. "By the way, you did not break me, Xander. I did that on my own a long time ago." Her words might have held bitterness, but her tone was gentle, as if letting him know she no longer saw him as the villain.

The instant she was gone, the hallway felt empty. Silas sighed and shifted, nails clicking on the hardwood. Xander touched the bandage around his palm and grimaced at the sting. Confession had not lessened that pain, but it had lifted something heavier inside his chest. He wanted to believe that, despite all the wounds, he and Emery might both find a way to heal.

He cleaned up the trail of sandpaper dust, reapplied a bit of pressure to the cut to ensure it would not bleed through, then headed outside. The workshop behind the house beckoned, his usual sanctuary. It smelled of sawdust and old varnish. This morning, it felt less like a prison and more like an invitation. All those times he had hidden here, drowning in guilt. Maybe today he could craft something out of hope.

A new piece of lumber leaned against the wall, untouched. A project for the front door that had been delayed by his own reluctance to face certain truths. He settled it across the workbench and ran his fingers over its grain. The surface was smooth, unscarred. A fresh start, in a way.

He reached for the chisel, ignoring the throb in his injured hand. One careful cut, then another, shaping the wood with slow, deliberate motions. His muscles knew this rhythm. He had used it for years, smoothing edges, refining corners, coaxing beauty from something raw and unfinished.

The difference today was the calm in his heartbeat. His thoughts were not solely about regrets or the fear of hurting Emery further. Instead, he pictured her leaning down to bandage his hand. He recalled the tremor in her voice that told him he was not the only one shaking under the burden of old secrets. He wanted to hold on to that shared vulnerability and see where it might lead.

He continued carving, letting the blade peel thin curls from the plank. Outside, the sun climbed, gilding the windows. A breeze drifted through the open door of the workshop, carrying the sounds of morning birds and distant traffic on the country road. Every now and then, Silas peered in, curious, then snuffled away, leaving Xander to his labor.

For the first time, Xander let the wood shape itself beneath his hands without that angry push to bury his mistakes under layers of sawdust. This would not be a punishment or a distraction. He wanted to create something that reflected the possibility of what came next. The letter had been read, the words finally spilled. Maybe that was step one of a steep climb. He felt that truth in every slow, measured motion of his chisel.

He set aside the tool and brushed off a scattering of wood flakes. Sunlight fell across his shoulders, a gentle warmth that reminded him of the first time he saw Emery's smile in that same bright glow so many years ago. A flutter of longing passed through him, but it did not feel as lonely as before. If they could keep talking, keep telling each other the parts they had kept hidden, maybe they could find a way forward.

He picked up the chisel again, resting the sharp edge against the plank. His heart drummed with quiet conviction. Each new cut promised to shape something meaningful, the same way honesty might carve a path between him and Emery. In that moment, he understood that healing was not a single choice or conversation. Healing required a deliberate act of rebuilding, one splinter at a time.

He cut into the wood, steady and sure, thinking of her last words. You did not break me. Maybe that meant they had a chance to mend what had been broken. He pressed the chisel forward, working carefully. The timber gave under his touch, revealing a graceful curve he had not even planned.

The motion sent a wave of relief through him, a wordless sense of acceptance that replaced the guilt he had carried for far too long. His gaze followed the curve, imagining the possibilities for the front door design. Possibilities. That was a good word for the day.

He exhaled and started carving again. For the first time in years, the work felt like healing instead of punishment.

CHAPTER

ELEVEN

EMERY

Travel Note: Lisbon taught me that sisters are both mirror and storm. You love them, you lose them, and if you are lucky, you find them again before the tide rolls out.
  —EW

Emery left the estate on foot just after sunrise, carrying nothing but her phone in one hand. She slipped the earbuds in but refused to play any music. Letting her mind run too wild might overwhelm her, and music could shift her mood in ways she did not want. Silence felt safer than any melody. She let the breeze and the chirp of cicadas become her only soundtrack.

At first, her legs moved tentatively along the pebbled drive leading away from the Westbrook estate. The crunch of gravel under her boots added to the early morning sounds. She tried not to think about the letter she had found or any of the tension she felt inside that house. Instead, she breathed in the salt-edged air of the

Lowcountry. The marsh was just beyond the bend, hazy with lingering morning mist, but she kept her gaze forward, aimed at the road ahead.

After a few minutes, her lungs settled into a patient rhythm. Each breath came more naturally, and soon she realized she was passing the old iron gate at the edge of a property that once belonged to a neighbor. She vaguely remembered childhood games of hide-and-seek there, her sister's laughter echoing. Today, even that faint recollection felt slightly out of place, like a postcard from another lifetime. A wave of nostalgia fluttered in her chest, but she did not slow.

She kept walking, turning onto a back lane that stretched past moss-hung oaks. They stood tall as guardians, flanking the path with silent grandeur. The lull beneath them felt thicker, like the world waited for her to acknowledge something she had been ignoring far too long. She refused to linger.

Her route wandered as she traveled through the quiet outskirts near the estate, a meandering loop of winding streets she had not visited since before her mother's funeral. House after house slept behind drooping willow branches and low stone walls. White picket fences gleamed in the dawn. A few yard sprinklers whirred, releasing arcs of water that sparkled in the early light. She trudged on, letting the blurred edges of her old life seep into her peripheral vision.

After half an hour, she came upon a wide gate of evenly spaced stone pillars, each topped by a carved crest she recognized instantly. This was the private school she and Laura had attended as girls, a place she had not thought about in years. The gate was still locked, as school was not yet in session for the day, and the campus beyond looked calm and almost eerie in its emptiness.

Emery stopped under a tree whose branches dripped with Spanish moss. A memory flickered: she and Laura, both in matching uniforms, once racing each other through the courtyard. She remembered the sweaty grip of her sister's hand, both giggling as they tried not to get caught by a teacher. Another memory threatened to bubble up, something about a detention slip, a scolding, and the secret way Laura had taken the blame for Emery. She inhaled sharply. The memory stung more than she expected. Laura. For so long, Emery had assumed the worst of her sister, yet these little recollections whispered a different story.

She shook her head and turned away, continuing along the sidewalk. The quiet in her ears deepened, blocking out every urge to dwell on the estate or on Xander's face when she had last seen him. Instead, she focused on her feet. One step. Then another. The day felt weighted with unspoken truths, and she was not sure if she was ready for them. Still, her muscles insisted she keep moving.

The next familiar place that called to her was a corner market. It was small, painted pale yellow and perched at the intersection of two narrow roads. A faded sign hung above the door, the letters chipped. She remembered standing there as a kid, watching her mother step inside to buy fresh okra and local produce every Saturday before noon. Margot always seemed so determined in her errands, tackling them with the same quiet fervor she poured into her writing. Emery could almost taste the memory of fried okra, tangy and salted, the kind her mother made on lazy weekend afternoons. The recollection made her stomach clench with longing and regret, but she did not go inside. She glanced at the sign a moment longer, then kept walking.

The sun was climbing higher now, painting each sidewalk crack in a sharper light. She tugged out her earbuds, pocketing them. Morning crickets had yielded to the subtle hum of the neighborhood waking up. A car rolled by, tires rumbling. Somewhere, a dog barked. She continued on, weaving past manicured yards and half-empty driveways. This was Charleston's quiet side, removed from the bustle of downtown, but still touched by the sticky warmth of late summer.

Eventually, the road curved back toward the large swath of land behind the estate. The family cemetery lay within that walled perimeter, a place Emery had intentionally avoided for years. Her pace slowed as she glimpsed the short brick boundary that circled the graves. Moss traced the mortar lines, the bricks slightly uneven from decades of heat and rainfall. The entrance gate, wrought iron with an ornate "W" at its center, swung open with the slightest push. She stared at the rusted latch for a few seconds, heart thrumming in her chest. Memories of her mother's funeral hovered at the edge of her awareness, the tears she had tried to control. She almost turned around. But this time, she did not. Gently, she stepped inside.

The cemetery was still, more than any she had felt on her walk so far. Old gravestones, some leaning, dotted the enclosure with the dignity of history. Several graves belonged to relatives Emery had never met, names etched in fading script. Her gaze wandered until it landed on one headstone that looked too new for this place, Margot Ellison Westbrook. She closed her eyes a moment, breath trembling as she moved closer.

Margot's name glistened in the soft light, the letters carved with care. Beneath the name was a single engraved magnolia blossom. Emery knew her mother had always adored magnolias, collecting their porcelain figurines, painting them in watercolors. A small bouquet rested in the tarnished metal holder attached near the base. The blooms were fairly recent, their petals only beginning to wilt. Emery guessed Laura had placed them there because Emery herself had never braved this place until now.

She knelt, the grass slightly damp against her jeans. For a while, she could not speak. Her mind whirled with every jumbled thought. She curled her hand through the grass, finally pressing her palm flat against the earth. It felt impossibly firm yet heartbreakingly fragile, like every-thing else in this world.

"I wish you'd told me," she whispered. Her voice quavered, swallowing her words as soon as they left her lips. She sat as still as stone, letting the moment wash back and forth. Her next sentences tumbled out in a rush. "I wish you'd said something about the pills, about your struggles. I wish you'd explained more about everything, this house, who my father was or is." She released a shaky exhale. "I spent so long hating you for leaving and then hating myself because I left too."

Her tears began a slow trickle. She felt them warm against her cheeks. Instead of wiping them away, she let them stay. She pictured Margot the last time they spoke, Margot's voice strained, her eyes holding both love and anger. Emery had been so caught up in her own hurt that she never considered the weight her mother carried. Now, kneeling at the grave, she realized how many questions she had never asked her mother, how many truths she might never fully understand.

"I swear, I can still hear you at night," Emery said. She turned her gaze to the engraved magnolia on the stone. "Sometimes, in dreams, I hear you calling my name." Her throat tightened. "They told me you had cancer, that it took you fast. I accepted that lie because it was easier, because I was too proud to question it. Then I left and never came back until well, until I had no choice."

She paused, letting the air settle. Her heart pounded, but she swallowed and forced herself to continue. "I found the letter, the one Xander wrote after your funeral. He told me the truth about how you died. I hated him for so long, but maybe I hate myself more, because I might have helped you. Maybe I would have stayed if I had known."

Her tears started coming faster now. The first sob surprised her, a raw sound that echoed in the quiet grave-yard. She pressed a fist to her mouth, trying to stifle it, but her body shook under the weight of old grief. She remembered her mother's laughter, sweet and fleeting, the way she smelled of jasmine perfume, the gentle hum of her lullabies when Emery was little. All of that ended here in this ground. Yet Emery felt it coursing through her, a bittersweet current she could not escape.

After several minutes, her sobs subsided to trembling breaths. She brushed her fingers along the carved granite, tracing the letters of Margot's name. "I still feel there is another story too. One about my father. My real father. Were you always planning to tell me, or did you hope I would never learn?"

Neither the headstone nor the breeze answered. A crow cawed somewhere overhead but flew away, as if fearful of intruding on a private confession. Emery stayed there a while, tears drying on her cheeks, letting the silence stretch until she felt calmer, drained. She stood unsteadily, knees stiff from kneeling so long.

"Goodbye," she whispered. Then, more quietly, "for now."

She closed the cemetery gate behind her, leaving that pocket of heartbreak behind. Her feet felt heavy as she walked back, the morning sunlight now bright and unblinking. By the time she returned to the estate's main approach, the day was truly awake. She could have gone inside, maybe faced Xander or rummaged through more of her mother's things. But her courage was spent. She needed a gentler space this evening, so she got in her car and drove to Callie's bungalow instead.

Callie's house glowed with that same unfiltered warmth Emery depended on. The jam prints of small, sticky toddler hands still smudged the storm door. A few tiny trucks and cars littered the front walkway, relics of the children's earlier play. The interior smelled faintly of melted butter and laundry detergent, a perfectly imperfect fragrance that Emery found comforting. She only nodded at her cousin, who seemed to recognize at once that something had changed in Emery's eyes. Without a single question, Callie pressed a glass of wine into Emery's hand and stood aside, letting Emery choose her own pace.

The kids were already asleep. Their quiet breathing drifted from a half-open door down the hall. Callie led Emery out to the back deck, where soft golden string lights glowed overhead. Cicadas droned in the shadows, and the air clung with sticky summer humidity. Emery sank into a wooden chair and wrapped a cotton blanket around her shoulders. She felt unsteady, as if the day's revelations had loosened something in her chest she normally kept locked behind walls.

Callie quietly dragged another chair close and sat, resting her elbow on the deck railing. The glass of wine in Emery's hand felt cold at first but warmed quickly in the thick air. She tasted it, a crisp white with a faint floral note. Then she stared at the swirl of it in the glass before letting out a heavy sigh.

"I visited Mom today," she said quietly. The porch lights moved in the small breeze. Callie said nothing, only gave a small nod, inviting Emery to continue. "I have not gone back there, back to her grave, since the funeral. I thought it would wreck me. And it kind of did."

Callie set her own wine aside and leaned forward. "You think it helped too?"

Emery exhaled slowly, letting her chin rest against the top of the blanket. "Yes. In a painful way. I realized how much I never asked her. And how much I am still afraid to learn."

They fell silent for a moment as nighttime birds chirped from a nearby magnolia tree. Callie placed a comforting hand on Emery's arm. "What is the biggest question you wanted to ask her?"

It took Emery a moment to find words. "I want to know if she was proud of me. If she ever looked at who I became and felt proud, not disappointed."

Callie's eyes showed sympathy. "I think she loved you as hard as she knew how. Sometimes love gets twisted with fear or secrets, but I doubt there was ever a day she was not proud of your spirit."

A tight heaviness lodged in Emery's throat, but she managed a small smile. "I have been angry for so long. Angry I did not get the truth, angry that I believed what made it easiest to leave. It is like I forgot how to be anything else."

Callie brushed a stray hair from Emery's forehead. "Try sad. Or relieved. Or even brave."

A weak laugh escaped Emery's lips. "One thing at a time."

They sipped their wine in the quiet, letting cicadas fill the space where words might have been. Callie asked no more questions. She simply offered the closeness of family, something Emery realized she needed more than she could admit. The darkness settled around them, warmer and gentler than daylight. After a while, Callie yawned and said she should check on the kids. Emery nodded, and Callie left her alone on the deck.

Emery stayed, cradling her empty glass and leaning back in the chair. The night deepened, and in the stillness, she sensed her mother's voice again, faint echoes of a lullaby sung long ago. This time, it hurt a little less to hear it in her memories.

Finally, she rose. She slipped into the guest room, rummaged in her bag until she found her journal. Its cover felt worn under her fingertips. The pages were crinkled from the humidity. She swore she could smell the faint trace of old coffee on its edges, a reminder of the many cafés she had visited around the world while writing notes about foreign places. Now her words felt different, more urgent, more personal.

Sitting cross-legged on the borrowed bed, she turned to a fresh page. She stared at it, debating whether to pour every emotion onto the paper or keep it short. Her pen hovered, and then she began.

Tell Dad I am sorry.

She stared at those words for a long moment, thinking of all the ways she had disappointed him, all the times she let him bear burdens alone. Then she moved to the next line.

Tell Laura I am listening.

She recalled the old private school gate, the memory of laughter, and the recent arguments overshadowed by confusion. Perhaps she owed Laura more understanding than final judgment, more open ears than accusations. Rain trickled against the window, so subtle she barely noticed at first. The quiet patter matched her heartbeat.

Inhaling, she wrote the third line.

Ask Xander if we can start again.

Her pulse fluttered. The pen slipped a bit, leaving a faint smudge of ink. Warmth coiled in her cheeks as she remembered the look in his eyes any time they spoke, both of them dancing around old hurt and new hope. She set the pen down and read the three lines again.

They glowed on the page with a kind of promise and a trembling uncertainty. But she felt the slightest trace of strength as she saw them in writing. She circled the last one. Twice.

CHAPTER

TWELVE

XANDER

Travel Note: On a solo trip to Patagonia, I realized survival is not about bravado. It is about not quitting. Grief is the same. You hike through it. You do not conquer it. You carry it forward.

—EW

Xander woke before the sun had fully risen, aware of an unsettling quiet that saturated the Westbrook estate. For several seconds, he stayed in bed, perched on the edge of his mattress in the caretaker's cottage. The usual morning sounds, birds chirping, the soft clang of cupboard doors in the distant kitchen, were absent. Even Silas, curled at the foot of the bed, lifted his head as though to confirm that the house beyond them remained still.

Xander stood and pulled on a faded gray T-shirt and jeans stiff from yesterday's work. As he stepped into the crisp air, he noticed the quiet inside the main house. No sign of Emery's voice drifting from the kitchen, no echo of her phone chiming. The hollowness gnawed at him. Over the last few days, he had grown used to her presence, even if they hardly spoke at times. Having her around at dawn had become a comfort he never imagined he would crave again.

He found a half cup of coffee left in the pot, still lukewarm. He drank it in a few gulps and headed outside to gather the supplies he had placed near the porch the night before: a can of deep-brown stain, a stack of sandpaper, a couple of clean rags. The porch rails still showed the patchy color where the old varnish had peeled. He intended to make them shine again. It was a modest project, but one he could finish before the summer's heavy humidity set in.

Silas padded behind him as he crossed toward the front porch. The boards creaked under Xander's weight, and he set down the stain bucket on a flattened cardboard box. The air smelled faintly of salt from the marsh, tinged with sweetgrass stirring in a light breeze. He could not see far into the distance because of the morning haze, but he sensed Shem Creek just beyond the oaks. Whenever he caught a glimpse of that water, he remembered being a teenager, thinking the creek was the edge of his world. Realizing later that Emery had become that edge, in every sense that mattered.

He wetted a paintbrush with the stain and applied it methodically, brushing along the wooden spindles of the railing. The repetition soothed him and sharpened his focus. He hummed a low tune, a habit he had developed as a child when he had no one to talk to in his father's quiet garage. Margot had once teased him about that hum, calling it his "work song." He still remembered how proud she had looked when he first installed a new screen door on the estate years ago. It stung to think how fragile that quiet pride had turned out to be. He shook the memory aside and kept working.

By the time he finished the first section, pale sunlight spilled across the yard. He stepped back to gauge the color. The stain was darker than he expected but in a rich, handsome way that highlighted the porch's original craftsmanship. He brushed off a speck of dust and steadied himself, letting that sense of purpose settle in his chest. He could not quite say why he felt unsettled this morning. In the days before Emery returned, quiet had been a constant. Now, it felt unnatural.

He looked at the marsh. Thin layers of fog clung to the grasses, but beneath the haze, he caught glimmers of sunlight dancing on the water. The light shimmered in a warmer shade than usual, as if the day itself might be offering him a small forgiveness. He exhaled, not entirely sure what or whom he was forgiving. Maybe himself.

Silas lifted his head suddenly, ears alert toward the driveway. A moment later, the rumble of tires on gravel reached Xander's ears. He wiped his hands on a rag and headed down the steps. A white delivery van pulled up near the caretaker's cottage. A man wearing a ball cap climbed out and slid open the truck's side door, rummaging for a package. In seconds, Xander recognized the shape: an oblong cardboard box with the distinctive label from a local antiques dealer.

"Alexander Langley?" the delivery man called. He set the box carefully on the ground.

Xander wiped the last of the stain from his palms. "That's me. Thank you." After signing the tablet he was offered, he carried the box back onto the porch. Silas gave it a curious sniff.

Inside was the antique doorknob set Xander had special-ordered weeks ago, hammered brass with intricate scrollwork. He had grand plans to install it on one of the upstairs rooms that still had a missing latch plate. He ran his fingertips over the metal, impressed by the subtle pattern. Once installed, it would look like it was part of the house's original design.

He set it aside for a moment, remembering his last real conversation with David. The old man had seemed so fragile, propped up in that hospital bed. Yet his eyes had cut through Xander's guilt with a clarity that left no room for denial. "If she comes back, do not lie to her," David had said. "She can handle anything but falsehood." The memory coiled in Xander's gut. He wondered if he had succeeded or failed. So far, Emery knew more than she used to, but maybe there was still more to tell. He was never sure how much air to offer her before it became distance.

Around midday, he finished the porch rails and cleaned his brush. Sweat soaked the back of his shirt, and he was about to head inside for water when he spotted another car pulling up. This time, it was Callie's small

SUV. She parked crookedly and hopped out, sunglasses sliding down her nose. In one hand, she carried a brown paper bag, grease spots hinting at a still-warm sandwich inside.

Xander met her halfway. "Hey," he said, aware of his own wariness. "Everything all right?"

"She needed air," Callie said simply. She glanced toward the silent house. "And space. Thought I would drop by."

He nodded and stepped aside so she could join him on the porch. He offered her a seat on the top step, but she collapsed into one of the wicker chairs. Silas trotted over, tail thumping as soon as Callie set the bag down. She fished out a wrapped sandwich and took a bite, not offering immediate conversation. Xander sat next to her. The sun felt hotter now, beating down on the half-stained railing. He contemplated moving the paint can into the shade but decided to wait.

Callie broke the silence after a few slow bites. "She left last night. Stayed at my place? No. She never showed. She must have gone somewhere else, cleared her head." Callie shrugged.

Xander's pulse fluttered in concern, but he forced himself to keep calm. Emery was not obligated to tell him every step of her day. He glanced at Callie. "So, you haven't heard from her either?"

"She texted me after midnight, said she was fine." Callie crumpled the sandwich wrapper in her fist. "She wanted to be alone with her thoughts, I guess."

He nodded and pressed his lips together. A part of him

wanted to chase Emery down, to fix everything. Another part remembered that forcing answers from her rarely ended well. He breathed.

After a while, Callie put the remains of her lunch into the brown bag and gestured to the porch swing. "You keep waiting for her to talk first, letting her slip away. Maybe that worked in the past, but if she comes back and you're still standing around waiting for her to make the next move, that's on you." She gave him a pointed look. "Know what I mean?"

He did, though acknowledging it made his chest tighten. "Yeah," he said quietly, meeting her gaze. "I do." He could not quite form more words. The truth was, he hated playing it cautious, but he also hated the thought of pushing Emery too far. He exhaled and nodded at Callie. She must have sensed the conflict in him because she patted his shoulder in a reassuring gesture and then stood to go.

"I better check on the twins," she said. "Text me if she shows."

He followed her to her car. Silas trailed behind, hoping for a final pat. Callie bent to scratch behind Silas's ears. Then she slid into her seat and drove off, leaving Xander alone again with the quiet.

He finished cleaning up the porch around mid-afternoon and decided to install the antique doorknob set upstairs. The second-floor hallway was cooler, courtesy of a box fan near the open window at the end. He knelt at the door, removing the old latch. The wood squeaked as he carefully fitted in the new hardware. It took time to line everything up properly, but he was diligent. This was the exact kind of detail he loved. By the time the knob was fully secure, the late afternoon light slanted through the window, painting amber squares across the floor.

He stood and tested the knob. It turned smoothly, satisfying in its click. He picked up his notepad from the hallway floor and jotted a note to re check the door's alignment tomorrow. Then he scribbled other tasks he hoped to handle soon, patch a small crack in the dining room crown molding, retouch the paint in Emery's bedroom window frame, restore an old mirror he had found in the attic. A quiet sense of purpose settled over him. The more he fixed, the less the house felt haunted by old secrets.

As evening descended, he went room by room with that notepad, scrawling final instructions for the contractors who would bring in a few last shipments of molding. The house remained silent. The glimmer of nightfall reflecting off the marsh was visible through nearly every window, a reminder of the Lowcountry's shifting tides. He wondered again where Emery was.

Eventually, he climbed the stairs to the attic. The door stuck a little, but he pushed through and turned on the single overhead bulb. Dust floated in the air. The space smelled of cedar and aged cloth. He walked around a stack of old furniture and pressed a hand to the trunk labeled *Margot – Personal.* He had avoided rummaging through it for weeks, never sure what he might uncover. Tonight, his hesitation felt less like fear and more like acceptance. He opened it.

The trunk lid opened with a faint creak. Inside, he found a box tied with a ribbon. He slid it out. The handwriting across the cardboard read Margot's Letters. When he lifted the lid, time seemed to slow. There was more than one letter. Ribbon bound bundles, some addressed to David, a few to other distant relatives. One envelope on top read simply *For Emery*. The sight of her name, scrawled in Margot's handwriting, made Xander's throat tighten.

He held it carefully and fought the urge to open it himself. He knew that would only betray David's last request. He closed the box but kept the single envelope in hand and set the rest back in the trunk. A thousand questions churned through him. Whatever was written in there could change how Emery saw her mother or how she felt about the past. Yet it was not his to decide. He placed the letter gently against his side and shut the trunk.

On his way down the attic stairs, the house cracked. The front door opened, the old hinges groaning. He heard footsteps on the foyer's hardwood. His pulse jumped. He stepped off the last stair and found Emery standing by the entry table. Her dark hair was damp, as though the evening humidity had settled on every strand. She looked at him, her eyes guarded but not cold. A layer of tension lifted from the air and was replaced by something simpler, more fragile.

He lifted the envelope, unable to hide the slight tremor in his fingers. "Your mom's trunk," he said, his voice quiet. "I found this. It was addressed to you."

Emery's gaze moved to the envelope. She reached for it, pressing it to her chest so gently, it made Xander's heart twist. "Thank you," she whispered.

He wanted to ask where she had been, if she was okay, if she had found the space she needed. But her expression suggested she might already be overwhelmed. So, he swallowed his questions and offered only a nod. She clutched the letter, and for a moment, neither of them spoke. Her eyes filled with a subdued gratitude that he did not dare interrupt.

With a quiet inhale, Emery moved past him, heading upstairs. Her soft steps faded along the landing. Xander realized he was still holding his notepad, the pages blank compared with the secrets she now carried in that envelope.

He crossed the foyer, stepping out onto the porch. The newly stained railing gleamed under the porch light. It smelled faintly sweet from the care he had put in just hours ago. He lowered himself onto the porch swing, which rocked under his weight. Years ago, he had carved his initials alongside Emery's on the underside of the seat. The memory of that moment teased at him with equal parts longing and hope.

He closed his eyes, letting the slight sway of the swing ground him. The evening air was warm on his skin, and he noticed it no longer felt oppressive. In some strange way, it felt like potential. He had spent so many nights thinking he was waiting for something to end. Something about tonight suggested that wait might be over.

His hand found the chain that kept the swing secure,

and he gave it a gentle push. The floorboards creaked, Silas settled near his feet, and Xander breathed in the gathering night. He imagined Emery upstairs, envelope pressed to her heart, reading a piece of her mother's soul. He did not know what truths might come to light or how it would alter the shape of their fragile reconciliation.

Yet for the first time in years, Xander did not feel like a man waiting for something to end. He felt like something might be beginning.

CHAPTER
THIRTEEN
EMERY

Travel Note: In Kerala, I once watched women paint the walls of a temple in absolute silence. Their brushstrokes held a reverence beyond words. Every sweep of color felt like prayer. Margot's letters feel the same way to me now. They are not explanations. They are not absolutions. They are an offering of a truth she did not know how to speak.

—EW

Emery woke to early light slipping through thin curtains that stirred in the faint breeze. Even before she opened her eyes completely, she felt the presence of the sealed envelope on her nightstand. It was a silent reminder of her mother. She had not dared to break the seal the night before. She allowed herself only to hold it close to her chest, a strange comfort warming her heart as she drifted off. When she finally blinked the tension of sleep away, the first thing she saw was that folded letter perched on top of a guidebook about Morocco. The sight made her inhale sharply.

She slid up against the pillows, the old headboard groaning at her movement. Bits of dust motes danced in the morning light. In the silence of her bedroom, she realized she did not feel the usual dread or heaviness pressing down on her. Something was different. Perhaps it was the way the house sounded more alive than haunted, floors creaking softly as if to greet the sun or a faint clink of dishes downstairs. She let herself believe that the day would not crush her, that she could stand to face whatever truths lay hidden in that letter.

A burst of song from a mockingbird outside drew her to the window. She stood and stretched out the knots in her shoulders. She noticed how bright the day looked. The marsh grasses in the distance swayed, pale green bristles catching the early golden light. She breathed in gratitude for those small details. Long ago, she would have scoffed at the idea of appreciating morning birdsong, but now she found solace in it. She had been chasing an ever-moving horizon for years, always stepping onto planes or trains, leaving behind older versions of herself. This morning, in her childhood home, she felt anchored.

Still dressed in a soft tank and pajama shorts, she decided to shower. The humid Charleston air clung to her, but she was oddly thankful for the familiarity of it. She undressed and stepped into the shower. Steam from the hot water swirled and reminded her of all the places she once traveled to escape this sticky climate. After she emerged from the bathroom, she felt lighter, cleansed by more than just water, cleansed perhaps by the budding resolve to see what lay on the other side of fear.

From a cardboard box in the corner of the room, she pulled out an old sundress. It was one Callie had brought over yesterday along with some other hand-me-downs. Emery laughed quietly at her reflection in the mirror. The dress was a pale green cotton print with a bow tie at the back. She tugged at the skirt and noticed it fell just above her knees. "Southern ghost chic," she murmured, recalling her own joke. She gave a half turn and decided it might suit the day, if only because it felt like something the house would approve of, a nod to the past without being swallowed by it.

They loaded up the truck a little while later, with Silas eagerly hopping into the backseat. The old dog's tail thumped rhythmically against the upholstery. Emery carried a simple tote with sunscreen, a towel, and a note-book. Xander filled a thermos with coffee and grabbed an extra water bottle which he slid onto the back floorboard. With no further discussion, they set out for Sullivan's Island.

The radio hummed with a classic rock station that drifted in and out. Emery let her gaze wander over the passing scenery. Live oaks, tall grasses, and the occasional flash of tidal creeks welcomed them. She realized how seldom she looked at these surroundings. For so long, she had associated every inch of Lowcountry terrain with heartbreak or regret. Today, the early sun gave everything a gentle glow, as if encouraging her to see it with new eyes.

The drive to the island was not long, about twenty minutes, but it passed in a dreamy blur of wind through open windows and measured sips of coffee from a to-go thermos. Silas panted happily. Xander occasionally tapped a thumb against the steering wheel. Not a single question was asked about the letter or about her father, David. Emery felt an odd relief. She was not ready to share that she still had not opened Margot's final words. She was not sure how to put that hesitation into the right language.

By the time they parked near the dunes, the beach was still relatively empty. A few families dotted the sand, setting up umbrellas. The breeze carried the brine of saltwater, and Emery's lips curved into a small smile as soon as she stepped out of the truck. Removing her sandals, she welcomed the sand beneath her feet. They walked along the shoreline, shoes in their hands, letting gentle waves lap their ankles. Emery closed her eyes and breathed in the tang of ocean air. Gulls circled overhead, their shrill cries mingling with the sounds of the surf. Each step felt strangely new, as if she had never really slowed down enough to appreciate the softness underfoot.

At one point, she glanced at Xander's profile. Sunlight played off his tanned skin, his posture easy yet cautious. She wondered if he felt the same subdued peace she experienced, or if the shift in their connection left him uneasy. She decided to ask the question that had been pressing on her mind.

"Do you ever wonder what would have happened if I hadn't left?" Her voice was not accusatory, only curious.

He stopped walking, turning his gaze to her. The

breeze ruffled his hair, and he let a gentle breath out before replying. "Every day," he said quietly, eyes reflecting a sincerity that caught her off guard. There was no bitterness in his tone, only a steady acceptance, as though his thoughts on that matter were as natural as the tide.

Emery swallowed against an unexpected wave of emotion. She stared at him for a moment, wanting to say so many things, wanting to apologize for the unspoken accusations that once filled the space between them. But the words refused to form. Instead, she nodded. That was enough for now.

They ambled on until a small beach shack came into view, advertising fish tacos on a painted wooden sign. Her stomach growled softly. She realized she was hungry again, so they placed an order and found a spot in the sand to sit. The tarp overhead provided some shade, but the sun's warmth still reached them. They unwrapped their food, the sweet smell of grilled shrimp, spices, and lime tang permeating the air.

Emery told him about traveling through Iceland during a season of perpetual light, about wandering Moroccan souks with a mild sense of awe, about the bright neon nights of Tokyo. She found herself talking more than she intended. Perhaps the environment, open sky, rolling waves, the reliability of Xander's presence, prompted her to share. He listened intently, occasionally asking a question that showed he was fully engaged. When she admitted that no matter how far she went, she always felt Charleston tugging at her, he offered a thoughtful nod.

"I used to see your byline sometimes," he said, his voice dropping lower. He picked up a small, opalescent seashell and turned it over in his palm. "Time, National Geographic. I would buy the magazine just to read your words. I tried to imagine you there in those crowded markets or on some frozen cliffside. I was proud of you, Em. But I was also so damn lonely, knowing you were seeing the whole world while I was just seeing the ghost of you in this town."

Emery watched his fingers trace the shell's delicate whorls. His honesty was a quiet blow to the chest, dismantling the last of her defenses.

"I was lonely, too," she confessed, the admission a near-whisper. "I thought if I saw enough, I could outrun the feeling. But every city started to look the same. I think," she paused, her voice trembling slightly, "I think I was just looking for a place that felt like you."

His gaze lifted from the shell to meet hers, and in his eyes, she saw seven years of waiting condensed into a single, heart-stopping moment of recognition.

"You were always going to be bigger than this place," he said softly, wiping taco sauce from his fingers. "You had that spark to see the rest of the world." He tried to be matter of fact, but a gentle undercurrent of pride colored his words.

She took a bite of taco, then paused to wipe a bit of salsa from her chin. She would never say it out loud, but his pride in her meant more than she expected. "Maybe I am bigger in some ways," she admitted. "But Charleston is etched on my bones, like the grain of wood you can't sand away. Does that make sense?"

He smiled, a brief upturn of the lips that felt as genuine as the day itself. "It does," he replied, and she believed him.

They finished eating in companionable silence, letting the surf provide a soundtrack. After discarding their trash, they slowly made their way back to the truck. The sun's rays had grown harsher, and Emery felt its heat prickle along the back of her neck. She was grateful for the shade inside the cab.

On the drive back, she dozed off, lulled by the gentle rumble of the engine and the satisfaction of a full stomach. She dreamed of nothing in particular, only drifting in reassuring darkness. When she opened her eyes, Xander was pulling into the gravel drive of the Westbrook estate. Late afternoon light cast everything in gold. The porch columns glowed in that radiance, and the open windows hinted at calm inside.

She mumbled a soft thanks as they parked. He glanced sideways at her, that unwavering gentleness in his eyes. "You looked peaceful," he said simply. "I didn't want to wake you."

She carried her tote inside, telling Xander she needed a moment alone. He did not object. She climbed the worn staircase, each step echoing with the house's old memories, until she reached her bedroom. The curtains billowed faintly from an open window. Warm air drifted in, scented with cut grass and hints of the marsh. On the nightstand, that letter waited.

At last, the time felt right. She set her tote on the floor and perched on the edge of the bed, her heart fluttering. Margot's handwriting on the envelope felt strangely intimate, like a whisper from across years. With careful fingers, she opened it. The paper inside bore shaky script, and each letter looked penned with great effort. She read slowly, no part of her rushing.

You were never a mistake. You were always the piece of me I wanted to protect the most and the one I understood the least. One day I will tell you the full story of how you came to be. Just know that the man you have always called Daddy may not be your biological father, but he is that in every other possible way.

The words hit her like a soft gust that stole her breath. It was not truly a confession about her paternity. She had long suspected the truth, had pieced together half-forgotten conversations and glimpses of old letters. Yet seeing it spelled out in her mother's shaky handwriting opened an old wound while simultaneously soothing it. Margot had not intended to hide this forever. Perhaps she ran out of time or courage or both.

Emery pressed the letter against her lap, noticing that her hands trembled. She did not cry. A strange calm enveloped her, similar to how it feels after a passing storm. She felt a subtle release of tension. *Yes,* she thought. *I suspected. And here it is.* No more lies, even if the revelation was incomplete. Margot might never give her the full story, but she had given her something important, an acknowledgement. An affirmation that Emery's father, David, was her father in all the ways that truly mattered.

She folded the letter carefully, set it in the envelope, and rested it on the nightstand again. From outside, she heard the soft creak of the porch swing. Her heart thudded. She pictured Xander outside, Silas probably at his feet. She felt a pull to go down there. She felt torn between staying in her room to absorb the letter's impact or stepping into that incomplete but healing presence that Xander offered.

She stood at the top of the stairs, resting her hand on the banister. The late sun lit the foyer in a long rectangle of pale gold. A slight breeze rattled the screen door. The porch swing creaked again. She leaned forward to see Xander through the open space of the door's glass. He was sitting there with a book in his lap; Silas curled beside him. The dog's tail flopped lazily. Emery wondered if Xander was actually reading or just holding the book as a shield for his thoughts.

She could have gone back to her room or closed the door, letting him remain unaware of her presence. Yet she felt a gentle nudge inside her chest. Perhaps it was the voice of her mother urging her toward truth and acceptance, or perhaps it was her own voice, newly unafraid. Whatever the cause, she found her feet carrying her down the stairs.

The porch boards felt warm even through her sandals. Each step made the old wood groan softly, announcing her arrival. Xander turned his head, marking her presence with a subtle shift of his shoulders. He offered no greeting, only a slight nod. Emery settled beside him on the swing, the seat rocking with the added weight. She placed her hands in her lap, noticing how her pulse fluttered. She did not speak. Neither did he.

Instead, they listened to the syncopated chirp of cicadas rising from the garden. The quiet between them felt expansive, tender, filled with mutual understanding rather than the friction of secrets. Silas raised his head to nuzzle her knee, then let it drop again with a sigh.

Emery let out a breath she had been holding. She would eventually tell him about her mother's letter. At some point, she needed to unpack everything she felt about the truth it contained. But at that moment, she preferred the quiet comfort of simply being together, watching the sky begin to show faint streaks of color that signaled evening's approach.

The swing drifted gently. Xander rested his book on the armrest. Emery stared out at the line of moss-laden oaks in the distance, letting the day's revelations melt into a calm acceptance. She felt his presence solid beside her, a reassuring warmth.

She closed her eyes, inhaling the scent of the marsh mixed with the faint toast of leftover coffee. She knew they both had more to say, more to resolve, but for that moment, they allowed themselves to exist in silence. It was not the tension of old resentments. It was the stillness of a new bond taking shape.

She leaned her shoulder against his, barely touching but enough to feel the strength of him, enough to let her heart settle in that gentle contact. He did not pull away. As the sky turned a dusky rose, she listened to the rustle of leaves laced by the southern breeze. The entire world seemed to exhale.

No words were required. Their unspoken truths flowed through the air with each creak of the swing. Emery closed her eyes again, feeling her chest rise and fall in time with the breath of the man beside her. Right then and there, that was all she needed.

No words. Just presence. And it was enough for now.

FOURTEEN

XANDER

Travel Note: I stood at the edge of the Cliffs of Moher once and swore I would never go back to anything that broke me. But here I am at Charleston's edge, in Xander's orbit, and maybe not everything broken stays that way.

—EW

The day lingered like a breath the whole house was holding. Early evening heat pressed against the screens, and the sky glowed with a bronze tint. On the front porch, Xander settled onto the swing, his body finally relaxing after a long stretch of tension. Something close to peace had returned to this place. Around the yard, paint cans, tarps, and a scattering of woodworking tools marked the remains of the day's efforts. Beyond the estate, the marsh shimmered at low tide, glinting gold where the sun still dipped low.

Emery stepped onto the porch without a sound. He didn't look directly at her, though her presence stirred something unmistakable in the air, like the electric promise of distant lightning, beautiful and dangerous all at once. She sat beside him, careful to leave enough space that their shoulders didn't touch. They both stared ahead, their eyes tracking the lazy movement of wind through the live oaks framing the driveway.

For a while, neither of them said a word. Silas stirred from his usual spot near the porch steps and wandered over, nudging his muzzle against the man's boot before settling across both their feet. The swing rocked gently beneath their shared weight, the chains emitting a faint creak. The smell of fresh wood stain from the railing mingled with the salt-kissed air. He drew a steadying breath. Words hovered, half-thoughts about the distance that had stretched between them, memories of her laughter echoing against these very floorboards. But before he could speak, she did.

"You still read paperbacks," Emery said, nodding toward the worn novel perched on the swing's arm. He'd nearly forgotten he'd brought it out.

Relieving that she hadn't opened with pain or accusation, he picked up the book, showing her the faded, dog-eared cover. "I like the feel of a story in my hands," he said, his tone easy. "Digital ones vanish too easily."

She studied the battered spine. "I used to tease you for being old-fashioned."

He managed a small smile. "You did. And I told you there's nothing wrong with old things, so long as they still hold together."

Silas pressed his warm flank against his ankle. A

silence followed, not uncomfortable. They listened to the rustle of Spanish moss, to the quieting sounds of the day's end. A squirrel darted along the porch rail, drawing a soft laugh from Emery as it paused to eye them before disappearing into the hydrangeas.

Their conversation stayed light at first, safe, easy. She asked about a cracked tile in the foyer. He explained that the tile came from a century-old artisan batch. It gave him something to focus on besides the thrum of her nearness.

"Dad always said that staircase was a character feature," she said, her voice casual but laced with old tension. "He wouldn't let Laura or me pry up the boards to stop the creaking."

He told me the same, he replied. Said a house without a creak doesn't have enough stories.

Her smile was small, soft, and something tugged inside his chest. He wanted to reach out, tuck that stray piece of hair behind her ear, touch her hand, but kept still. His palm pressed into the swing cushion instead, grounding himself.

The quiet stretched again, only broken by the thump of Silas's tail. He thought of all the time they had spent circling each other in this house. The words they had never said. He could feel her gaze on him, weighted, intimate, and a little dangerous.

What made you stay in Charleston all these years, she asked suddenly. Her eyes dropped to her hands after she spoke, as if bracing herself.

The question hit harder than he expected. He leaned

back into the swing, letting the wood slats take his weight, studying the lengthening shadows in the yard.

Because the people I loved were here, he said at last. His voice was rougher than he intended, but he kept it steady. Even if they were not speaking to me.

She let out a breath, tinged with sadness. That sounds a lot like punishment.

It was, he admitted. But not the way you think.

She tapped the armrest, absorbing the words. A breeze drifted by, carrying the scent of jasmine. He breathed in deeply. Maybe he had stayed out of loyalty. Or guilt. Or the stubborn hope that if he tended to the house and honored her father's wishes, maybe one day she would come back.

What if I had not gotten it all so wrong, she asked softly. What if I had not run in the first place?

He knew exactly what she meant, how she had misunderstood that moment with her sister, how grief had driven her away. A thousand small things had driven the wedge deeper since.

"I don't know," he said. "Maybe it would have turned out the same. Some things don't get rewritten, no matter how much we want to."

Her arms folded, her eyes distant. The sun finally slipped beneath the trees, casting streaks of purple and orange across the horizon. The cicadas raised a louder chorus, grieving the day, maybe, or welcoming the dark.

He looked at her again. There was tension at the edges of her mouth, but something softer, too. His hand lifted, almost without thought, and brushed a strand of hair from her cheek. His fingertips grazed her temple. She didn't flinch.

They stayed that way in the dimming light, breath mingling, the moment charged. Her pulse fluttered beneath her skin. When she turned slightly, her hair slid from his hand.

"I still think about that night," she whispered. "The fight with my mom. The way it all unraveled. So many lies. So much we never said. And then she was gone."

"I remember," he said, voice tight. "All of it." His hand found hers, gentle and sure. "I always thought you would come back. So, I waited."

Their eyes met. The pull between them grew taut. She glanced down at his mouth, just for a second. It was enough.

He leaned in slowly, giving her time to move. She didn't. Their lips brushed, tentative, rediscovering. The kiss deepened for a heartbeat, and in it, he felt all the unspoken pain, all the lingering hope. Her lips trembled against his, and he tasted salt. Whether from tears or Lowcountry air, he couldn't tell.

Then she pulled back, softly, carefully.

"I'm not ready," she said. Her voice wavered, but her meaning was clear. "I want this. But not yet."

Disappointment gripped his chest, but he nodded. "It's all right," he said, rough-voiced. "We can wait."

They didn't move. She didn't leave, and he didn't speak. The air around them thickened with everything unsaid, with the memory of what had passed between them. Overhead, twilight settled into a hazy purple, the porch light coming on. From the living room, a faint glow filtered through the curtains. The house bore silent witness.

They sat for a long while. When she finally stood, she looked like she might speak again but did not. Instead, she touched Silas's head and walked back inside. The screen door creaked shut behind her.

Alone now, he let out a long breath. His heartbeat with the echo of that kiss. Nothing was fixed. Nothing promised. But something had shifted.

Silas looked up, ears flicking. The man scratched behind them. "Go on, boy," he murmured. Silas followed Emery inside.

He stayed a while longer, listening to the chirp of cicadas and watching fireflies at the edge of the lawn. The scent of blooming jasmine wrapped him like memory.

Eventually, he stood. His legs felt unsteady as he made his way inside. The foyer was quiet. A lamp glowed in the hallway, casting soft light on scuff marks he always meant to fix. Tonight, he did not mind them. They were part of the house's story too.

On the second-floor landing, he heard the faintest sound behind her door, movement maybe. He paused, torn, but remembered her words. Not yet.

So, he went on into his own makeshift room he had now moved into here in the house, across from the linen closet, where the window let in humid night air and the hum of insects. He changed clothes, every muscle reminding him of the day's labor. But his thoughts were with her, with that kiss, and the way she looked just before she pulled away.

Lying in bed, he stared at the ceiling, shadows stretching overhead in strange shapes. The silence was no longer lonely. It was full. Full of possibility.

He imagined her one hallway over, not gone, not running. He relived the moment they touched, not for what it was, but what it might still become. And as he drifted toward sleep, he held onto that small, fragile spark.

Hope.

CHAPTER

FIFTEEN

EMERY

Travel Note: The Atacama Desert is so dry, even tears evaporate. But staying here at the estate, with him, feels like rain. Maybe I am not drying out. Maybe I am growing roots.
—EW

Emery stirred in her room long before the sun cleared the horizon. The morning air pressed against her skin in a damp warmth that she could not quite identify as simple humidity. She lay flat on her bed, staring up at the slow spin of the old ceiling fan. It creaked softly with each rotation, a comforting sound that reminded her of the house's living presence. Normally, she would have pulled the sheets over her head and pretended to ignore the world, but a growing sense of purpose thrummed beneath her skin.

She let the pillow fall away and sat up. The blankets rustled around her legs, and she was keenly aware of every shift of fabric against her body. Her mind raced back to the final moments of the previous evening. The faint press of Xander's lips lingered still, though the memory lacked the punch of a grand, sweeping kiss. He had approached her gently, as if unsure whether to bridge the space between them. She had not said yes, but she had not said no either. In that moment, she had found a small piece of clarity, a fragile awareness that maybe she could want this despite her wariness.

She stood, took a breath, and walked to the window. The faint marsh light colored the horizon in milky shades of gold and gray. From her vantage, she could see the edge of the front porch roof and a soft glow below, perhaps a lamp left on somewhere. There was a time when even passing near Xander felt like setting foot on dangerous ground, but that ominous sensation was shifting into something else. Not comfort, exactly, but something braver.

She showered and dressed with methodical slowness, choosing a simple cotton shirt and jeans. Her reflection in the mirror caught her off guard. A few nights ago, tension had hardened her features. Now her eyes looked steadier, as if a barrier had been lowered. She braided her hair over one shoulder and made her way downstairs, her footsteps carefully placed on the familiar squeaking boards.

In the kitchen, she paused at the threshold when she noticed a large ledger sprawled open on the table. She recognized it as her father's old property records, a ledger David had once used to keep track of land taxes, mainte-nance costs, and every detail he deemed relevant to the estate. Emery hesitated. It was not her custom to root through his things uninvited, but the pages were beckoning, faint pencil scrawls visible in the soft morning gloom. She stepped closer and pulled her bottom lip between her teeth.

The ledger's corners were yellowed by time. She ran a finger across the edges and found entire sections marked up in two different types of handwriting: her father's strong, blocky script and the looping style of her mother. Architectural notes peppered the margins toward the back. Xander's crisp penmanship had joined the mix, describing load-bearing walls and estimated material costs.

On a certain page, her mother's handwriting reappeared, faint but unmistakable.

Retain the wood grain. Keep the sense of history.

Below it, in pencil, a single statement jolted Emery's heart.

Don't lose her. Not again.

She couldn't be sure whether her mother had written it or if David had. Possibly, it was Xander's. The shape of the words was rougher, less elegant than Margot's script, but not exactly her father's style either. Her eyes traced the letters, and she felt her pulse surge. Someone had scrawled that message as a reminder, or maybe a plea. The words leapt out like a secret left in plain sight.

Her throat tightened. She stood there for an endless

moment, wishing she knew precisely whose plea this was meant to be. Then she shut the ledger slowly, not wanting to disturb any more pages. The kitchen felt charged, and she found herself pressing her hand against the cover of the book as if to draw calm from it. If she had read those lines a few days ago, she might have scoffed or fled the room entirely. Now, the note forced her to confront a stirring truth: she had already lost parts of herself once. She wasn't sure she could bear it again.

She tore her gaze away, noticing the shapes of random items on the counter, a basket of fruit, a lonely coffee mug left to dry. Without waiting for her usual mug of coffee, she headed out the door, knowing what she had to do. Morning air rushed to greet her as she walked to her car. The light had strengthened, turning the sky a hazy blue. She allowed the curve of the driveway to guide her. She wouldn't be able to settle until she saw her father again, until she spoke openly about what none of them had dared to confront before.

The drive to the hospital passed in a blur of oaks and quiet streets. Charleston traffic was mercifully light, so it took little time to reach the familiar building. She folded her hands on the steering wheel for a moment, inhaling. A part of her feared he might not be lucid enough for a serious talk. Another part dreaded that he would be too lucid, and that speaking candidly would tear open old wounds. But she'd promised to face the truth this time, not tiptoe around it.

She found David's room easily. He was sitting upright, reading the obituaries, newspaper pages rustling between his frail fingers. The pungent smell of antiseptic lingered, underscored by a faint lemony disinfectant. Despite the sterility, she found some comfort in the corridors, maybe because it forced everyone to be sincere.

David looked up and managed a soft smile. "You're early," he remarked, setting the paper aside. "I wasn't expecting you, not before your coffee."

Emery tried to return his smile, but her lips felt stiff. "Surprise visits are good for the soul, right?" She noticed a styrofoam cup on his tray, half-filled with weak coffee. "Planning your escape route?" she teased gently, tilting her chin toward his reading material.

He chuckled, the sound loosening some of the tension in her chest. "If you're reading obituaries, you might as well call it research," he said. "But I'm not going anywhere just yet." His eyes, still alert despite his exhaustion, lingered on her face. "You look like you have something on your mind."

She took the silent invitation to approach his bedside. The chair beside him was unoccupied, so she slid onto it and gripped the armrests. "I've been meaning to talk," she said. "About everything, I guess."

The corners of David's mouth tightened, though he nodded. "Feels like we should have done that years back."

She drew a shaky breath. "I read the letter," she began, letting her words hang. "About Margot, about what really happened. Also, I got hold of your ledger this morning."

"Find anything interesting?" he asked, a wry tilt to his brow. The dryness of his tone made her heart ache. He had always used humor to soften hard truths.

"There were sketches," she managed, "and a note in the margin. Something about 'not losing her again.' I don't know who wrote it, but..." She trailed off, uncertain how to phrase her confusion, how to say that she didn't want to be lost either.

David's features softened. "Your mother jotted down all kinds of little prayers, or sometimes Xander would scribble things when he went through my notes. Maybe it was your mother, or maybe it was him."

Emery's heart rattled at the unspoken message: maybe all of them had been praying, in one way or another, that the heartbreak wouldn't swallow her whole.

She cleared her throat. "We, none of us, were ever good at being honest, were we?"

He let out a low breath. "No, we weren't. The Westbrooks have a legacy of sweeping things under the rug until we trip on them."

She rubbed her palms against her thighs, remembering how she had screamed at Margot, the last real conversation they shared before her mother died. She had been certain she was the victim of countless lies, never imagining she might need to ask if her mother was hurting too. "I was cruel to her. And to you. Then I just left."

David shook his head as if to ward off her self-blame. "You were young, Emery. Furious, grieving. You still had a life to lead, as far as you saw it. Margot was gone, you couldn't fix that. But you still had your whole future, and maybe running felt like the best chance you had to breathe."

She swallowed, letting that truth settle. She didn't disagree, but it still hurt. "I'm sorry," she said, her voice unsteady. "Not just because I left, but because I didn't come back when you first got sick. I was scared of what I'd find. Scared I'd never escape these ghosts again."

He reached for her hand. Her fingers curled into his automatically, startled by the papery feel of his skin. "Don't leave me again, Emmy," he whispered. "I'm too old and tired to chase you around airports." His attempt at humor was gentle, but tears pricked at her eyes.

She squeezed his hand. "I won't go anywhere I can't come back from," she said, though her voice shook. "I promise."

They spoke for several more minutes, exchanging long-kept confessions about Margot's unpredictability, about how the family's attempt to wrap Emery in cotton might have done more damage than good. By the time a nurse came in to check David's vitals, Emery was blinking away tears that refused to fall. She pressed a careful kiss to her father's forehead, then excused herself to let him rest, feeling like the air in the corridors was slightly easier to breathe.

On the drive back, she wrestled with a restless energy. Instead of heading straight to the estate, she turned off onto a familiar side road that led toward the City Marina. Over the years, Charleston had changed. The dock was vastly expanded, and now large yachts crowded the water. She remembered a time when it had been quieter, just a few fishing vessels bobbing on gentle waves.

Parking, she wandered along the boardwalk until she

found a section near the pier's edge. She lowered herself onto a bench, feeling echoes of past visits. Once, as teenagers, she and Xander had lain in the bed of his old truck by these docks, spotting shooting stars across the sky. That memory felt half-dream, half-ache.

Boats drifted in and out. Marina workers looped ropes to cleats, and travelers disembarked, laughing or carrying their duffels. She watched them, removed yet oddly fascinated, as if studying a parade from behind glass. Eventually, she dug into her bag and slipped out a small leather-bound journal. She traced the corners of the cover before flipping to a blank page.

Her pen hovered, her mind swirling. The recent conversation with David weighed on her. The words that drifted out onto the paper almost surprised her:

I don't know how to be someone who forgives. But maybe I can be someone who tries.

She exhaled carefully and shut the journal. The admission felt raw. Fear was still there inside her, fear that opening the door to forgiveness might leave her heart unguarded. Yet she also felt a strange lightness, as if the act of writing it down birthed a tiny spark of hope.

By the time she returned to the Westbrook estate, dusk had claimed the horizon. Warm light shone through the downstairs windows. Usually, she would head upstairs, slip into pajamas, and attempt to write out her swirling thoughts, or maybe pretend to sleep until morning. Tonight, she halted by the study door. A narrow band of light seeped from beneath it.

She lifted her hand to knock, thinking of the kiss, the

half-step they had taken the previous night. Before she could waver, she nudged open the door. Xander was inside, reading by a table lamp. He looked up at the sound of her entrance, setting the book down. His eyes were calm, though she could see tension in the set of his shoulders.

She remained near the threshold, fingers grazing the doorknob. "If I told you I wanted to talk," she asked softly, "would you still be here tomorrow?"

His answer was immediate. "Yes," he said, his voice sure. "And the day after that, and the day after that. Whenever and wherever, I'm here."

Emery let out a breath she hadn't realized she was holding. She stepped into the room fully, closing the door behind her. The click of the latch seemed to echo. She caught his gaze, saw the sincerity in it, and felt the quiver in her stomach that told her she was crossing a threshold. She wasn't surrendering. Not yet. But she wasn't retreating, either. Their past was wounded, but something in her believed they could build a better present if they tried.

She took a few more steps until she reached the chair opposite him. She placed a hand on its back, steadying herself. The room smelled faintly of old books, warm lamplight, and the subtle spice of Xander's soap. She could see the fraying edges of the rug beneath the desk, a sign that so much of this house was still a work in progress. But for the first time since her return, her chest didn't feel tight from ghosts.

CHAPTER

SIXTEEN

XANDER

Travel Note: I once lived out of a duffel for three months and felt freer than I ever had. But there is something braver in choosing stillness. Restoration requires standing still long enough to see what can be saved.

—EW

Xander didn't sleep after Emery left the study. He remained on his back, gaze fixed on the slow rotation of the ceiling fan above his bed. The silence in the house felt gentler than it had weeks ago, not hollow. Tension still clung to the walls, but it no longer chafed him the way it once had. He knew she lingered just down the hallway, possibly restless in her own room. He thought about everything he hadn't said.

He had almost voiced it earlier. I miss you. I still love you. The words had formed behind his teeth, ready to slip free, but he had held them back. He had closed his eyes and tried to recall the feel of her presence, the faint scent of whatever citrus shampoo she used. A few hours earlier, she had stood in front of him, arms close to her sides. He had watched her expression soften when conversation drifted past the carefully drawn lines that kept them apart. Now, he imagined her somewhere upstairs.

He dozed in fitful increments, finally rising at first light. The early morning heat settled through the open windows, promising another humid day. Dressing quickly, he stepped outside, leaving Silas stretched across the foyer rug. The dog barely stirred, too lazy to follow at such an hour.

Xander chose to work on the side deck that ran along the estate's east wing. Thick ivy had crawled under the crawlspace supports, warping boards that once rested firm against the foundation. While dew still glistened on the grass, he knelt to pry out rotted planks, careful not to snap the weaker pieces. His muscles tensed with each tug. He relished the sweat gathering at his hairline. It distracted him from the images that had kept him awake.

By the time the sun climbed above the marsh, the entire underside of his shirt was damp. The earthy smell of loosened soil mingled with the tang of pine in the boards. He noticed a cloud of gnats near the edge of the deck and waved them off. Each breath tasted like salt and wet heat, a distinct Lowcountry brew that might cling to him forever.

He heard the porch door creak. His pulse quickened before he even turned. He already knew it was Emery. When he glanced over, she was stepping onto the porch with two cups of coffee in her hands. Her hair was pinned up, wavy strands escaping. She offered a mug without a word, letting him take it. He dipped his head in thanks.

They sipped in unhurried quiet, leaning against the house's worn siding. He admired how she held her coffee steady, despite the tension he occasionally caught in her shoulders. He tried to remember the last time they had shared a morning like this. It must have been ages ago, back when youthful excitement replaced the unspoken burdens they carried now.

Finally, she broke the calm. "You were always quieter when you were doing something with your hands," she said, her voice subdued. "Maybe that's why you never told me things that mattered."

He swallowed a mouthful of black coffee, the bitterness guiding him toward an honesty he had braced against for years. "Or maybe you never listened because you were always looking for a way out."

She didn't recoil, but her lips tightened. He set down his coffee, bracing for a swift retreat or a sharp retort. Instead, she exhaled and lowered herself onto the porch ledge beside him. She set her mug at her feet, as if choosing to absorb what he said rather than fight it.

"You're not wrong," she said, her tone surprisingly soft. "But I think I came back to see if I could unlearn that."

He felt a subtle relief ease the knot in his chest. He heard the wind move through the oak branches overhead. From beyond the yard, a distant boat horn wailed along the creek. He dared a glance at her profile, noticing how the sun outlined her cheekbones.

After a few beats, she leaned her back against the porch railing and drew her knees up. "It's strange to talk like this, like we're not dancing around old secrets."

"We have enough old secrets," he said. "Maybe it's time we let them breathe."

She gave a faint nod. "I was thinking about my father this morning. How he used to joke that every board in this house had its own story. Now I see how grief can twist those stories into something else. What did your parents leave behind for you? I never asked about them. I'm sorry."

Xander stared at the missing deck planks, inhaling the muggy air. He didn't often speak of his family, quiet, well-meaning people who had never quite understood his impulse to fix things others deemed beyond repair. "They were good folks," he began slowly, "but they had their own troubles. My father kept to himself, always working two jobs to pay bills. My mother, she was sweet, but she got ill. By the time I was old enough to do something, it was too late. They passed in close succession. I tried to manage, but I felt anchored here. And then your father gave me a job at the estate."

He continued. "He did not just give me a paycheck, Em. He gave me a place to put my grief. He said I could have the run of the caretaker's cottage and that the house had enough broken pieces to keep my hands busy for a lifetime. He knew I needed to build something to keep from falling apart myself."

She watched him intently. "I never knew the details."

"I didn't share many," he replied with a small shrug. "The pain dulled enough that I learned how to channel it into what I build. It's easier to restore a rotted beam than to talk about how you feel."

Her eyes moved over his face, sympathy shining through. "It makes sense. Maybe that's why you stayed after everything happened with my mother and then me leaving. You were used to staying."

He nodded but remained silent. Admitting how heartbreak had rooted him in place felt both obvious and raw. Before he could elaborate, Silas ambled onto the porch, tail wagging. Emery patted the dog's head, smiling softly. It was the first genuine smile Xander had seen from her that day.

Around noon, a rumble from the driveway caught their attention. A delivery truck pulled in, and a uniformed driver hoisted a large thermal bag onto the grass. Xander frowned, not recalling any order. The driver waved a farewell as he left.

Emery retrieved the note attached to the bag. *Feed each other. You need it.* She turned the card to him, and he recognized David's handwriting. A rush of warmth moved through his chest. It was so like David to offer gentle nudges, giving them chances to share more than short conversations and black coffee.

They carried the catered lunch to a shady spot under the large oak near the fence. The ground was soft with summer grass, and Xander offered Emery a folded tarp to sit on. He unpacked containers of lemon pepper chicken, roasted vegetables, and cornbread muffins. A crisp breeze stirred through the leaves overhead, bringing relief from the midday heat.

Silas flopped between them, tongue lolling. Xander felt a weight lift from his shoulders as Emery's cautious expression relaxed into shy contentment. They picked at the food, exchanging small talk about the condition of the house's windows, the best local place to get fresh shrimp, and how David must now be showing his paternal affection through food deliveries.

When they both had their fill, Emery lay back, resting on her elbows. "The silence is different here," she said, gazing at the sunlit yard. "Not the kind of quiet that makes you feel alone."

He knew what she meant. "I used to think every creak of the floorboards was the house longing for voices to fill its halls. Maybe it was just me."

She sat up and swept away a curl that had escaped her hairpin. "You used to roam the attic, right? I remember you once told me it was your hideout before I left."

He set aside the empty container. "Want to see it now? I finally cleared most of it last week. No more toppling boxes."

She nodded. Together, they walked through the house's rear entrance, boots echoing in the hallway. They passed the library doors, where faint lines of sunlight cast patterns on the floor. He led her upstairs and opened the creaky attic door. A rush of warm, dusty air enveloped them.

He turned on the single overhead bulb. The newly cleared space looked brighter, though the sloped ceiling remained cramped. She stepped over piles of spare molding and paused to run her fingers across exposed beams. Dust motes danced around her.

"It's smaller than I remembered," she observed, her voice low. "I used to think it went on forever."

He stood beside her, compelled by the soft aura around her shoulders. "This has always been my secret place," he said. "I'd come here when I needed to breathe."

She knelt near a line of labeled boxes. Old clothing, holiday decorations. Her hand rested on a trunk that read Emery – School. She glanced up at him. "Can I open it?"

He gestured for her to go ahead. She lifted the lid, revealing a stack of worn sketchpads. A flush touched her cheeks as she flipped through the pages. She had sketched city skylines, beaches, a tall figure that resembled him with cropped hair and broad shoulders. Another page captured the old baseball field behind her high school. She gave a soft laugh, and the sound grazed his heart like a gentle knock.

"Teenage dreams," she murmured, half-joking. "I never showed anyone these. Some are so bad."

He shook his head. "They're not bad. They're yours, and that's what makes them matter."

Her bronzed skin glowed in the attic's dim light. She closed the trunk and became suddenly shy. Xander wondered if she was recalling those afternoons when she used to sit barefoot on the porch, scribbling in her notebook, not letting him see. He wanted to gather these pieces of her and assure her that none of them scared him. Instead, he treaded lightly.

He gestured to the far corner. "There's old luggage

behind those beams, but I tossed most of the moth-eaten linens."

Emery nodded and stood while dusting off her jeans. They descended the attic stairs and returned to the main hallway with a shared quiet. Her shoulders appeared less guarded now, as if sifting through old sketches had given her permission to linger in the present.

Outside, the late afternoon sun draped the porch in golden light. They settled again on the wooden swing. His stomach fluttered when their legs brushed, his worn jeans against her faded denim. Silas padded across the porch and settled near the top step, giving them space.

Crickets began their early evening hum, and the air grew thick with that end-of-day humidity. Sometimes Xander's mind raced to find the next step, the right words. He looked at her profile. A delicate tension settled between them, so tangible it almost pulsed like another heartbeat.

He brushed his palm over his mouth. "Would you ever stay here," he asked softly, "if the house felt different? If it felt like a place you could rebuild?"

She hesitated, eyes on the horizon where the marsh grasses shifted. "Maybe," she replied. "If I felt different inside it." Her voice trembled on the last few words, but her expression remained calm.

He rested his hands on his thighs. He wanted to promise that he would do whatever it took to make her believe in this place again. He also knew that might mean letting her decide on her own, without pressure, without guilt.

Darkness settled in slow increments, and they kept

talking about little things: the best shade of paint for the hallway trim, the local painter who owed Xander a favor, the quiet that fell over the property when the tide rolled out. At one point, Emery tilted her head against his shoulder, a gesture so natural that it drew every breath from his lungs. Warmth flooded him.

He didn't kiss her. The urge persisted, stubborn and insistent, but he held still. He savored the feel of her closeness, the willingness she offered by resting against him. He listened to each inhale, each exhale, and acknowledged how powerful it was just to sit with her. *Wanting* was enough right then. Wanting was a promise of something they might build if they chose.

CHAPTER

SEVENTEEN

EMERY

Travel Note: In Berlin, I met an artist who welded glass into fractured iron. "I don't fix what's broken," she told me. "I make it honest." She held a torch to mismatched shards and fused them into stunning new forms. That is what we are doing here, I think. Making it honest.

—EW

Emery woke to her bedroom suffused with soft, bruised light, the edges of morning slipping through the thin curtains. She blinked in mild confusion, realizing she had slept later than usual. There was no echo of nightmares rattling her chest, no coil of dread tightening her stomach, as if her mind had granted her a small gift of uneventful rest.

She pushed aside the light summer blanket and took a slow breath. The air felt warmer than normal, a balmy feeling that made her feel at peace rather than weighed down. She stepped to the window to look at the marsh, noting the faint gold sunbeams shifting across the tall grasses. In the distance, an egret waded through brackish water. She listened to the soft breeze stirring the Spanish moss. Everything outside seemed calm, and for a moment, she let that calm seep into herself.

A slender notebook lay on her nightstand, the edges marked with a rainbow of small sticky notes. Her last written line from yesterday was scrawled in deeper ink, as if her pen had pressed extra hard. The phrase was incomplete, trailing off into white space. She considered picking up the pen to complete the thought, but her mood felt too fragile. Instead, she changed into a light cotton shirt and a pair of worn shorts, letting her hair hang loose around her shoulders.

Downstairs, the house stretched out in uneven patches of sunlight. She paused in the foyer. A wide mirror hung on the wall, its silver frame tarnished. With a gentle fingertip, she traced a faint mark in the mirror's corner, a lingering scuff from the days when she and her sister used to argue about who got to use the hallway for phone calls as teenagers. The memory of it made her chest twist.

She had avoided certain rooms since coming back, as if confronting them would wake the ghosts asleep in their corners. But she felt different this morning. Calmer. Ready, perhaps. She started with the formal sitting room on the right, letting her bare feet cross the threshold. The faint smell of lemon oil and dust clung to the furniture. A high, elegant ceiling soared overhead, and she remembered how every Christmas morning, the entire family would gather here. The memory glimmered: bright wrapping paper strewn on the carpet, carols playing from her mother's outdated stereo. Once, that normalcy had been enough to feel like love.

Emery ran her fingertips along a threadbare armchair. The cushion's fabric gave off a gentle rasp beneath her touch. She could almost see Margot perched there, straight-backed, a cup of tea near her elbow. The memory was vivid yet no longer unbearably painful. Exhaling, she slipped out of the sitting room.

She moved next to the library. Books lined the shelves, some with spines so faded she could barely read the titles. Margot used to read poetry aloud in this space, her tone sleek as velvet. Emery remembered the stillness that would settle over the room when her mother spoke, as if even the dust motes paused to listen. She turned her attention to the window seat where she used to sit. The cushion sagged where months of disuse had left an imprint. Despite the stale air, the library felt like a place of potential. If she closed her eyes, she could almost hear the pages turning and Margot's voice weaving one story or another.

Emery stepped into the main hallway again, following the wooden banister up the stairway. She lingered on the upstairs landing, hearing its familiar squeak. This was where she once overheard her parents arguing, hushed and urgent. Their words had carried through the thin walls, leaving her heart pounding at the door. Even now, recalling it made her shoulders tense, but she tried to remind herself that whatever had been said then was done. She wasn't a child straining her ears anymore. She was a woman here of her own choice, attempting to fill the silent spaces with truth.

She turned, noticing the pull-down ladder to the attic. Yesterday, Xander had shown her some of the reorganization he'd done, clearing away old boxes of holiday decor and carefully stacking them in corners. She felt an odd composure as she climbed the ladder, stepping onto the floorboards under the slanted ceiling. The pale light from a single dusty window illuminated the trunk she'd rummaged in. Taking a breath, she opened it again.

She sorted through a few old sketchpads, each capturing glimpses of her teenage imagination: stylized flowers, faraway skylines, a few bungled attempts at self-portraits. Her gaze snagged on one portrait in particular, a sixteen-year-old Emery with unrealistically perfect hair and an impossibly carefree grin. She couldn't decide if it was naive or hopeful. Maybe both.

She plucked the self-portrait from the sketchbook and folded it carefully into her pocket so she could put it later in her journal. She closed the trunk and rose. As she left the attic, she felt an odd stirring, some quiet acceptance of who she used to be, who she was now, and the space in between.

Returning to the foyer, she caught sight of something on the small wooden table by the stairs, a folded piece of paper resting alone, as if it had been deliberately placed there. She picked it up, heart tightening at the sight of her sister's handwriting.

I'm in town. Let me know if you're ready to talk.

A local area code and the name of a coffee shop were scrawled beneath it. Emery's chest went hollow. Laura. Just seeing her name in neat script caused conflicting emotions to jostle inside her, anger, hurt, and a strand of longing she didn't want to acknowledge.

She nearly ripped the note in half, an impulse flaring hot in her chest. But she heard the echo of her own voice from last night. She had told herself she was ready to stop running. Her fist tightened on the paper, and she swore under her breath. Then she grabbed her bag and her keys. She wasn't sure if she was truly ready but telling that to Laura in person seemed the only way to find out.

The coffee shop was a twenty-minute drive across old streets lined with live oaks. She rolled down her window to let the breeze wash over her face, though it did little to cool her nerves. She parked near a row of pastel storefronts and stepped inside the café. The smell of coffee beans and sweet pastries enveloped her. Laura was there, sitting at a small table by a window. She wore a crisp blouse, her dark hair pulled back in a smooth low ponytail. A shade darker than Emery's curls, the color drew attention to the sharp angles of her cheekbones and the deep-set brown eyes they shared. An iced tea glistened beside her elbow. She didn't stand, but she watched Emery approach with a guarded expression. Emery sat in the chair across from her, letting the silence settle.

"Surprised you texted me," Laura said gently, though her posture remained stiff.

Emery swallowed. "I almost didn't." She nodded at the iced tea in Laura's hand. "That was Mom's favorite. Half sweet, half unsweet, right?"

Laura let out a breath. "Yeah. Guess some habits stick."

A tense lull descended. Emery drummed her fingers on the table. The clamor in her skull felt louder than the coffee-shop chatter around them. She wanted to accuse, to scold, to ask a thousand questions about why Laura hadn't told her the truth about Margot. Yet the words felt slippery now that they were face to face.

Laura cleared her throat. "I don't expect you to forgive me. But I owe you an apology for how I handled things. I did what I thought was best at the time. Mother was in such a bad state and you," she paused, "I thought you couldn't handle it."

Emery's fists tightened on her lap. "So, you lied and let me believe Margot died from cancer. You even let me see you whispering with Xander. Did you want me to think you and he," her voice shook, "All this time, you let me run away with the worst assumption."

"You saw what you needed to see," Laura replied, her tone quiet. "But yeah, I let you believe it. Maybe I just wanted you to leave peacefully, focus on school, not get pulled into her decline. It was all so messy."

Emery's throat went dry. "Messy? It was my mother. And you watched me leave, watched me cut myself off from everything."

Laura's gaze moved aside. "Margot intended to tell

you everything about your birth father, about why she lied to you. I was afraid that truth would break you more than losing her already had. So, I kept telling myself it was better for you not to know all at once."

Emery stared at the tabletop, a swirl of emotions tangling in her chest. "Maybe you had good intentions," she finally said, voice unsteady. "But you took my choice away. Don't you get that?"

Laura's eyes shimmered, though she blinked hard. "I do. Now."

They sat in taut silence. Emery's chest crackled with leftover anger and a strange sadness. She wanted to accuse Laura of many sins, but she knew her sister had been suffering in her own way. The truth wasn't neat. It never was. Rubbing her forehead, Emery spoke softly. "It hurts. But it didn't kill me. And I guess that's how I know I needed to hear it."

Laura let out a shaky breath. "You don't have to forgive me instantly."

"I know." Emery rose, collecting her bag. "I can't do big declarations either. Not now."

They nodded at each other in a wordless truce. It wasn't a resolution, but it felt closer to honesty than they'd ever managed. Outside, the afternoon sun stung Emery's eyes. She drew in a lungful of muggy Charleston air, bracing for the tangle of feelings waiting. Her mind buzzed with half-formed thoughts about what came next for her and Laura, but she decided not to overthink. She only knew she was relieved to have some piece of the truth laid bare at last.

Back at the estate, she found Xander near the study doorway, tools spread on an old drop cloth. He was working on the doorframe, carefully fitting a piece of new trim where a crack had split the wood. The moment he saw her, his expression gentled. He didn't ask what happened, he only set down his hammer and offered her a glass of cold water. She drank half of it in three long gulps and let the coolness settle in her belly.

She exhaled a breath she hadn't realized she'd been holding. "Laura told me more about everything..." She paused. "It stings, but it didn't kill me."

Xander nodded, his gaze quietly steady. "That's how you know it was worth hearing."

Without another word, he led her inside the study. The walls still smelled faintly of fresh paint, but the overlay of old books and newly sawed wood gave it warmth. They sat on the floor shoulder to shoulder, the half-finished doorframe behind them. The boards in this room had seen so much history, Margot's penning of letters, David's silent pacing, Emery's own restless teenage footsteps. Now, the air felt different, as if it recognized a shift in her heart.

He didn't pry or push, he simply offered his presence. She leaned her head against the nearest bookshelf and let the tension drain from her muscles. Maybe it was the house's way of letting them breathe. She closed her eyes, still clutching the half-empty glass of water. Her mind moved through memories of the coffee shop, the tang of iced tea, and her sister's tremulous apology. It was all so far from clean or perfect. But it was real. Honest, in its jagged, painful way.

The boards beneath them creaked, as if acknowledging this fragile peace. Xander brushed a spot of sawdust from her knee and said nothing more. She reached out and let her palm rest against his forearm, appreciating how solid he felt. Here in this old room, the unspoken felt heavier than words, but it no longer terrified her.

They didn't speak again for a while. They just sat in the cool quiet of a room once filled with ghosts, now echoing with possibility.

EIGHTEEN

XANDER

Travel Note: I have shared rooms with strangers in Bali, wandered alleys in Granada, and danced alone in Tokyo, but nothing feels lonelier than sitting across from someone you once loved, waiting to be seen again.

—EW

Xander pressed a fresh length of crown molding against the top line of the study's wall. For a second, he focused on the texture beneath his fingertips, the newly sanded wood still carrying a trace of sawdust and let the dull ache in his shoulders ground him. The end of a project always felt like this, a mix of satisfaction and fatigue. He had removed the sample piece earlier in the week and shaped a replacement in the workshop behind the house. Now, under the study's warm overhead light, he installed the finished molding carefully.

Steps echoed behind him, soft against the polished floors. Emery leaned against the wall, her gaze tracking every moment of his work. She did not interrupt, yet he felt her presence acutely, like a gentle tug on his awareness. Each measured breath she took made him hyperconscious of the silence between them. Here they were, in a room once overshadowed by dust and broken trim, sharing an unspoken intimacy that had taken seven years to find again.

He swallowed and secured the molding with small brad nails. The tap of his hammer felt louder than usual, as if the study itself wanted to magnify every subtle shift between them. When he finished the final section and stepped off the ladder, he let out a breath he had been holding from the moment she walked in.

She spoke quietly, her voice carrying a low warmth that reached his ears and his chest at the same time. "You're doing a great job."

He lowered his hammer. A line of unspoken gratitude curled through him, but he decided not to voice it. He simply exhaled slow, releasing tension from his shoulders. He took a moment to observe the newly finished corners of the room. The crown molding balanced out the wainscoting Emery used to call "too fussy" whenever she teased him about his attention to detail. The sunken lines now gleamed, highlighting the polished floors. She seemed to examine every inch, as though searching for hidden meaning behind the pristine surfaces.

He stole a glance at her face. Her expression was unreadable, but her gaze lacked hardness. There was no resentment in the curve of her mouth, no anger in her posture. She might have been tired, but she was present.

After all the months he had spent working on this house, on her father's requests, on trying to convince himself that he was content to restore without confronting what he really wanted, seeing Emery watch him without a barrier in her eyes felt as close to calm as he had been in ages.

A soft shuffle sounded in the hallway. Silas appeared, sniffing at the newly painted doorframe. The dog wagged his tail once but did not bound forward. He seemed to sense that the moment echoed something delicate. Xander set the hammer aside, ran a knuckle behind the dog's ear, and walked out with Emery into the corridor. He noticed she stayed close to his side, her shoulder angled toward his, though she never quite touched him.

They parted ways briefly to ready themselves for the afternoon's trip to the hospital. He slipped back out to the caretaker's cottage for a quick shower to rinse away sawdust, then stepped back into the main house, combing damp hair that refused to stay neat. He found Emery in the foyer, leaning against the old banister with a thoughtful tilt of her head. The house appeared quiet, holding its breath for what came next.

A short drive later, he parked in the hospital lot. The building gleamed white in the bright day, and the humidity outside clung to them like an unwelcome blanket. Inside, they wound through the corridors to David's current room. Xander paused at the nurse's station, exchanging polite nods with staff members who recognized him from his many visits. He had grown used to the beeping devices and the antiseptic smells, always overshadowed by the knowledge that David's heart was as fragile as fine glass.

Emery slipped into her father's room first. Xander remained outside, leaning on the pale green wall. The nurse behind the desk offered him a sympathetic smile, and he returned it. Through the half-open door, he caught muffled fragments of conversation. Sometimes he heard Emery's voice stiffen with emotion, other times it softened until laughter bubbled up, faint but undeniable. That sound stirred an ache beneath his ribs. Hearing her laugh, a sign that she and David found a moment's peace in the face of everything, lifted something inside him. It also reminded him how fleeting time could be.

The nurse approached quietly, reminding him that David's vitals had mostly stabilized for the day. Where a few months ago he might have felt relief, now he simply felt the press of reality. Stabilized, but not cured. He thanked her, that same ball of concern lodged in his chest.

At last, David's voice sounded. "Xander, why don't you come in?" Xander eased the door open. David rested upright against pillows, a hospital tray with half-eaten lunch on one side. Emery stood next to the bed, eyes rimmed with tears she did not try to hide. Xander stepped in, the overhead lights reflecting off the plain tile floor.

David's gaze moved between them, warm but tired. "You still sanding the soul out of my house?" he asked, his tone laced with a teasing dryness.

A wry grin tugged at Xander's lips. "Trying to uncover it, actually."

"That place always had too many secrets," David said.

His gaze lingered on Emery, then returned to Xander. "You know what that house needs?" His voice rasped faintly. "New stories."

Xander looked at the older man for a moment, letting the words settle. In the hospital, he heard the mechanical hum of a nearby monitor, the distant squeak of a gurney's wheels, and Emery's quiet breathing. The idea struck him as both simple and profound, new stories. He offered David a small nod.

Emery leaned in, touched her father's hand, and passed him a cup of water. Then she said something softly. Xander did not catch the words, but David's face curled into a smile of genuine fondness. When it was time to leave, Xander placed a steady hand on David's forearm. He wanted to say more, something about how the house was shaping into the vision David had once described, or how he regretted the time Emery had missed. Instead, he squeezed lightly, then stepped back.

They parted from David with gentle goodbyes. In the hallway, Emery let out a slow breath. She looked at Xander, her eyes reflecting gratitude and worry. He offered the simplest reassurance he had, a nod, a slight rise of his hand. They walked out of the hospital side by side, footsteps echoing on the polished floor.

Outside, the mid-afternoon sun weighed down on them. The drive home was spent in a pensive quiet until they pulled onto the Westbrook estate's gravel driveway. The house rose before them with its tall windows and newly painted shutters. Late daylight cast patterned shadows across the porch, as though the place itself kept evolving with the layers of fresh wood and paint Xander had added. Silas greeted them with a sleepy wag of the tail from the front steps.

Emery suggested heading to the garden. Though the air was thick and warm, Xander agreed. The garden had become a shared task that brought them small joys, the rosemary patch, the half-wild bed of herbs, and especially a few vegetables they tried to salvage from the overrun corners. He spent the first ten minutes wrestling with a stray vine near the fence and shaking off inchworms that clung to the leaves. Emery crouched close and pulled weeds from around a drooping plant that might have been a pepper once.

She pushed her hair from her forehead, then brushed dirt off her palms. "I didn't realize how tall these weeds got," she said.

"They grow fast when no one's paying attention," Xander reached in to yank a stubborn root. "Kind of like regrets."

She tossed him a look, somewhere between amusement and partial agreement. Her voice turned light. "Do you remember when we tried to grow tomatoes and ended up with one sad tomato and a ton of basil?"

His eyes glazed over for a moment, and he leaned back on his heels. "I remember that tomato. And other things that looked like tomatoes but weren't." Xander suddenly got still but Emery didn't notice and kept on talking.

Her laugh surfaced, free and effortless. "That tomato looked like a ping pong ball and was very precious. The only one that survived. I think we pretended it was delicious to justify the hours we spent fussing over the garden."

Xander turned away, suddenly seeing flashes of a childhood before he knew Emery that weren't as perfect as the one she was remembering. He shook his head preferring to recall the teenage version of Emery, barefoot on the grass, stubbornly determined to coax life from poor soil. "That tomato was delicious. Mostly because it was impossible."

He watched her for a moment, a genuine smile touching his lips. The setting sun caught the wisps of hair that had escaped her ponytail, turning them to threads of gold. She had a small smudge of dirt on her cheek, just below her eye. Without thinking, he reached out. She stilled as his thumb came up to brush the dirt away. The gesture was slow, almost reverent. For a second, his thumb lingered on the warmth of her skin, and he saw her breath catch. Her eyes, wide and unguarded, locked with his. The playful energy of a moment ago dissolved into something deeper, more potent. It was the kind of simple, thoughtless touch that had been absent between them for five years, and its return felt important. He finally dropped his hand, and a current of heat passed between them.

Emery shook her head, but her eyes danced. They continued pulling weeds, working in a companionable silence. He felt the closeness in how easily they moved around each other. He would shift to toss a weed aside, and she would pass him a trowel without being asked. It was an unspoken rhythm, reminding him that once, they had believed they could do anything together, even if they only produced one tomato for their efforts.

As the sun dipped low, the sky turned orange and lavender at the edges. Long rays filtered through the live oaks, painting the back porch in golden patches of light. They gathered their tools and moved toward the house. Emery patted Silas's head before sitting on the porch steps. Xander retrieved a single lantern from the hallway inside and lit it with a flick of an old lighter. The gentle glow illuminated the outline of Emery's face, making her softness stand out against the coming twilight.

Silas settled at their feet, content. The breeze picked up, rattling the branches overhead. A faint scent of damp grass and honeysuckle mingled in the evening air. Xander lowered himself onto the top step, bracing his forearms on his knees, close enough to sense her warmth.

Emery spoke first, voice hushed as if the calm might break easily. "I don't know what this is." She paused, eyes drifting across the yard, the garden they had just cleared, and the quiet arch of the windows behind them. "But I don't want it to be over yet."

He studied the lantern's flame for a moment. The question in her tone made his pulse hitch, stirring a flash of hope he had tried to keep measured. "It's not over."

She turned to him, meeting his gaze unflinchingly. The remaining light made her eyes gleam, and the intensity in them caught him off guard for a moment. He knew how much fear and hurt she had carried. He also knew how quickly that fear could return if anything pushed too hard.

She exhaled softly and let her hand rest near his on the step.

Her words came slow, delicate. "You waited so many years."

Faced with the truth of those lost years, Xander let out a breath. He had no simple defense. "I didn't know I was waiting," he said, each syllable unsteady. "But I wasn't moving either."

Emery nodded, her eyes understanding. A chorus of cicadas began to sing in the trees, layering the dusk with a persistent hum. Her hand slid closer, brushing lightly against the back of his. He felt the careful shift, the warmth of her skin against his rough knuckles. It took only an ounce of courage to turn his palm slightly, letting their fingers touch more fully.

She did not flinch. Instead, she kept that contact, her expression open and thoughtful. Neither of them rushed to define what came next. In that soft glow, with the dog at their feet and the house behind them, they simply shared the silence of two people finding refuge in each other's presence.

He did not pull away.

CHAPTER

NINETEEN

EMERY

Travel Note: Cairo's streets taught me to inch forward through chaos, one breath at a time. Sorting family secrets feels the same, tangled but guiding you toward clarity.

—EW

Emery opened her eyes to a splash of sun filtering through the lace curtains. A bright birdcall drifted on the breeze, and the subtle fragrance of mint wafted in from the open window. She inhaled deeply, astonished that she felt at home in this room after so many past nights of unease. She let her fingertips brush the quilt's soft edge and realized she no longer felt like a stranger here. The house had not changed, but her heart had.

She rose, unhurried, and reached for the cardigan that lay draped over a wooden chair. Its pockets held a few stray pens and a folded snippet of paper she no longer needed to read. The hallway outside her bedroom looked the same as it did when she was seventeen, scuffed floorboards, fading wallpaper, but it no longer loomed with echoes of regret. She moved quietly, as though afraid of breaking the comfortable quiet.

Near the staircase, she passed the open door of her parents' old room. The sight of a rumpled bedspread brought her footsteps to a stop. *The Old Man and the Sea* lay splayed on top of a folded blanket, its spine strained where David must have left off reading before the last hospital visit. Her chest tightened. She could see him there, reading by lamplight and trying to distract himself from the weight of his illness, each turn of the page a small attempt at normalcy.

Emery placed her hand on the doorframe and breathed in the lingering smell of lemon oil. She wanted to believe David had more time than the doctors predicted, but that book on the bed reminded her that he was slipping away. She blinked back a surge of tears, then steeled herself and continued down the hallway to the attic ladder.

The attic was warm from the recent morning sun. A single beam of light cut the dim space, illuminating dust motes that hung in the air like tiny, suspended stars. Emery climbed carefully, aware of the gentle squeak each step produced. She had not been here in a while. Old trunks lined the eaves, some labeled with scrawled handwriting. One in particular caught her eye: M. W. – PRIVATE. She drew closer and lowered herself onto her knees.

She unlatched the trunk with a soft click. Inside, she discovered a fragile corsage surrounded by a handful of old photographs. The corsage looked brittle, with petals that had once been ivory, now tinged with yellow. She recognized one photograph that showed Margot in a sweeping white gown, presumably on her debutante night. A crown of radiant curls framed her smiling face. Emery's throat constricted. She never knew the story behind that night, never asked, and now it felt too late.

She rifled through more items, a few scribbled notes that appeared to be drafts of poems or lines from a letter. Beneath them sat an envelope. It bore her own name in Margot's looping script:

For Emery — To be read when it matters.

Emery felt as though her heartbeat echoed in the confined space. Her stomach fluttered with an anxious thrill. She settled cross-legged, set the envelope on her lap, and tore it open with more boldness than she felt.

The letter inside was handwritten, the words shaky, as if Margot's hand had trembled. Each sentence glowed with raw honesty. Emery read silently, her pulse racing.

You were not born from scandal. You were born from longing. I did what I thought would protect you. But I realize now that love without truth is harmful.

Margot confessed her affair with an older, powerful man who never intended to leave his own family. The letter revealed how Margot had loved him, how she believed that their child, Emery, would be safer if hidden under the Westbrook name. David had agreed to raise Emery as his own rather than drag painful truths into the light. Margot's tone was apologetic, layered with regret. Emery read it again, this time out loud in a whisper, letting her tears fall freely.

She felt a swirl of emotions, astonishment, relief, and loss. Her mother had carried this secret with all the weight of an anchor, and Emery felt her own soul lighten now that the truth had surfaced. For so many years, Emery had grappled with rumors, half-truths, and illusions. Now, the truth was messier than any rumor, yet it offered clarity she had never had before.

When she emerged from the attic, she held the letter close to her chest. She needed air, needed sunlight. She slipped downstairs, her bare feet padding across the carpet runner, and paused at the front door. Once outside, she found the porch bathed in gold. The humidity clung to her skin, but a breeze off the marsh cooled her cheeks. Xander stood near the railing, sipping coffee, his posture as still as the porch columns behind him.

He turned at the sound of her footsteps. The moment their eyes met, he set his mug down. She walked forward and extended the letter without speaking. The tension in her chest felt almost painful, but she knew ignoring it was no longer an option.

Xander took the paper carefully from her grasp. His

gaze shifted across each line, and he exhaled softly when he finished reading. He folded the letter gently and placed it on the small table behind him. He did not rush to speak but let the gravity of it settle.

She broke the silence first. "You knew some of it already?"

His voice was low. "I did. I never had the full story, but I suspected Margot had reasons for keeping that secret."

Emery drew in a shaky breath. "Why didn't you tell me?"

Xander studied her, empathy in his gaze. "It wasn't mine to share. It was your mother's truth and David's. They kept me at a distance, and I respected that line. I didn't want to make another wrong choice, not after everything we've all been through."

Her breath stuttered, gratitude and anger tangling as she looked out at the marsh where reeds swayed gently in the breeze. "Do you have any idea who he was? My biological father?"

He shook his head. "I only know it was someone in your mother's past. David probably has the details, but the way Margot spoke about him, it felt like she wanted to leave it hidden. She must have changed her mind if she wrote you this letter."

Emery pulled her knees close. The boards felt warm through her thin sleep pants. She held out a hand, inviting Xander to sit beside her. "I thought it would shatter everything," she murmured. "All these months, I've been afraid to learn the truth about my father. Turns out, I feel more complete, like at least I know who I was all this time."

Xander lowered himself and rested one calloused hand over hers. The softness of his expression steadied her racing heart. "Your mother's choices weren't fair to you," he said, voice gentle. "But I understand why she believed she was protecting you. David loves you in every way a father can. I think Margot knew that."

Emery felt the prickle of fresh tears. "David is my dad. Nothing changes that. But I wasted so many years thinking I had no real father left. Now I see he was here all along, waiting for me."

Xander's thumb traced a slow circle over the back of her hand. She felt her pulse thrum at the contact. His warmth, his steady presence reminded her of all they once had. She gazed at him, struggling to piece her words together. "I left because I was lost, because I hated the feeling that I didn't belong to anyone anymore. But then I stayed away because if I came back, I would have to face who I might become in this house."

"Who do you think that is?" he asked quietly.

She hesitated, letting the breeze stir the loose strands of her hair. "Someone strong enough to stay, I guess. Someone not afraid to love the people here. And that scared me more than running did."

His grip on her hand tightened slightly. His eyes shone with something between longing and relief. "You never had to prove yourself to me. I've been here, waiting, just hoping you'd look at me and see there can be more than old ghosts between us."

She felt her breath catch. A memory flickered, the two of them as teenagers on these very porch steps, shoulders touching, hearts fluttering with the newness of love. Now, years later, they had more scars, more regrets, but a deeper understanding of each other.

He reached for her other hand, and she let him gather both in his. "You're the first woman I ever loved," he said. "The only woman I've ever loved."

Her heart pounded at the laid-bare confession. She recalled a time when she doubted every word he spoke, when her bitter assumptions stood in the way, but now she recognized an unguarded truth in his voice. He had never truly stopped caring about her.

She rose, and he stood as well, still holding her hands. The porch seemed to push in around them. She stepped forward, closing the space between them. When she lifted her chin, her tears clung to her lashes. "I never admitted it," she whispered, "but losing you broke me in ways I wouldn't face."

She saw his own tears at the corners of his eyes. He leaned in slowly, giving her a chance to move away if she wanted. She remained still, heart racing. When their lips finally met, the kiss carried more emotion than all their words combined. It was not timid or uncertain, it was an embrace of shared pain and hope. She let her fingers curl around the back of his neck, and he pulled her against his chest with firm, sure arms.

The soft taste of salt and coffee lingered on his mouth. A gentle tremor passed through her. This was different from the strained glances and wary conversations of recent weeks. This was surrender, a choice made without fear.

He broke the kiss, breathing unsteadily, and pressed his forehead to hers. She kept her eyes closed, letting the warmth of his breath fan across her cheek. Every breath they exchanged felt like a promise: We are still here.

Then in one swift movement, he scooped her into his arms. A small gasp left her lips, but she didn't resist. She looped her arms around his neck, laughter bubbling up as she felt his strength. He carried her across the threshold of the front door and into the house. She realized with a swirl of anticipation that she did not feel the old panic. She did not feel the urge to run.

They passed the foyer where so many tense greetings and half-hearted farewells had taken place. He mounted the stairs, step by step, with her cradled in his arms as if she weighed nothing. The house felt like it held its breath for them, and she let her fingers slide along the collar of his shirt, feeling the warmth beneath. Her heart pounded with each footfall on the old wooden steps.

In the upstairs hallway, he turned toward her bedroom. She did not flinch. She did not tell him to stop. He eased open the door with one hand and nudged it shut behind them. The room was lit by the morning sun that streamed through gauzy curtains, a glow that made every-thing seem softer.

She watched his face as he set her gently on the edge of the bed. Her face felt warm, her breaths still uneven from the kiss. He knelt in front of her, hands resting lightly on her thighs. The last of her tears dried on her cheeks, replaced by a trembling anticipation she could not control.

She combed her fingers through his hair, and he closed his eyes, leaning into her touch.

"Emery," he murmured. "We can slow down if—"

She placed her fingertips over his lips, silencing the question. "I don't want to slow down," she said. Her voice trembled with honesty. "I'm ready to choose this."

He swallowed hard, eyes lit with tenderness and desire. Then he stood, guided her further onto the bed, and kissed her again, deeper this time. Their shared urgency hummed between them. She tugged at the hem of his shirt, heart thudding with each new inch of skin she discovered.

The world beyond her bedroom fell away. There was only his warmth, his quiet hum of contentment whenever her hands roamed and the gentle press of his mouth against hers. Memories of their past heartbreak wove into the present, but instead of pulling them apart, it became a kind of tapestry connecting them more painfully, beautifully.

Sunlight streamed across rumpled sheets as she let him slip her cardigan from her shoulders. He trailed soft kisses along her collarbone, and she caught her breath, overwhelmed by the certainty that she was exactly where she needed to be. She had spent so long fearing the truth, fearing her own capacity to care, but now she realized that allowing love was the bravest step of all.

He cupped her face, brushed her lips, and ran his thumb over her cheek. "I love you," he whispered. "I never stopped."

She pressed her forehead to his and whispered back, "I love you too."

He kissed her gently at first, then with unguarded passion. The tension that once bound them in silence now freed them to speak with touch rather than words. Their quiet laughter mingled with low murmurs as they explored the tender edges of each other's hearts and bodies. She felt tears threaten again, but this time they were tears of a release she never thought possible.

When he lifted her fully into his arms, she surrendered to the moment, letting him guide her deeper onto the bed. The door was closed, the house silent except for the muffled call of a bird outside the window. The rest of the world ceased to exist.

She let her fingers trace every line of his shoulders, every ridge of muscle that trembled beneath her palms. His breath came heavier, and she pressed her own lips against his neck, tasting the faint salt of sweat and longing. The weight of his body over hers was comforting, a promise that she no longer had to bear everything alone.

He whispered her name, voice thick with emotion, and she responded with a nudge of her hips and a gentle sigh that lined up their hearts. She felt the last defenses fall away as acceptance filled her. They moved together, exchanging slow touches and fervent kisses. Every sense sharpened, the warmth of the sunlight, the soft rustle of sheets, the scent of his skin.

She pulled him closer, more certain than she had ever been, and gave herself over to the love they had both denied for so many years. Xander kissed her tears away, cradling her cheek before lowering his mouth to hers again with tender urgency. He whispered words of comfort and devotion she had never let herself crave until now.

In that quiet sanctuary of her old bedroom, they made love, and the house around them no longer felt like a fortress of ghosts. It felt like home.

CHAPTER
TWENTY
XANDER

Travel Note: In the Arctic Circle, silence is a living thing. Here, it is the same between me and Xander. But sometimes silence is not the end of the story. It is the invitation to start again.

—EW

Xander ran a gentle hand across the porch swing's wooden armrest, letting the warm afternoon air settle around him. The sun was high, and the soft hum of cicadas vibrated along the edges of the estate. Emery slept beside him, her head tilted back against the top slat. He noticed how the sunlight caught in her hair, making a fine halo of loose strands around her face. He did not mind that she had drifted off. He quietly guarded the moment as if it were a delicate piece of stained glass that he refused to let anyone shatter.

He kicked one foot lightly to set the swing in motion. The rhythmic creaking joined the chirping of birds perched somewhere beyond the porch rail. In his mind, he compared the house now to the one he had first walked into months ago. Then, the corridors were quiet in a different way, haunted by a sense of abandonment and regret. That day, he had pressed his palm against doorframes, half expecting the walls to cave in from all the unspoken grief sealed in them. Now, he sensed the foundation of the estate was shifting in a better direction. Renovation was not just about new wood and fresh paint but the gradual exchange of old ghosts for new possibilities.

He glanced at Emery again. Her breathing was even, shoulders rising with each inhale. He could still feel the echoes of the conversation they had shared earlier, the one that ended in lingering smiles. She had made a passing comment about never expecting to find real peace here. Now, she was dozing like she owned the world. He closed the worn paperback in his lap, an old architectural guide, and let it rest on the seat between them. When he quietly exhaled, the tension in his body ebbed. He was not the same man she had left behind seven years ago, and he sensed she was not the same woman who stormed away. That thought gave him something close to joy.

Eventually, she began to stir. Her lashes fluttered, and she opened her eyes, taking a moment to orient herself as though she was not quite sure where reality ended and sleep began. She stretched, arching her back and rolling her shoulders. He felt the swing jolt under her movement. Out by the creek, a breeze sent small ripples across the water, and the sky stirred with the suggestion of coming clouds.

She rubbed the back of her neck. "I don't even remember falling asleep," she said. Her voice was drowsy, huskier than usual.

Xander smiled and moved the paperback aside. "That's how peace sneaks up on you."

She nodded, a slow, thoughtful gesture. Then she stood, leaning on the porch railing and looking out at the garden. He recognized the subtle shift in her expression. He had spent enough time around her to read the small signs she gave off. Sometimes, when her brow furrowed, she was thinking of something complicated, her father's health, the place she wanted to make in Charleston, maybe a new project. He waited, letting her find her footing. She turned back with a grateful look, as if to say thanks for letting her sleep without feeling rushed.

They went their separate ways after that. He headed to the front hall, a bright space full of morning rays when the sun was on the right side of the house. The carved paneling along the entryway had begun to show age years ago. He had stripped and sanded so much of it that he could practically feel the woodgrain in his sleep. Yet it still needed finishing touches, especially along the carved edges that curled like scrolls. He set out his tools, sanders, chisels, soft cloths, and got to work. Each small pass of sandpaper reminded him that restoration demanded slow patience. It never happened in a single, dramatic flourish.

Partway through, he heard Emery's low voice carrying from the other side of the foyer. She was on the phone.

Although he did not want to listen, certain words carried in the stillness: "Charleston pitch," "travel column," "too personal." He ran a rag over the freshly sanded wood, but even that was not enough to mask the murmur of her conversation. She sounded both eager and hesitant, as though she were finally letting her writing reflect everything this house had brought to the surface. She ended the call with a promise to send a draft soon. He wondered if she would show it to him first or keep it quiet until she felt ready. Either way, he would not pry. If traveling the world taught her anything, he suspected it was how to reveal truths on her own schedule.

She appeared in the doorway, a grin forming at the corner of her mouth when she saw him. "You look like you lost a fight with a cedar tree," she teased, eyeing the wood shavings in his hair and on his shirt.

He raised one brow, pressing a hand through his dark hair to shake some of the debris loose. "You should see the cedar," he replied. He found comfort in the gentle banter, the way they had fallen back into a rhythm that was playful without feeling strained.

Later that evening, they settled into the kitchen together. They had not cooked side by side in a long time. He recalled them laughing in front of a cluttered stove when they were teenagers, fumbling with saucepans and measuring cups. Tonight was different. She rummaged in the cabinets for spices while he cubed chicken and chopped vegetables. The space felt large but not empty. Every time they reached over each other, their arms brushed. Each small contact sent a pleasant warmth up his spine.

She bumped his hip when he was washing rice, and he bumped her back gently. The normalcy in it struck him as precious. They were no longer the anxious, guarded strangers who had circled each other in the foyer weeks ago. They were two people who had dared to speak their truths, and something beautiful had taken root because of it.

At the table, they shared an easy dinner. The overhead light glowed softly, and Silas lay at their feet. Emery turned her fork slowly in her food before asking, "Did you ever leave Charleston?"

He wiped his mouth on a napkin. "Briefly," he said. "A few small projects led me out of state for a time. But I always ended up back here. The house needed me, and your dad, well, he needed someone he could trust."

Her gaze showed understanding. "Did it ever feel like a weight?" she asked, sounding curious rather than accusatory.

His breath caught. He remembered the days he had spent alone, pulling at rotted trim, painting walls, haunted by old misunderstandings. "Only when I thought I was the only one carrying it."

She nodded, eyes solemn. He sensed she understood more than she let on. Before long, they finished dinner, and he stacked the plates in the sink. She insisted on drying, so he rinsed. Their shoulders bumped again, and they both laughed. Eventually, they abandoned the chore half-finished. They turned off the lights and moved to the porch to sit in the fading glow of dusk.

He settled on one side of the swing while she curled up in the far corner. He could see the sky beyond the marsh, a darkening canvas with faint flashes of lightning at the horizon. The summer storms had a habit of rolling in dramatically, then clearing just as abruptly. For a while, they watched the scattered flashes and listened to thunder move across the distant creek.

"I want to stay," she said. Her voice trembled slightly from honesty, not from fear. "But not as a visitor. And not just in this house."

He turned to her, letting the gentle sway of the swing slow to a stop. "Then stay," he said. "Not for me. Not for the past. But for what's next."

In the lantern glow, he saw her lashes flutter. Maybe she was holding back tears, or maybe it was just relief. Her hand reached for his, fingers curling around his. The simple warmth of her skin against his made him inhale sharply.

"Then let's figure out what next is," she said quietly, "together."

He felt a surge of gratitude that threatened to close his throat. He thought about the nights he waited for her to return, the half-finished letters he never mailed, the times in his workshop he imagined hearing her step outside. Now, she was here, and she was asking to rebuild something with him, for real. He squeezed her hand gently and opened his mouth to speak, but she spoke first.

"What comes next is you and I in bed naked together," she teased, her tone softly amused. A wry grin tugged at the corners of her lips. He realized his heart was hammering. He could barely keep from looking at her mouth when she spoke. She laughed, and the sound vibrated all the way through him. "Don't you think we've both earned that kind of peace?"

He set his palm on her hip. "Seems we have," he said, feeling heat flare across his cheeks. Her boldness did not scare him, it thrilled him. He stood, scooping her up with an easy lift. She let out a breathy laugh but arched closer, her arm winding around his neck. He loved how she felt against him, solid yet full of promise. Without hesitating, he carried her up the stairs, trailing faint footprints of flour left on his jeans. The old house groaned softly under their shifting weight, but it was not a protest, it sounded like an exhale of acceptance.

In her room, she reached back to close the door. The last sliver of hallway light vanished, and he noticed how the darkness made every breath between them more pronounced. Her hands gently pressed on his shoulders, guiding him. He set her on the near edge of the bed, feeling his own heart pound. They had made love before, but every moment since their reconciliation felt like a fragile new start, one that could vanish if they let their old fears get in the way. Yet tonight, she did not seem afraid to let him see the softness in her gaze.

They undressed each other slowly. His hands grazed the hem of her shirt, peeling it away inch by inch. She tugged softly at his belt, letting it drop to the floor. The air was warm on his skin, punctuated by the distant whisper of thunder. Each article of clothing falling away was a small surrender to something that had been building for years. He pressed his lips to the hollow at her collarbone, feeling a quiet tremor run through her. In that moment, he whispered her name, letting old longing bleed into new devotion.

They moved to the center of the bed, sinking against pillows that smelled faintly of magnolia. He noted how her breath caught when he traced a line along her shoulder with his fingertips. Everything about this felt heightened, the quiet of the house, the press of her body against his, the knowledge that they had finally stepped fully into the present. He bent lower, lips grazing her ear, and whispered every wish he had never voiced aloud. He told her how he pictured them finishing the estate together, how he imagined nights on that porch swing, how he wanted to be the one she turned to whether storms were raging or the sun was shining.

She melted into him, each kiss deeper than the last. Her fingers raked through his hair, pulling him closer. He asked if she was all right, and she answered with a soft, content hum that made his pulse quicken. He lost count of how many times he said her name. They became a tangle of limbs and quiet promises, their murmurs filling the spaces that had once been silent. If the house had any ghosts left, he imagined they might be smiling at this triumph of love over regret.

He whispered all his desires and longings to her, voice unsteady yet honest, and she leaned in until no distance remained. In that tender moment, she melted completely in his arms.

CHAPTER

TWENTY-ONE

EMERY

Travel Note: A camel driver once told me outside Petra, "The desert gives you back what you leave behind." This house is like that, full of the echoes we buried, ready to return them when we are ready to listen.

—EW

Morning light formed a crescent along the faded wallpaper. Emery's pulse raced, but not from nightmare or panic. For once, it came from a sense of purpose bright and clear. She sat up, pushing aside the soft sheets, and looked around the space that had once felt more like a stranger's room than her own. The walls carried old scuffs, faint ghosts of poster tape, and the memories she had finally stopped running from.

Sliding out of bed, she tugged on worn jeans, then chose one of her favorite cotton shirts. The shirt bore a slight tear near the hem where she had once wriggled past a broken fence on the outskirts of Havana while scribbling notes for a travel piece. She still remembered the salt-sweet air that day and the sense she was free to roam anywhere. Now, she realized that freedom had always been inside her, waiting for her to come home.

She fastened a slim silver bracelet around her wrist, one of her mother's old pieces, tarnished yet still delicate. She admired the etchings in the metal. The swirling patterns reminded her of vines or perhaps waves that shaped themselves around the Lowcountry shores. Her mother had left behind more than secrets, she thought. She had left Emery little fragments of memory. Emery inhaled, steadying herself, and stepped into the hallway.

Every door in the house remained closed except one. The study was partially open, revealing a sluice of early sunlight across polished hardwood. She heard a quiet rustle of pages. When she entered, she found Xander barefoot, his shoulders relaxed even as he read a well-worn historical text by the window. Sawdust streaked the edges of his shirt from the day before. He had apparently woken early as well. Neither of them spoke.

Emery padded across the room and placed a gentle kiss on the crown of his head. She felt him tense for a moment before leaning into her touch, warm acceptance in that small movement. He glanced up, eyes questioning, but she only gave him a small smile. A silent promise passed between them. They were past pretense. She left without explaining and heard the soft glide of paper as Xander closed his book behind her.

Down in the foyer, she spotted Silas dozing near the base of the staircase, golden fur spread like a plush rug.

The dog lifted his head but did not rise, content to let her pass. She wondered if even Silas could sense her urgency. Then she slipped out the front door, the morning brilliance greeting her with a surge of humid air and the gentle stir of a breeze coming off the marsh.

Her car waited in the driveway, an unsung sentinel waiting to carry her into the city. As she backed out, she glanced at the grand porch columns receding behind her. An ache settled in her chest, not of loss but of commitment. She had something she needed to say, now that she finally knew how.

She made her way down the old road toward Charleston, weaving past tall oaks draped in Spanish moss. The shadows across the road reminded her of the times she had driven these routes before, but always with a coil of dread in her chest. Today, her heart thudded with conviction. Morning sun glared across her windshield, revealing a clear sky. Sometimes the day began with an edge of possibility so bright it was almost startling. She followed it all the way to Roper Hospital.

Inside the lobby, she greeted the nurse by name, then navigated the corridors that now felt familiar. She hated that this place had become so routine, yet a small part of her was grateful for every day David had left. When she stepped into his room, she found him propped up against a thin pillow, ear bent toward a small Bluetooth speaker on the bedside stand. A soulful saxophone played a gentle jazz tune, soothing and reflective.

"Didn't expect you before breakfast," David

murmured, his voice rough but welcoming. The corners of his mouth turned up just enough to show he was pleased.

Emery's response caught in her throat. She pulled a chair close and sat, resting her hands on her denim-clad knees. He muted the speaker, letting the last notes fade beneath the rhythmic beep of medical monitors. He waited, gaze steady. The bandage around his arm from recent treatments looked stark against his pale skin.

She drew a breath. "I read the letter."

A flicker passed through his expression, neither shock nor relief, but something that acknowledged the weight of what she had found. "I wondered if you would," he said quietly. His voice still held a quiet authority, even from a hospital bed.

Emery hesitated. She had spent so long believing in illusions that telling the truth now almost made her tremble. "I need to know," she said, voice low, "did you ever resent raising a child who wasn't biologically yours?" She felt her chest constrict the moment the words left her lips.

David's eyes seemed to soften further. He reached up with shaky fingers to turn off the speaker entirely, and for a moment, they could both hear the hum of the hospital's air conditioning. "Never," he answered. "You were mine before you ever took your first breath. Nothing about that changed, not for a second."

She had intended to remain composed, to speak calmly, but tears welled too quickly. She tried to blink them back, yet they escaped, sliding across her cheeks, dripping onto her faded shirt. She could not recall the last time she felt tears that were neither angry nor full of blame. These tears carried acceptance and a mourning for all the time she had lost. David did not reach for her. He simply let her cry, his face reflective and loving.

After a few moments, Emery wiped her cheeks with the back of her hand. Words felt unnecessary, so she settled for slow breaths until her chest loosened its knot. David turned slightly, wincing, and reached for the drawer beside his bed.

"I want you to have something," he said, withdrawing a small package wrapped in tissue. He held it out with trembling hands, urging her to take it. Emery swallowed a fresh wave of emotion as she accepted the bundle. Carefully, she peeled back the tissue to reveal a graceful silver locket. She recognized the filigree design, Margot's old piece that Emery had once glimpsed in a photograph of her mother at a dance recital. She had never seen the locket up close before now.

"She wanted you to have it when you were ready. She never told me, but I believe it was a gift from someone she had once loved." David explained. He sank back against the bed, weariness dragging at the edges of his features.

Emery ran her thumb along the locket's surface and noticed a faint tarnish near the clasp. "Thank you," she whispered, voice tight. She wanted to say more, to ask obvious questions. But in this moment, she finally understood the depth of love that lay beneath secrets, but her words remained tangled behind her gratitude.

David nodded and closed his eyes as if the conversation itself had taken all his energy. She stood and leaned over to press a soft kiss to his temple. The faint jazz music came from the speaker, its notes a comforting hum in the background.

She stepped into the hallway and let the door sigh shut behind her. She paused, blinking under the fluorescent lights. There was no meltdown, no dramatic upheaval inside her. Instead, a strange serenity wrapped around her heart. She gripped the locket in her palm, partly wishing her mother could see this moment.

The drive back to the estate felt dreamlike. She stopped once, outside a small white church with tall spires, the church she used to attend as a child so many years ago. The morning sun dazzled the stained-glass windows. Emery pulled over and cut the engine. She rested her forehead on the steering wheel, staring at the old wooden structure.

"I forgive you," she whispered. Her voice trembled, uncertain of which forgiveness truly mattered. Perhaps she spoke to Margot, perhaps to David, or to herself. She only knew that speaking the words freed something deep inside her chest. It felt like exhaling a burden she had carried across continents.

When she arrived at the estate, she parked near the front garden. The humidity pressed around her as she saw Xander in the distance, kneeling among the tomato plants that had stubbornly refused to thrive. He wore a faded cap, hair escaping in tufts, and he was tugging at a few weeds with methodical patience.

She approached quietly. He glanced up when she was a few steps away. Sweat shimmered on his brow. He managed a small smile that made her stomach twist with the warmth of recognition. In the stillness of the garden, birds darted overhead, and the rustling of the live oaks sang in the background.

"You keep trying to grow impossible things," Emery said softly, nodding to the stubborn tomato plants. She remembered how they had joked once about how the soil might not support them, but they kept trying anyway.

Xander raked a hand across his forehead, leaving a smear of dirt at his hairline. "You're standing here, aren't you?" he replied. A hint of hope laced his tone, as though he were referencing far more than just the plants.

She took a shaky breath and knelt beside him. The dirt pressed gently against her knees. She placed her hand over his, feeling the warmth of his calloused fingers against her own. "I want to stay." She repeated those words she had once murmured, but this time there was no fear, no doubt. "I'm done running."

A breeze rippled through the garden, carrying the scent of rosemary. Xander's eyes brightened with something, perhaps relief or gratitude. He didn't speak. Instead, he let his free hand curve along her waist until she leaned closer against him. For once, no tension coiled in her belly. She felt only solidity, a sense that the two of them were exactly where they should be, in a place that had once been haunted by memories but now held the promise of new beginnings.

That evening, Emery found her bedroom both soothing and invigorating. She had changed into soft cotton shorts and a loose blouse, the day's perspiration washed away. The open window let in a balmy breeze.

She lit a small bedside lamp, enough to illuminate the journal resting on the nightstand. Her father's words still echoed within her, as did the confession that he had never once regretted loving her. She blinked back tears that threatened again, although these tears felt gentler.

She flipped to a blank page in her journal, inking the date at the top. Her pen hovered, then pressed firmly onto the paper. Charleston's skyline and crossing oceans filled her mind, but none of that seemed as urgent now as the revelation that she had changed. She started writing.

Charleston did not change. I did. It stopped being the place I ran from and became the place I turned back toward. That has to mean something.

She sat quietly, letting the night wrap around her. Outside, the cicadas hummed low, and somewhere down the hall, she heard floorboards creak. Probably Xander moving about, checking a repair or turning off a hallway light. She breathed out slowly, letting the pen slip from her fingers. Tonight, she no longer felt the raw ache of an undone conversation or the bitterness of betrayal. Instead, she felt a tenderness for everything that brought her here, good or bad.

She tore off a small sliver from that page, folding it into a tiny triangle and reading the words once more before slipping it inside the locket that now belonged to her. The tarnished silver glinted in the soft lamplight, as though welcoming a new secret. Carefully, she placed the chain around her neck. The cool metal settled against her skin, above her heartbeat.

Rising, she moved to the old mirror atop her dresser. The glass was slightly warped, producing a faint waviness at the edges. Emery saw her reflection, hair loose around her shoulders, eyes still carrying a hint of red from earlier tears. Yet what she noticed most was the subtle glow in her expression, a soft calm she had carried back from the hospital, from the garden, from the conversation that morning in the study.

She lifted a hand to the locket at her collarbone, thinking about the folded note inside. The reflection looking back at her no longer appeared weighed down by grief or regrets. The edges of her mouth turned up in something like a smile.

She did not look haunted anymore. She looked here.

TWENTY-TWO

XANDER

Travel Note: In Santorini, I watched a stranger trace their name into wet sand only to watch it vanish. I think we are all trying to write permanence into impermanent things.
—*EW*

Xander stood near the counter, mug in hand, his gaze fixed on Emery as she sliced peaches into a ceramic bowl. Early light spilled through the large kitchen windows, illuminating each dust mote drifting in the air. She hummed a tune he vaguely recognized, something with a lazy, crooked rhythm. It was not so much the song itself that affected him, but the way her voice caught now and then, sounding as if she were testing the melody without a care for perfection.

He swallowed and set his mug down before his suddenly unsteady hand made a mess. There was a new steadiness in her posture, the sun revealing faint high-lights in her hair he had never noticed during their younger years. Yet her movements were unhurried, almost languid, as though she no longer had anything to outrun. He could not remember the last time he had seen her so at ease doing something so ordinary. His heart felt strangely tight, and he told himself to keep breathing.

Her locket caught the sun each time she lifted her knife. It was a subtle flash of silver, but he noticed every glint. He knew that piece of jewelry held more than a photograph or a random snippet of note, it held part of her mother's truth. He had seen Emery clasp it around her neck the morning she finally admitted she would face the past on her own terms. Watching it sparkle reminded him of how much pain she had opened herself up to and how brave it was to wear that pain as an emblem, not a wound. He felt proud of her. He felt protective of her. He felt everything he had once pushed aside.

She finished slicing the peaches, ran her palm over the side of the knife to tap the excess fruit into the bowl, and looked at him. Her eyes crinkled with a small smile. "Hungry?"

He forced a grin in return. "Ravenous. Peaches taste better when someone else cuts them for me." His voice came out steadier than he expected.

She took a spoonful of fruit, offered him a bite, and he leaned forward to taste it. Sunshine spilled onto his shoulders, warming him in that quiet moment. The sweetness of the peach burst across his tongue, and a surge of something he only now recognized as contentment spread through him. He had not felt this calm in a long time.

They ate breakfast together, leaning against the

counter as if it were the most natural thing in the world, no grand gestures, no forced exchanges. When the dishes were rinsed and the kitchen was mostly cleaned, they drifted outside. Silas trotted at their heels. Xander glanced at Emery to see if she wanted to hold his hand, but she merely brushed her palm lightly over his forearm as they walked through the foyer.

They stepped onto the front porch, descending the worn steps into the garden. A gentle breeze stirred the rosemary plants, releasing that sweet, herbal fragrance. They headed toward the hedgerows that bordered the marsh, the air thick with humidity yet somehow made bearable by the promise of open skies. Birds rose from the grasses, their cries faded by distance. Neither of them spoke.

He loved how the house looked from this vantage, proud columns framing the porch they had painstakingly restored. He also remembered with some bittersweet pang the day he replaced warped boards in the deck so that he could keep imagining Emery stepping across them without risk of a stumble. Perhaps that was what he had done all these years, fix everything he could for the day she returned, in case she ever wanted to stay.

The crunch of gravel underfoot accompanied their leisurely stroll. Emery paused by a blooming hydrangea, her fingertips tracing a blossom. She glanced at him with a look that asked no questions yet seemed to hold every question in the world. In that silence, Xander felt more at home than he had in years.

They circled around the far side of the property and

headed back past the carriage house. He realized he missed the quiet days he used to spend in there, hammer in hand, weeding out rotten wood and layering fresh paint. There was more to do, there always would be in a home this old, but at least he no longer felt the weight of doing it alone.

By the time the mid-afternoon heat descended, they decided to drive into town. He stood behind Emery in the foyer as she collected her purse and an old notepad, something she had begun carrying around again. This time, she left the front door wide open, a small detail yet one that felt significant. No more shutting herself in or out. He let out a breath he had not realized he was holding.

They took Xander's truck, windows rolled down. The air rushed in, warm against their faces. Emery insisted on picking the music, a playlist of old jazz and nostalgic songs she had compiled sometime during her travels. He tapped the steering wheel in rhythm, glancing at her out of the corner of his eye and finding an unguarded smile on her lips.

Their destination was a small warehouse near the downtown waterfront, where Xander had placed an order for reclaimed floor tiles for the upstairs laundry area. The building was nondescript, situated in a row of similar loading docks. He parked, hopped out, and helped Emery down from the cab. She offered a quick thanks, still carrying that notepad. Inside, the musty smell of stacked crates and cardboard boxes greeted them. Half a dozen industrial lamps lit the long aisles.

A wiry man with graying hair approached. "Xander Langley?" he asked.

Xander nodded. "That's me. I'm here about the vintage tiles."

The man beckoned them to the back and explained the difference between the finishes. Xander let Emery handle most of the questions. She bent over a crate of tiles and ran her fingertip across the faint patterns etched into the ceramic. She asked thoughtful questions about the original location of the tiles, raising details about Charleston's historical design that made Xander realize she had listened more closely to his architectural ramblings than he ever suspected. The older man seemed impressed. Xander felt pride.

He watched her in that moment, her curiosity, the way she inspected each piece as though she were analyzing not just shape but history. He wondered how many sides of herself she had cultivated in all those places around the world. During the lost years, she became someone deeper and more vibrant. Now he was the beneficiary of that growth. It filled him with a swelling sense of gratitude tinged with regret for the time he missed.

They left with the crates loaded into the bed of the truck. As they buckled in, Emery turned to him and exhaled softly. "I'm thinking of writing about Charleston after all. But not for the column."

He pulled onto the main road and glanced at her briefly. His grip on the steering wheel tightened. "For what, then?"

She shrugged and set her notepad on her lap, flipping

a page. "Maybe for me. I've been working on something more personal. I don't know if it'll ever see the inside of a publisher's office, but I want to put it on paper. Feels necessary."

A prickle of hope tightened his shoulders. "You deserve to tell your story however you want."

She reached across the console and laid her hand over his for a brief moment, letting her cool fingertips rest against his skin. She said nothing else. Neither did he. The gesture was enough.

Back at the estate, the sky turned from pale blue to a simmering gray, boiling clouds rolling inland from the harbor. By the time Xander carried the last set of tiles indoors, fat raindrops smacked the porch steps. Thunder grumbled low. Emery popped her head out from the foyer, a rueful smile on her lips. That was all the warning they got before the storm unleashed its fury.

Lightning crackled somewhere close, illuminating the windows. Rain battered the roof with punishing force, making the old house groan. Within minutes, the lights blinked once, then blinked again, and everything went dark.

Xander cursed under his breath and rummaged for a flashlight in the kitchen drawer. The beam cut through the gloom, revealing Emery collecting matches and a handful of candles that had sat on a side table for weeks. She lit them one by one, the small flames casting soft arcs of brightness across the walls.

"I'd better check the fuse box," he said. "Might be the main breaker again."

Emery nodded, leaning forward to shield a candle's flame from a draft. "I'll set up some candles in the dining room so we can at least see each other's faces."

He followed the narrow hall to where another breaker panel lurked behind a door. Sure enough, a circuit was blown. Rain hammered the roof, drumming an angry beat. He flipped switches, muttering to himself about how the wiring could have been replaced decades ago if only the budget had allowed. The estate's bones were strong, but the veins and arteries were another matter.

When he returned to the dining room, he found Emery waiting with two half-burned candles in mismatched holders. A pair of wine glasses stood on the table along with a half bottle of red she must have scavenged from the kitchen. She turned at the squeak of his shoes on the hardwood, lifting one glass and extending it toward him with a crooked smile.

"Dinner by candlelight?" she asked, the playful note in her voice echoing off the silent walls.

He let out a low chuckle. "I was thinking of reheating the leftovers, but I guess that's out. Microwave's dead."

She nodded, opening the fridge door just long enough to grab the container of leftover pasta and some cheese. They would not stay cold for long in a power outage, but it hardly mattered. They settled for cold noodles and a shared hunk of bread. The wine tasted surprisingly good, maybe because of the way the storm enclosed them in a private world of flickering candlelight and whispered conversation.

Rain hammered the windows in pulse-like waves. At

times, thunder jolted so close it vibrated the floor beneath his feet. She teased him about how he could fix crown molding but never figure out how to keep the electricity stable during storms. He teased back, reminding her that some corners of the estate would always be older than both of them.

Eventually, they fell into a gentle quiet. The wine gave him enough courage to say what pressed on his mind. "I think you're different now. Softer, maybe. Something about you is less guarded."

She raised an eyebrow and set her glass on the table. Her expression held a hint of cautious amusement. "And you?"

"Me?" He shrugged, feeling warmth creep into his cheeks. "I'm hornier."

Her laugh rang out, echoing against the candle lit walls. She nearly spilled her drink.

"All right, I wasn't expecting that honesty."

He reached across and caught the base of her glass, steadying it. "I'm sorry, I guess I could say I'm also less afraid to speak my mind. But it's the truth. You in my life again, it does things to me."

Her laughter softened. "Yeah, maybe we're both less afraid."

He set his plate aside, letting the fork clatter. Outside, the winds quieted, though rain still pattered. Candlelight reflected in her eyes, showing the hesitant hope that lived there. He drew a breath.

"I'm still afraid," he admitted slowly. "Sometimes I

worry I'll let you have all my happiness, and then you'll," he paused, "you'll walk."

She stood, her silhouette sharp against the candle's glow, and moved around the table. Her bare feet made no sound on the floor. He pushed his own chair back, his heart thumping. She stepped between his knees, leaned down, and placed her palms on either side of his face. In that moment, her eyes were unwavering.

"I'm not walking." Her whisper resonated in his chest. She kissed him, softly at first, her lips warm and tasting faintly of wine. He breathed her in and let the tension in his body slip away, then eased his arms around her waist, pulling her closer. When they finally separated, she rested her forehead against his.

"This time," he murmured, voice husky, "we stay."

"This time," she agreed.

TWENTY-THREE

EMERY

Travel Note: I have rewritten the same goodbye in twenty cities. But the hardest ones are the ones I never said. Maybe this house, this story, this man is where the sentence finally ends.

—EW

Emery stirred from sleep at the first hint of dawn light. She took in a slow breath, noticing how the sheets still held warmth from her body and how vividly she remembered Xander's touch from the night before. Her heart fluttered at the recollection of that last, lingering kiss. But now, all was silent. She braced one hand on the mattress and sat up, letting her gaze move across her bedroom's dim interior. The corners of the old wallpaper caught the faint glow that seeped in through the window.

When she planted her bare feet on the floor, she found it cool and comforting, as though the house itself tried to offer reassurance. She stood, stretching to ease the slight stiffness in her limbs. Rather than dressing immediately, she walked to the window in her thin cotton sleep shirt to watch the marsh awaken beneath a blooming sun.

Below, she spied Xander. He stood near a wide patch of grass that ran up against a line of oaks. Silas trotted around him, wagging his tail with eager devotion. Xander balanced a fresh cup of coffee in one hand and a small tin of dog food in the other. At first, he did not realize she was watching, but then he lifted his head as if drawn by her presence. He spotted her shadow against the window and raised his mug, lips curving in a half-smile. Emery felt her chest grow warm, answering his greeting with a soft lift of her hand. The simple connection, the way he acknowledged her without speaking, reminded her that she no longer woke up alone, not truly.

She showered and took her time dressing, choosing pale linen pants and a sleeveless top. The humidity already pressed in, promising a warm day. Once she was downstairs, she discovered a plate covered in foil on the kitchen counter. A scrawled note in Xander's compact handwriting read: "I made eggs. If they're cold, reheat them. See you when you're back." She lifted the foil and smiled at the simple breakfast. He had even sprinkled a little pepper on top, the way he knew she liked. She felt a stir of gratitude and amusement at the same time.

With the morning pushing forward, she hurried to eat, not meaning to rush but aware that she had planned to visit her father earlier than usual. She gathered her purse and keys, gave Silas a brief rub on the head, and drove to the hospital. By the time she stepped into David's room, sunlight streamed through a narrow window onto freshly mopped linoleum. The faint scent of antiseptic clung to every surface, forcing Emery to remember how impermanent everything could feel in a place so devoted to the fragile line between life and death.

David was dozing, a biography splayed open across his lap, its pages shifting in a stray draft from the open door. A nurse looked up when Emery slipped inside, then offered a gentle nod as she left the room to give them privacy. Emery eased a chair beside the bed, trying not to wake him. She set her bag on the floor and pulled out one of her travel journals. She glanced at the cover: scuffed corners, a faint coffee ring on the back, and a small text sticker reading "Lisbon" stuck beside a doodle of a magnolia blossom.

She opened it to pages she normally kept under lock and key, pages filled with confessions she had rarely shared even with herself. Carefully, she read in a soft whisper. She skipped her more polished travelogues and settled on her raw, unfiltered scribblings. Her voice shook slightly as she spoke of how desperately alone she had felt in Venice, walking the labyrinth of canals at dusk. She read aloud about the anger that coiled in her gut in Hanoi, how it mirrored certain frustrations she had carried from home. She faltered only when she reached a passage on Amsterdam, describing her heartbreak, her sleepless nights, her inability to shake the feeling that she was unmoored from everything she used to love.

Halfway through the journal entry, she heard David

stir. His eyes fluttered open. She paused, turning her gaze to him. He wore a faint smile, though she could see how exhaustion clung to the lines around his mouth.

"That's good," he said, voice hoarse. "It sounds like you stopped pretending you were fine."

Emery lowered the journal to her lap and met his eyes. She fought the urge to apologize, for what she couldn't be sure. Sorry for not being here sooner, sorry for running, or maybe sorry for letting him believe this charade lasted so long. Instead, she leaned forward and brushed her lips against his forehead in a gentle kiss.

"I'm trying," she said. She felt his hand shift slightly atop the sheet, and she placed her own over it, just for a moment, grounding herself in the simple comfort of contact.

He drifted again before long, lulled by whatever medication kept his pain at bay. Emery left him a short note on his bedside table, promising to visit soon. Then she stepped into the corridor. The lights buzzed overhead as she walked, each step echoing on the tiled floor. Though she felt her chest ache with the heaviness of his condition, she also noticed a strange peace inside her. They both understood time was precious. She was learning not to waste it.

Back at the estate, the midday heat greeted her. She parked beneath the shade of a sprawling oak. The house stood quiet except for muted hammering from somewhere further down the hall, indicating that Xander was finishing some minor repairs. Instead of seeking out its source, she climbed the staircase to her mother's old bedroom.

Margot's closet had become something of an uncharted territory. Emery had poked around before but never allowed herself sustained exploration. This time, she stepped inside and clicked on the overhead light. The small space smelled faintly of her mother's perfume, though the scent had diminished over the years. Linen blouses and silk scarves still hung from wooden hangers, some covered in a thin layer of dust at the shoulders.

Emery began carefully taking items down. A patterned linen blouse with subtle pineapples along the hem, a floral shawl that Margot wore on spring evenings, a perfume bottle half-full of rose scent. Each piece felt like a window into the mother she had both adored and misunderstood. Emery folded them into a neat pile, whispering small apologies under her breath, apologies for leaving everything untouched for so long.

After a few quiet minutes, she spotted a small rectangular box hidden behind a row of dresses that smelled of cedar. She set the dresses aside and lifted the box, easing it open. Inside, she found a yellowed Polaroid. The photograph showed Margot seated on the steps of the porch, holding baby Emery in her arms. Margot's head was tilted back in laughter, her hair gleaming in the sun. Emery felt her breath catch. She turned the Polaroid over and saw a message scrawled in faded ink: Worth every secret.

She trailed a fingertip over the words. There were so many secrets, she thought, ones that scarred this house for years. But maybe they were worth it if they led to love, to protection, to the chance that Emery could be raised by a father who cherished her despite not being hers by blood. She pressed the Polaroid gently against her chest, wishing she could have asked her mother about the meaning behind that short sentence.

Eventually, she put the photo into her purse and resisted the urge to search further. She needed fresh air. A restlessness welled inside her, urging her to leave the estate for a bit. She changed into comfortable sandals, got into her car, and drove toward the harbor. After a short navigation past the peninsula's winding streets, she arrived at a wooden pier overlooking boats bobbing in the water. The harbor glimmered under the afternoon sun.

At the dock's edge, she leaned against a railing. A breeze stirred her hair, and the briny scent of the tide filled her nose. She thought of other harbors around the world, places she had berated her heart by writing emotional goodbyes in battered journals. Somehow, standing here felt different.

She retrieved that same journal she had read to David from her bag, flipped it open, and let her pen hover. Then, with a calm exhale, she began writing.

Grief is not the end of the story. It's the soil. If you stay still long enough, something always grows.

Her handwriting trembled a little, but she finished the sentence. She closed the journal and focused on the water, letting the cries of gulls and the creak of boats center her.

She felt the shift inside her, like a gentle acceptance that sometimes the worst storms left behind the most fertile ground.

An hour or so later, she met Callie downtown near St. Phillip's Episcopal Church. They each carried cups of iced coffee, condensation trailing down the plastic in the warm air. They found a spot on the worn steps that faced a bustling square. Tourists wandered around with cameras, and a few locals chatted on nearby benches. It was a scene of everyday Charleston, bright, humid, alive with quiet charm.

"So," Callie said, leaning an elbow on her knee, "what happens now?"

"Now?" Emery echoed, stretching her legs. She studied her shoes, scattering specks of city dust with a small shuffle. Then she lifted her gaze. "I think I build something here."

"With him?" Callie asked, raising an eyebrow pointedly.

Emery's thoughts leapt to Xander, the gentle way he lifted his mug that morning, the quiet acceptance in his eyes whenever she spoke of her family. She closed her eyes briefly, picturing him. "With myself first," she said. "Then maybe with him."

A small grin spread across Callie's face. "That sounds like progress," she teased. "I was beginning to think you would never admit it."

They sipped in companionable silence for a moment. Emotions appeared behind Emery's eyes, relief for having at least some clarity, sadness that her father's time was running short, and a cautious hope for whatever might lie ahead. But it felt right. She was home, in a sense, and she could not deny that the city's weight on her chest had lessened. It was still there, that gravitational pull of memory, but now it felt less like a burden and more like a truth she could carry.

When she returned to the estate that evening, she noticed a warm glow from the library windows. She walked inside and found Xander crouched by a long table. Stacks of design samples and paint swatches were labeled in neat rows. He glanced up at her approach and brushed sawdust from his hair. A subdued smile softened his mouth as he stood.

"Are these for the new floors in the west corridor?" she asked, nodding at the array of materials. The library smelled faintly of old paper and fresh paint, a combination that felt oddly soothing.

He nodded and dusted off his hands. "I'm finalizing a few details. There's a chance we can salvage a second-floor balcony if we shore up some of that old wood. It might be a lot of work, though."

Emery stepped closer, letting the old floor creak beneath her. "I want to do it," she said. "I need to rebuild something I used to be afraid of. The old balcony was always rotting, and I avoided stepping on it. But now I want to fix it myself or at least try."

He studied her face, searching for any sign of hesitation. Seeing only resolve, he nodded. "All right," he said simply, no doubt in his voice. "I'll help if you want me to, but it's good if you take the lead."

"Thank you." She exhaled, a subtle tremor leaving her body. She knew this was her way of taking back a piece of the house that once weighed so heavily on her. Restoring it would be part of restoring herself.

Xander opened his mouth as if he might say something more, but then he just offered a small smile. A reassuring sense of trust passed between them. Emery felt her pulse quicken at the realization that he wasn't questioning her capability. He wasn't rushing to do it for her. He was letting her control her own narrative.

They talked briefly about timelines, about who she might call for certain supplies, and how to safely navigate the structural issues. Then she drifted upward to her bedroom, the promise of tomorrow's tasks humming in her thoughts. Despite her lingering worries about her father, she felt anchored by her own determination.

In the low glow of her bedside lamp, she flipped open her journal one last time. Her heart pounded softly, recalling how the day began with her still warm from Xander's presence. She knew grief lingered like a silent echo throughout the halls, and David's condition remained uncertain. She allowed herself a small, hopeful smile and wrote the final line of the day, letting each word carry the weight of her decision.

I came back for a funeral. I think I'm staying for a life.

TWENTY-FOUR

XANDER

Travel Note: In Florence, I wept inside a cathedral not for the faith, but for the beauty someone believed was worth preserving. Xander's hands do that too with houses, with hearts.
—EW

Xander woke in darkness. The early morning settled around him, and for a moment he lingered in bed, listening to the quiet rhythm of the house. The sheets still held a faint trace of Emery's scent from yesterday's warmth. He breathed in, feeling a gentle pull in his chest, then rose and padded barefoot across the hall. Careful not to disturb her, he pushed open the back door and stepped onto the porch.

Silas immediately lifted his head from a rumpled old cushion. The dog's tail thumped once, then he ambled over, brushing his muzzle against Xander's leg. Fog clung to the marshes in thick swirls, making the yard look like a dreamscape. Out beyond the garden fence, pale sky began to merge into sleepy gray water, and the wooden planks under Xander's feet carried the memory of the heavy rains from days past.

He settled onto a chair with his coffee mug in hand, though he had yet to fill it. Emery had teased him the night before about how he always seemed to wake up craving coffee and fresh air in equal measure. She was the only person who noticed such a detail. Gazing out over the marsh, he let his thoughts drift. He had rebuilt portions of this very porch in recent weeks, reinforcing the beams that had warped after too many storms. A few older boards were left untouched because Emery insisted they carried family history in their knots and scratches. He could not deny that some things, though imperfect, told stories too precious to discard.

His gaze slid to the porch swing on the far side, a relic of long-ago evenings. He had replaced the ropes, sanded the seat, but kept the faint initials carved into the wood: E and X. Those letters felt like promises made when they were too young to understand them. He stood and stepped closer. The swing swayed slightly, inviting him to sit. Instead, he rested his hand on the back of it and looked out again into the milky morning mist. He wondered if other people felt this same quiet reverence at dawn, the sense that time itself paused to breathe.

Eventually, he returned inside to brew coffee, the dog at his heels. Steam rose in soft curls as he filled two mugs. He glanced at the doorway, half-hoping Emery might wander in, hair mussed, wearing the old sleep shirt she favored. He was not sure when he started yearning for these small moments, but they had become as necessary as the planks under his boots. When she did not appear immediately, he left her mug on the counter and took his own back outside.

This time, Silas curled up by his feet. The horizon began to lighten, and Charleston's humid warmth crept up around him like an embrace. After a while, a creak behind him signaled her arrival. Emery stepped onto the porch in shorts and a loose sweater that hung off one shoulder. Her hair was still tangled from sleep. She mumbled a greeting and stretched like a cat, then nudged Silas aside to lean against Xander's chair.

"You're too serene for this hour," she murmured.

He half-smiled. "Maybe I'm just enjoying the quiet before the day starts. You slept well?"

She nodded, eyes flicking to the swing but not addressing it. "Better than I expected. Thanks for making coffee." She took a sip from his mug and made a face. "Still too bitter, but I'll forgive you."

They shared a few more beats of silence. Somewhere in the distance, a heron glided across the marsh, its silhouette ghostly in the fading fog. This felt intimate, as though they stood at the threshold of something that could be either comforting or terrifying, depending on how they chose to see it.

After breakfast, they walked into the study and spread out a bundle of sketches on the large wooden desk. The old chandelier overhead was still draped in a dusty cloth from the last painting session, but enough morning light filtered through the windows that they could see clearly.

Emery twisted her hair into a messy bun and secured it with a pencil, then studied the lines on the page.

The plan was to refurbish the upstairs balcony that overlooked the side garden. It had been left to rot for years, and Xander had always stepped around it with caution. But Emery had grown determined to rebuild it, insisting it was "part of the house's soul." She pointed to a corner of the blueprint.

"So, if we remove that section of railing, do we lose all of it?" she asked.

He peered closer. "We might just reinstall a new corner piece. The wood's decayed there, but the original hardware is salvageable."

She nodded and twisted her pencil in a slow circle. "I want this to be my project, but I need you to check my steps. I'm confident I can attach new boards, but I worry about messing up the structural reinforcement."

He tried not to smile, remembering that at one time, she had left these walls without looking back. Now she was leading a repair that called for careful attention to detail and faith in her own hands. "You'll be fine. I'll offer advice, but you'll do most of the work. Sound fair?"

She looked at him, and something in her gaze burned with quiet determination. "I don't want you to carry me through this," she said. "I want you to walk beside me."

He set down the blueprint and turned to face her fully. "I have no interest in saving you, only standing next to you while you save yourself."

A shade of relief crossed her features, and she leaned over the desk, closing the distance between them. Her kiss was slow, warm, and tasted of the honey she had drizzled onto her toast earlier. "Good answer," she whispered.

Not long after, they wrapped their notes and headed out to pick up reclaimed wood from a salvage yard West of the Ashley. The sky was a bright wash of blue by then, dotted with a few low-hanging clouds promising afternoon heat. Xander drove with windows down. The breeze whipped strands of Emery's hair across her face, and he occasionally glanced her way, struck by how quickly her guarded expression had softened in these recent days.

She asked him about the years he spent on his own, working on smaller projects around the city, living quietly in Charleston while she was off circling the globe. He told her about the first few months, how he buried himself in tasks that kept the estate from falling apart completely, half-hoping she might return at any moment. Time passed, and she did not return, so he simply kept going, building a life out of sawdust and early mornings.

"I thought about leaving," he admitted. "Sometimes, it felt like Charleston's history was woven into every pore of my skin. It reminded me of you, of your mother, of everything that went wrong."

She shifted in her seat, eyes flickering to him. "But you stayed."

He nodded. "I guess I always felt like there was more to do here, not just patching up walls, either. Maybe I was waiting for the chance to do something right."

When they arrived at the salvage yard, the sun beat down relentlessly, so the musty interior of the warehouse felt like a refuge. They walked through narrow aisles stacked high with old doors, chipped window frames, and scattered beams. Emery pointed out a set of banister pieces that looked promisingly sturdy, then nodded toward a bundle of half-sanded boards. Xander tested them for knots and splitting, taking care to show her how to tap for hollowness. After they agreed on a price with the yard owner, they loaded the planks into his truck bed.

On the drive home, she asked, almost shyly, if he had ever seriously dated during her absence. His hands tightened on the wheel, but he answered quietly, "I tried once or twice, but it never felt right. My heart was still here."

He could not look at her or he might have stopped the truck and kissed her right then. The admission sat in the air, heavy and tender. Finally, she reached across the console and briefly laid her hand on his forearm.

"I'm glad you stayed," she said in a low voice.

He turned onto the long drive leading to the estate, noticing how the new gravel crunched beneath the tires. Overhead, oak branches laced together, filtering sunlight through Spanish moss that shimmered in the breeze. Xander felt something gradually ease inside him, a sensation of returning to a place that no longer hurt the way it once had.

That evening, once the sun dipped below the tree line, they began installing the first boards of the balcony floor. The air felt dense, hot in that sticky Lowcountry way. Emery wore cut-off jeans and a faded tank top. She used a crowbar to pry up a rotten plank, grimacing at the musty smell that rose with it. Xander stood beside her, measuring a replacement piece, checking how it would align with the existing joists.

They worked side by side, sweat beading on their necks under what little light spilled from the upstairs hall. Emery hammered nails with more force than necessary, and when they finished that section, they were both flushed and breathless. Silas dozed at the top of the stairs, his head resting on his front paws.

"Clumsy but effective," Emery said, assessing the boards they had installed. She was laughing between words, cheeks bright from the effort. "You think we did it right?"

He pressed his sole against the floor, testing. It held steady. "I think it's perfect for day one. We'll tackle the next set of boards tomorrow."

Her eyes sparked. "Perfect might be generous, but I'll take it."

They tidied up the tools in comfortable companionship, then parted ways to shower. Xander chose the downstairs bathroom, letting cool water run over his shoulders. He rubbed at the line of sweat and dirt along his arms, thinking about how easily they had fallen into rhythm. Even their banter about how to hold a hammer or line up a plank felt like the reflection of something deeper. They were learning to trust each other again.

When he finished, he dressed in clean jeans and a threadbare white T-shirt. He could still catch the faint smell of cedar clinging to his skin from earlier in the day. He found Emery in the study, perched on the floor with notebooks stacked against the shelves. She wore a robe that gapped slightly at her collar, hair pinned in a damp knot. Her bare feet skimmed the rug as she reached for a dog-eared architectural reference book.

"You look like you're studying," he said softly, crossing the threshold.

She peered up, eyes warm. "I have a lot to learn." Then she patted the spot beside her. "Sit with me?"

He settled down, shoulder to shoulder, backs nearly pressed to the row of books behind them. She closed her references, letting her robe slip a fraction, and exhaled slowly. The lamp on the desk provided just enough glow to wash them both in soft light. Beyond the window, cicadas started their nightly chorus.

"This," she said after a time, "still scares me."

He turned his head, regarding her carefully. "Good. If it didn't, it wouldn't matter."

Her expression changed from surprise to acceptance. Moisture lit her eyes, but she did not cry. Instead, she shifted so their legs touched, tangling her foot with his. "Then let's matter," she whispered.

His hand came up to cradle her cheek, and she leaned in, breath hitching. He captured her mouth in a kiss that held no question of the past or the future, only the tangible, living moment. She made a soft sound against his lips, and he angled closer, feeling the heat of her body through his thin shirt. Time blurred. When they finally pulled apart, her fingers coiled in the fabric at his shoulder as though reluctant to let go.

Neither of them bothered with elaborate speeches. No more confessions seemed necessary. They wandered upstairs together, sharing a companionable silence broken only by occasional jokes about how sore their arms would be in the morning from all that hammering.

In her bedroom, the remnants of day clung like an afterglow to the sheer curtains. He paused near the door, uncertain for half a second whether she truly wanted him to stay. But she tugged on his hand, guiding him inside. With the door closed, the world outside magnified every small movement, the soft rustle of sheets when she turned back the covers, the quiet shuffle of his feet as he removed his boots for the second time that night. Later they lay side by side, a gap of inches between them, staring at the ceiling fan rotate in a slow circle. She turned onto her side at last, propping her head on one hand. "Xander," she said, her voice low and steady. "Thank you for letting me lead earlier."

He slid his arm under her neck and drew her closer. "It's your house. Your life. I'm here because I want to be."

She reached up, tracing a light path along his jaw. Desire flared, but it was a gentle, comforting warmth rather than the desperate spark of long-buried longing. At some point, her eyelids fluttered shut, and she let out a long sigh that seemed to ease years of tension.

He pressed a kiss to her temple and felt her body melt against his. No barriers stood between them now, only the soft sigh of acceptance. Outside, the cicadas droned in a steady lullaby, and Silas snored somewhere in the hall. The old floorboards overhead groaned as the house settled.

For the first time in years, Xander did not feel like he

was hovering on the edge of something, waiting for a door to slam or an argument to erupt. Instead, he felt only the sweet, solid presence of this woman who had once been a stranger in her own home. Now, she had chosen to stay and chosen him to stay as well. That night, they fell asleep in the same bed. No declarations. No explanations. Just the quiet, sacred peace of two people who finally stopped running.

CHAPTER

TWENTY-FIVE

EMERY

Travel Note: I watched the sunrise in Nairobi with a Maasai woman who braided her daughter's hair and said, "This is our way of telling them they belong." I think I am learning how to belong too.

—EW

Emery stirred awake in her bedroom, the faint light of dawn filtering through gauzy curtains. At first, she kept her eyes closed, savoring the warmth of Xander's body draped over her side, the slow rise and fall of his chest reassuring her that he was there and that she was here, exactly where she was meant to be. For once, she felt no rush to fight the creeping consciousness. Silas's gentle snoring from the floor sounded like a soft hum, an offbeat lullaby in an otherwise still house. Emery smiled as she blinked at the ceiling. She let herself remain in Xander's arms for a few more breaths, memorizing each second.

Finally, she gingerly lifted his arm from around her waist and slipped free, trying not to jostle him too much.

A subtle ache lingered in her muscles, reminding her of how close they had been the night before. She didn't mind the twinge. It felt like proof of belonging rather than mere soreness. Her fingers moved instinctively to the locket at her neck. She traced its edge, feeling the cool silver, remembering the note tucked inside it, a small secret between her and her mother, in a way.

She stood and crossed to the bathroom. Warm water from the shower soon misted the mirror and chased away any lingering grogginess. Under the steady drum of the showerhead, Emery let her thoughts flow. She pictured her father's smile from two days before, the way he had pressed her hand in his hospital bed when he told her, "You were meant to carry it forward." She pictured her mother's grave, still unvisited this week, and made a silent promise to go. Steam curled around her face like a protective shawl.

When she emerged and dressed in a soft linen shirt and jeans, she noticed the bed was neatly made. Xander was gone, as was Silas. The morning sun angled through the half-drawn curtains, turning dust motes into floating sparks. She felt unhurried, more at ease than she had in years.

Footsteps and a faint clatter of cookware guided her to the kitchen. Xander stood by the stove under the glow of a single overhead light, moving with casual competence as he coaxed scrambled eggs to fluffy perfection. The smell of bacon and freshly brewed coffee made her stomach let out a small, appreciative growl.

He glanced over his shoulder, catching her entrance. "Morning," he said softly. "Coffee is ready if you want it. I thought you might be hungry."

Emery slid onto a stool by the counter. "You look like a man determined to have a productive day," she teased, eyeing the spatula in his hand.

A lopsided grin spread across his face. "Well, it started with a productive night, so I think I can relax just a bit." He lowered the heat on the stove and looked at her, resting one hip against the counter. "I hope you're feeling okay."

She felt a pleasant warmth in her cheeks. "I'm good. Better than good." Her gaze fell to the plate Xander placed in front of her. She forked a small mound of eggs, impressed by how tender they looked. "You've become quite the chef."

He shrugged. "Figured cooking for two might be a skill worth learning. Silas is no critic, he'll eat almost anything."

At the mention of the dog, Emery looked around. She spotted Silas sprawled near the pantry, tail wagging drowsily. She slipped off the stool and knelt. She scratched behind his ears. "You chose the right morning to hang out in here, buddy," she cooed. Then she retook her seat and sipped her coffee. "This is nice," she whispered, more to herself than to Xander.

They ate in easy quiet, the kind of silence that felt comfortable rather than strained. Outside, a breeze rustled the bushes lining the porch and carried in the distinct scent of salt and late-summer heat. When they finished, Xander rinsed the dishes and nodded toward the front door. "You want to sit outside a while?"

She followed him onto the porch and stepped into balmy morning air. The boards under their feet gave a familiar creak, and she smiled at the memory of how those same boards used to unsettle her, a reminder of time wearing everything down. Now, she found that tiny noise comforting, like the house was offering a morning greeting.

They settled on a pair of wicker chairs that faced out toward the marsh. Dappled sunlight warmed the porch. Silas curled at Xander's feet, content. Emery leaned back and closed her eyes and drew in a long breath through her nose. She felt the humid air cling to her skin.

Xander broke the silence. "I want to finish some trim work in the library. After that, I was thinking about the new balcony railings for the second floor. If we get that done, we'll be on track to start repainting the upstairs hallway next week."

He sounded excited but in a subdued way, like anticipation mixed with genuine pleasure. She watched him as he spoke, noting the way his gaze wandered to the yard, likely planning out each task that lay ahead. "You've come alive in this house," she said softly. "Though I guess it's not just the house anymore."

He caught the meaning in her words and nodded. "I stayed for the estate at first. Now I stay for more than that."

She let his words settle against her heart for a moment, then traced the fringe of the woven chair. "My father told me he is ready to go ahead and sign the house over," she said quietly. "He thinks I need it. Or maybe he thinks the house needs me. And Laura already has too many houses of her own." Xander angled to face her, curiosity lighting his eyes. "How do you feel about that?"

She exhaled, considering her answer. "Terrified. Like if I tie myself to this place, I will wake up one day and not recognize who I have become. But also, I want to do it. I want to see it flourish."

He reached over and took her hand gently. "Staying does not mean stopping," he said. "It means planting your feet long enough to bloom."

Emery felt her throat tighten. She squeezed his hand back. "Thank you," she murmured. She could not manage more words in that moment, but she hoped he heard her gratitude anyway.

They lingered on the porch, watching the morning brighten into full day. When the sun climbed higher, Emery excused herself to dress for an errand. She slipped away from the house with a quiet sense of purpose she had not felt before, driving in the direction of the small cemetery at the back edge of the property.

She parked by a low stone wall. A scattering of gravestones dotted the sun-washed grass, overshadowed by mossy oaks. She walked under those branches until she found the headstone marking Margot Ellison Westbrook. It was simple, her mother's name etched deeply in granite, a tiny magnolia carved underneath.

Emery knelt, feeling warmth radiate through her jeans from the ground. She touched the base of the headstone and swallowed hard. For a long time, she sat and remembered the many questions she had never asked while her mother was alive.

Finally, she lifted the silver locket she always wore now. She pressed it against the stone. "I wish we could have talked about this more," she said aloud, her voice wavering slightly. "About who I am, and who you wanted me to be. I wish you could tell me why you chose lies over honesty. Maybe you thought it would hurt less."

A gentle breeze brushed past, ruffling the loose strands of her hair. She set the pendant carefully at the foot of the grave. "You loved me enough to lie," she whispered, "and maybe too much to stop. But I am going to try to love you with the truth. I hope that is enough."

A single white petal drifted from one of the overhanging magnolia tree branches, landing in her lap. She gazed at it, not sure if it was coincidence or something more. Whatever it was, it felt like grace. She stayed there a while longer, letting quiet tears come and go until she felt lighter.

When she returned to the estate, she headed upstairs to her mother's old desk. Dust coated the surface, and she coughed softly as she opened the drawers. For a moment, she hesitated. She dreaded the possibility of finding more secrets, more half truths. But she pressed on, scouring each compartment until she reached a narrow one at the bottom.

Inside lay a stack of pages clipped together. The title

page read, *A Charleston Woman by Margot Ellison West-brook*. Her mother's handwriting looped elegantly in the margins. Emery flipped past the first page and saw the dedication. *To my daughters. For the truth I never found the words to tell.*

Her pulse quickened as she realized what she was holding, her mother's unfinished memoir. Here was another story. Another chance for answers, or at least for understanding. She pressed the manuscript to her chest and let out a trembling breath, half excitement, half sorrow.

That evening, she found Xander on the porch, a dim candle on the low table between the wicker chairs. Cicadas droned in the humid darkness, and the smell of fresh paint lingered on his clothes. She settled beside him and gave him a solemn look. "I found something," she said, placing the manuscript on her lap.

His eyes moved over the title. Slowly, he reached out and touched the edges of the pages. "Her memoir?" he asked.

Emery nodded. "There are only fragments. Some chapters are nearly complete, while others are just notes. She dedicated it to me and Laura."

They spent the next hour looking through the document, reading a passage here and there under the unsteady glow of candlelight. Some pages bore entire paragraphs about Margot's childhood, others contained only scribbled outlines. Most were unsettled reflections on love, regrets, and fierce devotion to her family. It felt like unraveling a thread that had been knotted for years.

When they finally paused, Emery closed the manuscript and rested a palm against the cover. "Do you think she'd want me to finish it?"

Xander's gaze was gentle. "I think she's been waiting for you to try," he replied.

They fell silent as the night wrapped itself around the porch. Silas dozed by the door, stirring only when the faint rustle of leaves signaled a breeze. Emery touched her mother's manuscript again, feeling a surge of determination. She glanced at Xander, his features softened by candlelight, and felt the certainty that she was ready.

Later, in her bedroom, she propped her journal on her knees and clicked on the bedside lamp. She stared at a blank page for a few beats, a light hum of nerves dancing in her chest. Then she set her pen to paper, writing the words that had hovered in her mind since discovering her mother's memoir.

I came home thinking everything was gone. What I found was everything waiting.

Her hand shook slightly as she added the final punctuation, and her eyes burned briefly with unshed tears. She closed the journal and smoothed her palm over the cover, letting her chest rise and fall as the heaviness settled into something else, something close to hope. In that moment, she allowed herself to believe she was on the brink of belonging, truly belonging, in a way that no plane ticket or foreign city had ever offered. The lamp dimmed once, but the light remained steady. She exhaled in relief, welcoming the calm that had taken root. Silas snored softly on the rug near the door, and from downstairs came the faint scrape of Xander tidying for the night. She could feel the gentle hum of the house, old timbers and all, as though it were breathing beside her.

CHAPTER

TWENTY-SIX

XANDER

Travel Note: I spent one Christmas in Buenos Aires writing postcards I never sent. It is not enough to write the words. You have to deliver them. I am ready to say what matters out loud.

—EW

Xander stirred in the first glow of dawn. He lay on his side, one arm tucked beneath the pillow, eyes drifting to the silhouette in bed beside him. Emery slept with her hair half-fanned across the sheets, her cheek pressed into a pillow still imprinted with the shape of dreams. He studied the line of her jaw, the delicate curve of her shoulder, and the way the sheet had slipped just below her collarbone. It was a slow, reverent moment. He memorized every inch of her because, after all these years of half-truths and misunderstanding, he was finally allowed to keep what he saw.

He could tell it was close to sunrise because a faint

gray light touched the edges of the curtains. Emery's breath changed in slow intervals. He noticed her chest rising and falling, each inhale a quiet reassurance that she was there, that she had chosen to remain by his side. In another time, he would have anticipated her leaving, braced for the disappointment of an empty bed before dawn. This morning, that notion felt distant. She had promised she would stay, and he let himself believe her.

When he carefully slid out of bed, he took great care not to jostle the mattress. He caught a glimpse of her eyelids shifting, but she didn't truly wake. She exhaled softly and settled back into peaceful sleep. Silas was curled near the doorway, tail thumping once against the floor when Xander moved. Xander gave him a silent nod, and the dog blinked in acknowledgment, as though saying he too wanted a few more minutes of rest.

Downstairs, the house greeted him with its familiar morning creaks. He noticed the gentle whir of a ceiling fan turning in the parlor. The air smelled faintly of old books and pine-scented floor polish. It was a scent he had come to associate with second chances. In the kitchen, he ground fresh coffee beans and turned on the machine, stepping away to check the windows while he waited.

He walked each hallway methodically, a mental list forming in his mind. He examined the frames around the tall windows that faced the marsh, running a hand along the fresh paint. They seemed to have held up well against the previous night's humidity. Next, he moved to the wide front porch. The boards there were new, carefully laid during the weeks of tension and hope that had marked his and Emery's slow reconciliation. He tested the last rail he had replaced. No loose spindles. He stood for a moment, enjoying the mild weather, the feeling of something like peace.

Coffee called him back inside, but he decided to do one final inspection before drinking his fill. He headed into the dining room. The big windows let in pale morning light, revealing how well the new curtains matched the color scheme Emery had picked. He grinned. A few months ago, he never would have guessed he'd be poring over curtain fabrics with her, let alone enjoying it.

In the kitchen, he poured a mug of coffee and filled a second one in case Emery woke soon. Steam curled upward, and he breathed in the comforting bitterness. He sipped slowly, leaning against the counter, aware of how different this ritual felt now. Once, he might have made only one cup, convinced she would be gone or uninterested. That time was over, and the evidence of it sat in a full mug, waiting patiently on the counter.

He decided to step outside for a real look at the marsh. Silas followed, nails clicking against the floorboards as Xander opened the screen door. The morning sky was brushed with lavender and pink, a pastel promise that the day might be gentle. He strolled toward the edge of the garden, where rosemary grew in unruly clumps alongside neat rows of sage and thyme, Emery's attempt to transform neglected soil into something alive.

He nearly walked past the rosemary bush before he noticed the nest. He paused and crouched, parting the fragrant leaves just enough to see. Inside, two tiny blue eggs nestled together, perfect in their fragility. Something stirred in him as he stared. He had never thought of rosemary as a hiding place for new life. The nest seemed almost symbolic, a small beginning of something fresh in the midst of all that was old. With a gentleness close to reverence, he stood, careful not to disturb the nest or brush the plant too forcefully. A hint of a smile touched his lips as he continued his inspection.

Back inside, Emery's coffee remained untouched on the counter. He lowered the heat on the coffee maker so it would not grow stale too quickly. Then he headed upstairs to shower, taking each step quietly. The water was a welcome wake-up, washing away the sawdust smudges lingering from the previous night's drafting session. He kept imagining her waiting in bed, but when he emerged in a clean shirt and jeans, ready to face the day, she was still curled in the covers. Let her sleep, he thought. She deserved the rest. They both did.

He left a note on a slip of paper near her mug in the kitchen.

Em, had to run a quick errand. Back soon. Coffee is yours.

-X

By the time he stepped outside again, the sky had brightened. He climbed into his old truck, the engine rumbling beneath him, and merged into light morning traffic. Charleston woke slowly, but it always seemed to greet him with that strange blend of old and new. He parked near Roper Hospital and made his way to the front desk. The hallways were faintly lit by overhead fluorescents, the smell of antiseptic drifting in the air. His footsteps echoed as he moved toward David's room.

He was not sure what to expect today. Sometimes David was bright and chatty, eager to discuss the estate or the writing retreat Emery had recently started talking about. Other times, he was drowsy, eyes half-lidded, too weary to converse. This morning, David appeared awake, sitting propped against pillows. His movements were more delicate now, but his gaze remained clear.

"You're early, Xander," David said in a raspy but steady voice. "When I saw the clock, I half-expected the nurse to say you would not be here until afternoon."

"I wanted to see how you were feeling," Xander replied. He crossed the room and sank into the chair beside the bed. "Emery's still asleep at home."

David's thin lips twitched in something like a smile. "Let her rest."

They exchanged a few remarks, lightly touching on the weather and some minor questions about the estate's progress. Xander mentioned the final coats of stain on the porch railings and the new shutters they had installed the previous week. David nodded, eyes trained on Xander with a sharpness that defied his weakening body.

"I want you to stay," David said abruptly. "Not because of the house. Not because of her. Because I think you belong here as much as she does."

Xander's shoulders tensed. He exhaled before answering. "I've always belonged to her. I just didn't know what to do when she left."

David's hand shifted beneath the blanket, as though he wanted to reach out but couldn't quite muster the energy. "So don't leave now. People run, but legacy is built by the ones who come back and keep standing." His voice was soft yet carried the weight of a lesson hammered by time.

Xander leaned forward in the chair, elbows propped on his knees. His voice came out quieter than usual. "I won't. I mean it. I plan to stay."

David nodded once and closed his eyes, letting that affirmation settle in. Xander remained at the bedside a bit longer, speaking in low tones about the new idea for the estate. He mentioned that Emery wanted to open a retreat for writers and artists, and David's face lit up with something that looked like pride. After a while, a nurse stepped in to check David's vitals, quietly suggesting he needed rest. Xander offered David a final nod. He stood and left the room, feeling a subtle surge of relief and responsibility rising together in his chest.

Driving away from the hospital, he realized how strange it felt to let hope outweigh dread. He used to come here worried about everything he might lose. Now, the hope felt unfamiliar but not unwelcome. He headed across town, passing the Ravenel Bridge entrance on his left. A wave of old memories threatened to grip him, memories of how leaving or staying once felt like a gamble. He focused on the road and continued.

He stopped at the local preservation office in a nondescript municipal building partway between the hospital and the estate. The corridors smelled of old paper and echoes of city planning debate. The clerk greeted him by name and handed over a thick envelope containing forms for grants, historical site nominations, and cultural programming in Charleston. These were the official steps toward turning Emery's dream into something real. He thanked the clerk, tucked the envelope under his arm, and walked back outside into soft, late morning sunshine.

With the forms in hand, he drove to a hardware store to meet an old carpenter friend, Gus. Together they lingered over architectural sketches laid out across the tailgate of Xander's truck. He walked Gus through the concept of expanding the carriage house into a working demonstration workshop, where visitors and aspiring preservationists could learn. In the old days, Xander might have hesitated to invest in such an ambitious plan, but now every word he spoke was laced with a fresh sense of direction. He wasn't just preserving the Westbrook estate. He was in essence helping build a future for it.

Gus nodded approvingly and jotted notes on the corners of the papers. The day was warm, and the tang of sawdust from a nearby lumber yard captivated them both. They talked about cost estimates, potential volunteers, and how quickly they might complete the renovations. When they parted ways, Xander shook Gus's hand firmly, feeling a renewed surge of energy that carried him back to the truck.

By the time he arrived home, the sun had reached a gentle afternoon brightness. Emery's car was in the driveway. He stepped out and scooped up the envelope of grant papers. Silas spotted him from the porch and loped over, tail wagging in a slow, steady rhythm that always reminded Xander of loyal acceptance.

Inside, he found Emery in the living room, barefoot and flipping through a stack of mail. She glanced up, and her tired eyes immediately sparked with something bright.

"You were gone a while," she remarked, not accusing him but curious.

He set down the envelope of forms on a nearby table. "Met up with Gus about that expansion. Also stopped by the hospital to see your dad."

Her expression shifted to concern. "How is he?"

"Weaker," Xander admitted, "but determined. He told me not to leave."

Her lips parted in a silent sigh, then she stepped closer to him. She lifted a hand to the back of his neck and pulled him in for a soft, unhurried kiss. The contact was gentle but spoke volumes, a thousand silent affirmations passing between them. When she pulled away, her forehead rested briefly against his.

"I'm glad you're here," she whispered.

They settled in the study after a while, side by side on the old couch that was now covered in a new slipcover Emery had found. She flipped through some of her notes for the residency idea. Xander thumbed through the grant documents, explaining each form. She listened, occasionally interjecting with questions about budget or timeline. He noticed how she radiated excitement, and it made him marvel at how different she was from the distant woman he once feared would vanish forever.

Come evening, the two of them drifted onto the front porch, letting the screen door rattle shut behind them. Xander brought a rough sketchpad with him, one corner dog-eared from frequent use. He had been up late the night before, drafting a potential floor plan for the renovated carriage house, scrawling creative additions in the margins. He saw a faint smear of pencil on his thumb, a mark of his labor. Emery sat beside him, hugging her knees to her chest on the swing. She rested her chin on them, watching him with open curiosity.

"You're not building things anymore," she said, her voice low and thrumming with admiration. "You're building something."

He set the pad aside and turned to her, feeling the quiet stir of summer wind. "With you," he said simply.

She took his hand and twined her fingers through his. "For us."

Fireflies began to appear in the growing twilight, spots of golden light that hovered above the flowerbeds and beyond, into the garden. Xander thought about the eggs in that rosemary bush, how they sat so delicately hidden, with everything they could become. He mused that this house was like a nest too, holding them as they decided how to hatch a future they had once been too afraid to admit they wanted.

He closed his eyes for a moment, inhaling the scent of warm earth and faint blossoms. Every broken piece of their past had led them here, he realized. The heartbreak, the misunderstandings, the guilt, each crack had let in a little more light. The arms of live oaks stood against the sky, and the final glimmers of sunset faded into a deep cobalt overhead.

They lingered until the stars began to appear, pinpricks above the marsh. He felt her hand in his, and it gave him the comfort he had lacked for so long. When the night claimed the porch, they went inside, exchanging quiet smiles that spoke more than words could hold. The dog padded after them, nails clicking across the floor. In the study, Emery checked a draft she was working on and set it aside.

Xander murmured something about feeling restless and headed upstairs, returning a few minutes later with a folded piece of paper. He slipped into Emery's bedroom and set the note in the drawer of her writing desk, careful not to disturb the stack of journals she kept there. His heart beat with a mixture of tension and absolute resolve. This note was brief, but it mattered because he had learned that writing words was not enough. You had to let them reach the person they were meant for.

He glanced at the note one last time.

I'll still be here in the morning. I hope you will be too.

—X

CHAPTER

TWENTY-SEVEN

EMERY

Emery awoke with a gentle sense of awakening coursing through her, although she had no plans to rush out of bed. Light filtered in through the curtains, turning the edges of the room gold. She stayed still, letting herself absorb this newfound calm. Thoughts of the past few weeks hovered in her mind, restorations half-finished, truths half-told, and a heart that felt more settled than it ever had. She swallowed and let the quiet hold her.

When she finally rose, she walked across the floorboards of her childhood bedroom, aware of how three weeks ago this space felt like a stranger's domain. Now, it felt like hers again. She rubbed her arms, remembering how the night air the previous evening had been thick with humidity and hope.

Quietly, she put on a soft cotton dress, then combed through her hair just enough to tame the tangles. Her reflection in the mirror looked calm, though a faint tiredness lingered in the corners of her eyes.

Heading toward the hallway, she paused at her desk. She had started placing her notebooks and pens there, a silent vow that she would make this desk part of her morning routine. She noticed the drawer was slightly ajar. Yesterday, it had been closed neatly. Now, the gap reminded her of a half-offered secret. Curiosity made her tug it open.

Inside lay a slip of paper, folded once. The handwriting across the top read "Emery" in Xander's unmistakably neat script. She inhaled, her pulse quickening. Gently, she lifted the note out and opened it. Three lines, written carefully:

I'll still be here in the morning. I hope you will be too.

—X

For a long moment, she stood near the desk and pressed the note to her chest. The warmth of those words filled her with something close to gratitude. She recalled all the times she had left places behind, chasing temporary solace around the globe. She had never considered whether anyone else might be waiting. Silencing the sudden flutter in her rib cage, she read the words again, then folded the note. She hoped he knew that she planned to stay.

Barefoot, she made her way downstairs. The estate remained quiet except for the muffled sound of wind through the nearby marsh. She stepped onto the front porch, drawn by the scent of coffee. Outside, Xander waited, dressed in worn jeans and a loose T-shirt. He offered her a mug without a word. She took it, their eyes meeting briefly in a gentle understanding. There was no urge to fill the silence, the morning itself felt sacred enough.

They sat side by side on the porch steps. The railings still smelled faintly of fresh wood and stain. In the distance, mist hovered over the marsh like a thin veil, drifting lazily as the sun rose. Emery sipped her coffee, appreciating the mild bitterness. She glanced at Xander, who kept his gaze on the horizon. Neither spoke about the note she had found. They did not need to.

Eventually, they finished their coffees. The sound of Silas padding over broke the quiet. He nudged Emery's hand, and she gave him a gentle rub behind the ears. She felt more at peace than she had in years. She stood, brushing off her dress, and took one last look at Xander before heading back inside to tackle the day.

By midmorning, she had relocated to her mother's bedroom, though part of her still hesitated to call it that. At some point, she couldn't remember when, her parents had separate bedrooms. Boxes rested on the dresser and bed, some half-labeled, some still sealed. The jewelry box sat in the center of the bedspread, a carved wooden container that smelled faintly of cedar and perfume. She stared at it for a few seconds, bracing herself.

She lifted the lid, unveiling a modest collection of necklaces, rings, and loose brooches. She separated the pieces into piles, one for Laura, one for herself, a few for donation. Several pieces looked familiar from childhood memories or old photographs. She recalled Margot wearing them at parties or family gatherings. The recollection stirred a pang of longing, but it was gentler than before.

At the bottom, a stray pin caught her attention. It must have slipped behind a stacked pair of earrings. She pulled it away. The pin's base had stuck to the wooden panel beneath, as if glued by time or disuse. To her surprise, the panel shifted. She pressed lightly, and it lifted, a false bottom.

Her breath caught in her throat as she gently lifted the board that concealed the false bottom. Beneath lay an envelope and an older photograph. She picked up the photo first, a dignified-looking man in a tailored suit. The edges of the picture had begun to yellow, and the man's expression was reserved, his gaze direct. Emery felt a primal sense of recognition, though she had never seen his face before.

Her pulse quickened. She turned the photograph over. No name was scrawled on the back, just the faint outline of a year. She set it aside and reached for the envelope, which displayed her name, Emery. She swallowed hard, her hands trembling as she opened it. Inside were several pages in Margot's handwriting. The first line made her heart skip.

My dearest girl,
There are things I never told you. Not out of shame, but because I was never sure you were ready. Maybe I was not ready either. You come from a long line of women who love deeply, even when it hurts. I only hope you learn to love with open hands...

Emery's eyes darted across the page, tears rising before she realized she was weeping. She had suspected for a while, ever since other letters had revealed parts of the truth. But seeing Julian Ashcroft's name in her mother's handwriting made everything concrete. She pictured an entire life lost to secrecy and heartbreak.

Her mother's testimony spelled out how Julian had left, how David had chosen to raise Emery as his own, and how Margot had kept quiet, possibly out of fear or indecision. Reading each word felt like walking through a door she could never close again.

By the time she finished the letter, her tears had turned into soft sobs. She pressed her forehead against her palm, letting the grief pass through her. After a minute, she calmed enough to fold the pages neatly and place them inside her journal she had retrieved from her bedroom. Then she wrote a simple line: I know now. And I am still here.

Resolute, she turned to a clean page in her journal. The emotional weight of the day compelled her to write a letter not to her mother, not to Xander, but to who she had been seven years ago. Carefully, she scribbled phrases about forgiveness, about running away, about the illusions that had driven her to constant travel. She thanked her younger self for surviving but reminded that version of herself that survival was not the same as living. The act of writing it down soothed her, as if she were releasing a final breath of regret.

By early afternoon, Emery found herself driving into downtown Charleston, a collection of loose manuscript pages and notes tucked into a folder beside her. The city's familiar streets thrummed with midday energy. Students and tourists bustled along sidewalks, and the pastel hues of the old buildings glowed in the sunlight. She parked near a narrow road off King Street, then walked the rest of the way to the house of a friend who was a publisher. A lazy ceiling fan spun on the friend's sunroom porch, providing mild relief from the heat.

Inside, they sipped sweet tea. Her friend listened attentively as Emery explained the concept: a project that wove Margot's partially finished manuscript with Emery's own reflections, not simply as a memoir, but as a dual reckoning. It was about telling the story Margot had not been able to finish and confronting the truths that Emery herself had once fled. Emery paused at the end of her pitch, fingers fidgeting with the condensation on her glass.

Her friend leaned forward, eyes bright. "Emery, this is not just a good idea. This is your voice finding its shape."

The words reverberated in Emery's chest. For the first time, she felt real excitement about writing, not as an escape, but as a way to face what mattered. She smiled at her friend gratefully, and they clinked glasses in a small toast. She spent another half hour brainstorming potential structures before gathering her notes to leave. Outside, the air smelled of honeysuckle and car exhaust, that oddly comforting Charleston blend.

She drove back to the estate with the windows rolled down. The late-afternoon light spread across the marshy landscape, painting the reeds and water in soft gold. A sense of belonging crept in, a quiet hum in her chest she had never expected to feel again.

That evening, Emery joined Xander on the back deck. Strings of small white lights were hung above them like a scattering of stars. A gentle breeze carried the scent of rosemary from a nearby herb planter. They ate a simple dinner of grilled fish and vegetables, their conversation unhurried. Occasionally, he would glance at her and smile in that quiet way that made her heart shift.

When their plates were cleared, Xander turned off the overhead lantern, leaving only the string lights. She rose from her seat, stepping closer to him. He slid an arm around her waist, and she rested her head against his chest. Together, they began to sway in a slow dance, guided by no music except the nocturnal chorus of cicadas and rustling leaves. Their bare feet brushed the wooden boards in a languid rhythm. Emery's pulse thrummed, half from the closeness of his body, half from the sense that everything she had run from was finally behind her.

Her voice came out as a whisper. "I am not afraid anymore."

He responded by holding her tighter. "Then we are exactly where we are supposed to be."

She closed her eyes, let the warmth of him center her, and felt each inhale pass between them. His heartbeat was steady beneath her cheek. There had been a time when this moment would have been too much, too close, too real. Now it felt like a promise. She gently slid her hand up to cup his jaw, pressing a soft kiss to his cheek. He exhaled, turning his face until their lips met. The tender press of his mouth against hers left nothing to question.

In her bedroom, she changed into a loose tank top and pulled on soft cotton shorts. The room was moonlit, the partial glow drawing faint silhouettes on the walls. She moved to her writing desk, where she sensed the day's events still swirling in her head. Setting her journal on the nightstand, she opened it to a fresh page. For a moment, she stared at the blank space, unsure of how to capture the fullness of everything she felt.

Finally, she let the pen flow.

Tomorrow, I will begin again. And this time, I will stay.

She studied the words, feeling each letter deeply. No more running, no more silent regrets. She closed her journal and set it carefully on the nightstand. Outside, a faint breeze rattled the window, but the rest of the house felt quiet as if it were breathing with her. Smiling at herself, Emery switched off the lamp, settled against the pillows and let her grateful heart find rest in the darkness.

CHAPTER

TWENTY-EIGHT

XANDER

Travel Note: I once learned a dance from an old man in Oaxaca who said, "We don't do this to forget. We do this to remember who made it with us." That's what this porch feels like tonight.
—EW

Xander roused before the horizon gave any hint of dawn. Silence stretched through the estate's halls, stirring only when Silas let out a soft snore in the nearby sitting room. Xander lay still for several breaths, listening to the old dog's gentle rumble, a faint tick from the cooling pipes, and somewhere downstairs, the lingering echo of the porch swing that never seemed entirely motionless. Moonlight seeped around the edges of the shutters, revealing Emery's sleeping form on the bed beside him.

Though he and Emery had fallen asleep hours ago, he still caught himself marveling that she was here, that she had chosen to stay in this place. Her face in the half-light

259

appeared peaceful, lips parted in the calm that had taken so long for her to embrace. He resisted the urge to reach out because he might wake her before she could soak in more rest.

He slid from the sheets with careful movements and pressed bare feet to the wooden floor. The old boards gave a slight groan under his weight, but Emery did not stir, only made a gentle sound in her sleep that brought a faint smile to his lips. He found his jeans draped over a chair, pulled them on, and padded quietly downstairs. The house, once so heavy with ghosts, now felt like it was inhaling and exhaling with them, a living thing that had decided it could hold new possibilities.

He stepped into the kitchen and flipped on a single overhead light. Tall windows framed the shimmering silhouette of the marsh beyond. In another hour, the glow of day would flood this space, but for now he welcomed the soft quiet. He scooped fresh coffee grounds into the machine and let it start its slow drip while the aroma built into something comforting.

Silas meandered in with his tail wagging. The old golden retriever bumped his head against Xander's leg, and Xander gave him a gentle rub behind the ears. It always warmed him to see how the dog never lost faith in morning routines. For Silas, consistency was everything, a steady pat on the head, a quiet reassurance that daybreak always came.

Xander poured a mug of coffee and carried it out to the front porch. The distant call of a marsh bird echoed through the predawn stillness. He set the cup on the porch railing. It was a ritual he'd grown used to, waiting for her, holding space for the day they would greet together.

Taking a seat on the porch swing, he felt the slight sway beneath him. Once upon a time, that small creak might have left him tense. Now, it felt like a lullaby to nerves that had finally begun to rest. He let the damp coastal air wrap him in a peace he never expected to feel in these walls.

Yet he sensed a charge in the air, as if they stood at the boundary of something unnamed. The thought made him rise again. He wandered, coffee mug in hand, picked up a flashlight that hung on a hook, and went down the front steps and around the side of the house. Dew clung to the grass. He followed a winding path to the place where they had first tried to coax tomatoes from the stubborn ground.

A wave of quiet pride washed over him as he turned on the flashlight to survey how his meager seedlings were doing. He crouched next to a green bush. Weeks ago, it was barely a handful of leaves. Now, nestled among those green stems, a single tomato peeked out, small, bright, and undeniably growing.

"Look at you," he murmured. He imagined Emery teasing him for talking to a plant. But the sight filled his chest with hope. If something could flourish in this abandoned garden, then all the heartbreak, the misunderstandings, and the secrets that once weighed them down might yield something good too.

He placed a palm lightly against the earth, feeling its warmth, then stood. He made a short circuit around the house, noticing details he had carefully restored, the spindles of the front porch railing, the window sashes in the sunroom, the fresh boards that now anchored the back deck. This was the last day he would view the property as a project in limbo. Soon, fresh plans would carry them beyond mere restoration and into something bigger. He walked toward the workshop that had been his sanctuary for months, but the impulse to linger on the porch drew him back.

When he returned to the porch, the air smelled of morning, a blend of salt breeze and brewing coffee. The horizon streaked with the first faint line of pink. He settled down again on the swing. This time, he removed a drafting pad from beneath the seat. He had stashed it there recently, itching to articulate a new blueprint beyond the standard tasks.

Turning on the flashlight again to give him some light, he placed the pad across his knees and opened it. The blank page urged him to begin, so he guided his pencil in swift, deliberate strokes. He sketched the shape of the estate's main building, a broad rectangle hinting at old family architecture, then drew an extended structure off to one side, a cluster of rooms that would become small studios and writing nooks. In the margin, he wrote a note, *Common area: library plus lounge.* He smiled to himself. Emery had once said she dreamed of opening the house for expressive gatherings where people could write, share stories, or simply feel safe. It was an idea that had freed him from merely restoring old bones and invited him to build something new instead.

He was so absorbed that he did not notice Emery's

footsteps until she stepped onto the porch. She wore an oversized shirt that brushed her thighs, hair was mussed around her face, and she carried a mug of coffee. Even half asleep, she moved with a gentle grace that made him want to hold her. She paused to sip, eyes closed as she savored the coffee's warmth.

He set aside his pencil. "You could have stayed in bed longer," he said quietly, though his voice revealed he was happy to see her.

She shrugged, a small smile playing at her lips. "You forgot that I like to watch sunrises too. Besides, I smelled coffee."

He chuckled and waited as she approached, then let her sink next to him on the swing. The old porch boards were still cool, and a faint breeze ruffled the hair at her temples. She tucked her body lightly against his side, pressing her cheek to his shoulder for a moment.

"You're carrying that pad around again," she said, nodding toward his sketches. She peered down at the lines inked across the page, her dark eyes keen. "Planning something secret?"

He exhaled. "Not exactly secret. More like something I'm ready to show you." Gently, he lifted the pad so she could see.

She scanned the rough blueprint, rectangular hallways branching into separate wings, dotted with small boxes labeled "study," "guest suite," "reading alcove." A faint excitement shimmered in her voice when she said, "So you're serious about the writing residency?"

"I am," he replied. "I want a place that's more than a

house trying to bury its ghosts. I want it to be a place that welcomes new life. Writers, artists, anyone searching for a quiet corner to create."

Her hands slid over his, still resting on the sketch-book. "This is good," she murmured. "You're good, Xander."

He studied her face for a moment. A doubt edged his gaze, not about the plans themselves, but about the two of them. "Are we good?" he asked quietly.

"We're not perfect," she said. She set her coffee aside and met his eyes with a frankness that sent warmth through his chest. "But we're true."

He nodded. Sometimes honesty was enough. The morning lengthened, an unspoken agreement that they had said what mattered. They both turned their attention back to the horizon. The sun was climbing, painting edges of clouds in gold.

She nudged him. "Oh, if you ever get bored, we can always pick another fight about light fixtures."

He pretended to scowl. "Don't even start. I can still remember that argument about brass sconces in the entryway."

She laughed, the sound low and authentic. "I had a dream last night," she said, shifting closer. "We were older. Wrinkled, maybe. Still sitting on this porch, arguing about which antique will fit best in the big hall."

"Were we still using the porch swing as a second office?"

"Absolutely," she teased. "Nothing ever changes that."

He leaned down to press a light kiss to the top of her

head. "If that's how the future looks, I can handle more lamp and sconce debates."

They fell into a companionable silence as birds began to stir in the oaks overhead. The house felt awake now. It waited for them to finish their quiet moment. Xander's hand found Emery's, and he gave it a small squeeze. She sighed contentedly and traced the outline of a half-finished window sketch on his page.

Eventually, she stood with her empty mug, reaching to gather his as well. "I'll go refresh these," she said. "You keep sketching."

He watched her disappear inside. The screen door rattled behind her, then stilled. In her absence, he felt the emptiness of the porch for just a moment. The breeze carried the sweet scent of wet grass and lingering night blooms. She would be back, and that knowledge reassured him more than any promise they had ever spoken out loud.

He turned his attention once more to the blueprint, adding careful notes in the margins: "Max occupancy," "Workshop materials," "Guest capacity." Each pencil mark felt like a tiny vow to her, to himself, and to every piece of this home that deserved a second life.

He remained there until the sun rose high enough to wash the porch in warmth. By then, Emery had returned, sat beside him once more, and observed while he made finishing touches. They shared breakfast eventually, simple toast, jam, and new coffees, before the day coaxed them into separate tasks. She insisted on sorting through books for what she called a "rotating library" to occupy the new reading lounge. He headed upstairs to check a remodel detail he had left half-done the previous afternoon.

By late morning, the house started to give way to the normal rhythms of footsteps, phone calls, and the hum of activity. He found himself wandering into Emery's room, where she had arranged her desk by the window. It looked as though she had stepped away for a moment. An open journal lay across the surface, and a small, carved paperweight pinned down one corner against a light breeze from the window. Her pen was left angled on top, as if she had paused in mid-thought.

Xander felt a need stir in him, a wish to leave her something she could lean on whenever doubts arose again. He retrieved a blank piece of stationery from the nearby drawer and sat on the edge of the bed. The late morning sun cast tree-filtered shadows on the floorboards. His heart thudded quietly as he wrote:

If we forget, we begin here. On the porch. With coffee. With light. With choosing each other again.

He let the ink dry, drawing in a slow inhale, then read it back. So much of their story had hinged on words unsaid, letters never sent. This time, he wanted his words to remain in her hands. He folded the page and wrote her name on the outside and left it on her desk.

Stepping away, he caught his own reflection in the mirror above the desk. He saw a man who had been weighed down for years by things he could not name. Today, that weight felt bearable. Hopeful, even. He ran a hand through his hair, exhaling.

Satisfied, he left her room and drifted down the hallway, seeking her out for no other reason than to see her smile. He found her on the upstairs landing, kneeling beside a chest labeled with half-faded script. She looked up, confusion mixed with curiosity. "I did not know about this trunk," she murmured.

"You will find new surprises all the time in this place." He offered a calm grin. She reached for him, and he helped her stand. Their hands remained linked, an unspoken question in her eyes.

He gently tugged her hand. "Come on. Let us take a break from rummaging through old boxes."

They made their way back to the bedroom they now shared, the door standing ajar in quiet welcome. Sunbeams fanned across the floor in bright ribbons. Emery set down the handful of old letters she had carried from the trunk. She opened the closet, rummaged for a spare blanket, then changed her mind and left it. Instead, she walked to him, face soft.

He wrapped an arm around her waist. "Have I told you today how proud I am?" he said. "For everything you have done, for staying to build something out of all this."

She slid her hands up his shoulders. "If you only knew how much that means to me."

She guided him toward the bed, and a quiet settled over them. The estate outside went on with its daily tasks, wood settling, Silas shuffling around, the distant call of a bird, but here, for this moment, they had time. No squeaking floorboard or lingering ghost intruded as they eased onto the mattress together.

TWENTY-NINE

EMERY

Travel Note: I once heard that in Chiang Mai, they send lanterns to the sky, each carrying a wish. Tonight, I do not need fairytale fragments. I just want to hold his hand in this quiet and know that I stayed.

—EW

Emery closed her journal and exhaled. She let her fingertips rest on the notebook's worn edges, as if tethering all her scattered nerves to the page. The day had brought a gentler light, but her heart felt heavier than it had in weeks. She smoothed a stray curl behind her ear and rose from her desk, aware that she was running late. She had promised her father she would return after lunch.

She found Xander in the hallway, wearing a faded T-shirt and carefully setting aside a stack of lumber samples. He looked up at her approach. The morning had already been busy, a supplier drop-off, a brief discussion about the second-floor balcony, and a shared half-smile over coffee.

In another lifetime, small domestic routines would have felt out of reach. Now, they felt like a fragile promise.

He studied her face and frowned. "You look like you hardly slept. Are you sure you want to do this alone?"

She managed a small smile. "He gets tired faster these days, but I think I need the time with him. By myself."

Xander opened his mouth, but no words came. His gaze said enough, concern, regret, affection all at once. Gently, he reached for her fingers, giving them a light squeeze. "Tell him I said hello."

Emery squeezed back, then slipped out to the porch. Silas nosed her leg as she passed, tail wagging in a comforting rhythm. The sun was mild for Charleston this time of year, thin clouds drifting across an otherwise clear sky. She breathed in the warmth of late afternoon, then climbed into her car. Her father's voice, the memory of it, drove her onward.

She made the trip into downtown Charleston, weaving through streets she had once avoided. She could have recited every turn by heart, but today the roads felt different. She did not grip the steering wheel in dread. Instead, she let each stoplight, each traffic lull, cradle her in some tentative calm. She parked near Roper Hospital and walked inside, bracing herself against the lingering antiseptic smell that still pressed at her senses.

When she reached her father's room, she paused just outside the door. Through the narrow window set in the frame, she saw him reclined against his pillows, the over-head lights dialed low. His eyes were closed. A book rested on his lap. Some days were better than others. She had learned that his energy came and went like the tide. She stepped into the room carefully, hoping not to wake him if he was resting.

But David stirred at the sound of her footsteps. His eyes fluttered open, and a slow smile curved his lips. "Emmy," he said softly. His voice was weaker than yesterday. She heard an echo of the man who once carried her on his shoulders across the old orchard behind their estate.

"Hi, Dad," she replied, closing the door behind her. She set her bag on the small table by the window and approached the bed. Her gaze traveled to the book lying across his lap, Margot's unfinished manuscript. She swallowed a knot in her throat. This was the project that connected them all, Margot's words, Emery's determination, and David's unwavering faith that they would preserve it.

His fingers trembled lightly as he brushed the pages. "I wanted another taste of your mother's writing. I did not get far."

Emery gently pulled a chair closer. The fabric of the seat crinkled as she settled down and drew the manuscript into her hands. "Shall I read it to you?"

He nodded, relief in his eyes. Emery cleared her throat and began. The words wove a picture of Charleston's old beginnings, a swirl of personal anecdotes about a city Margot had loved fiercely yet never fully escaped. Halfway through a paragraph about the first night Margot spent in the Westbrook estate as a newlywed, Emery's voice caught. She glanced at David, worried she might upset him, but he seemed calm. He was listening with the rapt focus of a professor enthralled by a favorite student's presentation.

The room's ambient sounds, the soft beeping of the monitors, the shuffle of feet in the hallway, fell away, leaving only her mother's words bridging past and present. She finished one page, then another, until her eyes blurred a bit with emotion she tried to hold back. Finally, David made a gentle motion with his hand, and she lowered the manuscript.

A hush settled between them. His breathing sounded more labored than usual. He offered a faint smile, then reached for her hand. "Emmy, you should finish it."

She felt every ounce of meaning in that simple statement. Finish it. The one task that once felt impossible, like stepping into her mother's shoes and risking heartbreak all over again. She started to protest, but the lump in her throat strangled any words. She leaned toward him, her eyes stinging. "I—"

"You have your own voice now," David whispered. "It should carry hers across the finish line."

Tears welled, and she did not bother brushing them away. He squeezed her hand, gentle but firm. Emery recognized the bittersweet pride in his expression, the same look he used to wear when she brought home a new travel magazine feature. The difference was that now it was about more than a clever article. This was legacy. This was reckoning. She stared at him, wanting to say so much, but no single sentence felt big enough.

Before she stood to leave, he whispered again, softer than before, "I am proud of you, Emmy. Not because you stayed. But because you grew roots where you once only saw escape."

She pressed her lips together, tears slipping down her cheeks. Her heart felt too full. She bent over and kissed his temple, lingering there long enough to give herself the solace she needed. He closed his eyes, and she knew it was time for him to rest. She left quietly, clutching Margot's manuscript against her chest.

In the hallway, she stopped beside a row of vending machines, letting herself breathe. David's words spiraled through her mind, "grew roots." She had always thought she had no place in Charleston. This city was where she had fought with Margot, where she had misunderstood Laura, and where she had stormed out with a heart shredded by loss. Yet the more days she spent here now, the more it felt like home. She wondered if home was not something you built in one swoop but something you let take shape over time.

Leaving Roper Hospital behind, Emery took a winding route through downtown. The sidewalks bustled with late afternoon crowds. A group of tourists paused on a corner, snapping photos of pastel-colored buildings. She caught the smell of roasted coffee beans drifting from a nearby shop. A breeze fluttered the hem of her light linen cardigan, and she inhaled the scent of salt air. For the first time in years, she walked these streets without feeling like a stranger.

She passed Marion Square, where an early evening farmers' market was wrapping up. The red glow of the setting sun gilded the statue at the square's center. A wave of nostalgia pulled her toward the café where she had once seen Laura unexpectedly. That meeting had been tense, full of unspoken accusations. Now, she longed to show her sister something else, the Emery who had decided not to run.

When she reached the café's entrance, she paused. The memory of that day flickered in her mind, how she had gripped the back of a chair, fighting the urge to flee. Instead of stepping inside, she scrolled through her phone until she found Laura's number. She hesitated, thumb hovering above the screen, then typed out a text:

I am still your sister. If you want to meet me at the house tomorrow, I will be there with coffee.

Emery read it twice, pressed Send, and exhaled. Maybe Laura would decline. Maybe she would not respond. Laura never stayed in one place too long and always surprised everyone whenever she would show up. She had gone to NYU and had married a successful venture capitalist. They had a jet and houses all over the world that they constantly flitted between. Emery loved the vagabond nature of her sister but didn't know how truly happy she was since they hadn't spent any real time together since their mother's funeral. But Emery felt lighter just knowing she had extended a hand. With that done, she turned on her heel and continued walking, letting the day's last light guide her back to her car.

She arrived at the Westbrook estate as dusk settled. The front porch lamps cast a warm glow along the columns. She spotted Xander in the upstairs window, an outline against the amber light. Silas trotted around the garden, sniffing at a few new planters. The rhythmic chirping of cicadas hummed through the night air.

After parking, she let herself in through the foyer, setting Margot's manuscript carefully on the foyer table. Her limbs felt heavy from the hospital visit, but a sense of calm pushed back on her fatigue. She called up the stairs, "Xander? You there?" Her voice echoed in the corridor.

He emerged from the second story, saw the expression on her face, and extended a hand. "Do you want to go to the balcony? We have at least another hour of decent light."

Emery nodded. She climbed the stairs, feeling the reassuring creak of the wood that she and Xander had replaced. It was the same route she used to take as a child, but the weight of old memories felt gentler now. He led her out to the second-story balcony, a space they had rebuilt together from rotted boards into something sturdy, even elegant. The air still smelled of fresh-cut lumber, mingling with the marsh's tang below.

They stood side by side against the new railing, gazing at the fading light spreading across the horizon. Soft purples and oranges blended into an opalescent sky, the marsh reflecting hints of gold. She watched a flock of birds skim across the water, their silhouettes painting graceful arcs against the clouds.

"Your dad doing all right?" Xander asked quietly.

Emery inhaled, letting the hush fill her chest. "He is weaker. I read some of Margot's manuscript to him. He told me to finish it."

Xander nodded, his gaze drifting over the yard. "That sounds like him."

She brushed her palm across the balcony's rail and smiled faintly. "It still surprises me how this house no longer feels like a cage. For the longest time, I was convinced it was an anchor dragging me under." She thought of all the nights she had spent awake, haunted by regrets and secrets. "Now, it actually feels like a book I want to write. Like I can shape it into something new."

A small grin tugged at his lips. "Start with this chapter," he said, leaning closer.

She turned toward him. "Then you are in the first line."

His answering smile carried a blend of relief and tenderness. He slid an arm around her waist and drew her closer, until her cheek rested against his shoulder. They watched the sky deepen into darkness spreading over the expansive lawns below. The house behind them creaked as if in contentment, no longer straining under the weight of unspoken sorrows. She could feel Xander's heartbeat steady under her ear, each pulse a small reminder of how far they had come. Eventually, they retreated inside, hand in hand.

In her bedroom, Emery opened the nightstand drawer, where she kept her journal and some of the private letters from Margot and Xander. She turned to a fresh page in her journal, pen scratching softly across paper as she composed a new travel entry.

Grief does not close cleanly. It lingers in the spaces we dust and the gardens we plant. But so does love. And home. And the future.

She let the ink settle, each sentence ringing with the truth she had begun to accept. She read it again, then carefully tore the slender page from her notebook and folded it. She placed it beside the letters her mother had left behind, as well as Xander's notes, those gentle anchors she had once been so afraid to read. All the ghosts she used to fear were now brushing against her fingertips, woven into words instead of sharp regrets.

CHAPTER
THIRTY
XANDER

*Travel Note: In Dubrovnik, I once wrote that I feared perma-
nence. But now, as I place these pages in this desk drawer, I
realize I have never built anything worth staying for.
Until now.*

—EW

Xander shifted awake in the muted glow of dawn,
the first-floor study where he sometimes slept on
the pull out still wrapped in half shadow. Silas lay
sprawled across the floor near the foot of the bed. The old
golden retriever's chest rose and fell in calm rhythm, a soft
counterpoint to the faint scratch of a pen drifting from
upstairs. That sound had become familiar these past
weeks, Emery's morning ritual of writing before
addressing anyone or anything else.

He took a moment to orient himself. The estate's
walls, once so steeped in tension, now felt secure. He
remembered when the halls groaned with emptiness, and

though he had tried to fill every gap with new paint or well placed nails, the quiet had haunted him. Now the silence seemed alive, a vessel for the future they were creating.

With care not to disturb Silas, Xander rose and pulled on a worn T shirt and jeans. He stepped into the corridor and pressed his palm lightly against the wood paneling. Months ago he worried if he could complete this project. Now each board seemed to breathe acceptance. He walked until he reached the library, where a few leftover boxes from the renovation still waited to be cleared out. He paused, remembering how Emery once paced this exact spot, face drawn in confusion, the day she returned. He exhaled gratitude that she was still here.

A soft click from upstairs signaled Emery taking a break from writing. He smiled to himself, envisioning the slender pen in her hand, the slight crease of concentration between her brows. A year ago, he would not have dared imagine her back in Charleston for more than a weekend, let alone living under this roof. Now their names appeared side by side on nearly every document he was drawing up for the house's next stage. Mine and hers, he mused, merging seamlessly.

He made his way to the study, a room whose once cracked molding had been meticulously repaired piece by piece. Early sunlight streamed through tall windows, illuminating the large oak desk near the wall. Stacks of papers lay spread across it. Atop the largest stack was the finalized grant application for the residency they planned to host inside these walls. It bore both their signatures, thick black ink that felt weightier than any vow Xander had ever made.

For a moment he stood there absorbing it. The sunlight revealed tiny grooves in the desk's surface, evidence of its long history. Margot once wrote at this desk, and now Emery did too. Gently he flipped through the top pages. A note in Emery's handwriting suggested adding a small reading alcove in the second-floor hallway. Another note, in his own script, proposed building a skylight in the attic for natural light. Where his pen strokes ended, hers began. The synergy made his chest swell with a sense of rightness.

He glanced at the clock and decided he had enough time to take a quick walk through the garden before Emery beckoned him to share whatever morning tasks she had planned. With the folder tucked neatly back in place, he left the study, heading out through the foyer and onto the porch.

The humidity hugged him the instant he stepped outside, greeting him like an old friend. Just beyond the wide steps, the garden burst with green. In the early hours, dewdrops clung to rosemary stalks and leftover wildflowers. He spotted the patch of tomato plants near the fence; the very ones Emery had teased him about for so long. He walked over to them and examined the leaves. Tiny beads of moisture glittered under the rising sun, and a single ripe tomato caught his eye. He remembered how that first green tomato was a small triumph in barren soil. Now their small row produced fruit regularly.

Silas trundled out behind him. The dog gave a

curious sniff at a patch of damp grass, then eyed the tomatoes as if checking whether they too needed his supervision. Xander patted Silas's head, content in the shared hush. This was the sort of morning he used to dream about, calm, purposeful, and unhurried by heartbreak.

A soft voice from the porch drew his attention. Emery stood there wearing gray shorts and a light T-shirt. Her hair fell loose around her shoulders. She had two coffee mugs in her hands and wore an expression of gentle invitation.

"Good timing," he said, strolling back over to her.

She stepped down one stair and extended a mug toward him. "I wasn't sure if you'd started any yet."

He took the cup and inhaled the comforting bitterness. "I wanted to walk a bit first." Then he sipped. "Thank you."

They settled on the porch side by side, leaning against a column. For a moment, they just drank in silence, letting the morning saturate them with warmth. Finally, she turned her head to him and said, "Laura's coming today. We... I told her we'd meet around noon."

A nervous pinch settled between his ribs, recalling the tension that had lingered between the sisters for years. Yet he remembered hearing both of them laugh the last time Laura visited, a hopeful sign that old wounds were healing.

"You're sure you're okay to see her?"

Emery's lips curved into a small smile. "I told her I'd be here. I meant it."

He nodded. "Then I'll be in the workshop. If you need me, just call."

"Thank you," she said, setting her mug aside to wrap her arms around his waist. The gesture was casual yet intimate. Physical closeness no longer felt tentative with her, it felt earned, a soft reward for all the times they doubted this day would ever come.

They parted soon afterward. While Emery headed inside to do her final preparations for Laura's arrival, Xander walked across the yard to the old carriage house. It had been converted into his personal workspace, the walls lined with half-finished carpentry projects, shelves of paint cans, and a cluster of tools neatly organized by function. Sawdust tinted the air with a faint sweetness. He grabbed a fresh piece of driftwood he had salvaged from the beach on Sullivan's Island, a smooth, gently curved log that fit comfortably in his grip.

He turned on a small fan and set to work. The sound of sandpaper on wood comforted him with its familiar rasp. Drifting inside from an open window came the sound of voices. He caught the rise and fall of Emery's tone, bright as sunshine, and Laura's, slightly hesitant at first but softening as they spoke. Xander could not make out their words, only the timbre. He let himself savor the relief of it. Perhaps the past was finally loosening its grip.

He focused on the piece in his hand, shaping it into a small arch that could cradle a vase of fresh flowers once it was finished. His mind drifted through memories of how many times he had stood here, hating the weight of secrets and dreading Emery's absence. Now, hope had replaced dread. With each stroke of sandpaper, the wood's surface smoothed, exposing clean patterns hidden just beneath the pale driftwood grain. It felt symbolic. He would coax this piece into something beautiful, letting the natural shape guide him.

Occasionally, the pitch of laughter outside spiked. Emery's laugh was the one he recognized best, a bright sound that had been missing for so long. He could not help smiling. The knot of tension in his chest unwound bit by bit. Whatever the sisters discussed, it was forging new ground. He reached for his carving knife and began to refine the edges.

Time blurred pleasantly. Eventually, the voices faded, and he heard a car engine start. He set the driftwood aside and walked to the open window. Through the trees, he glimpsed Laura's car rolling toward the exit. There was no slam of doors, no raised words. That had to mean good things.

He wiped the sawdust from his hands on a rag, then walked back toward the main house. The sun rode low in the sky, stretching gold light across the grass. He found Emery leaning against the back steps, her head tilted, letting the last of the day's warmth graze her face. Silas lounged at her feet, wagging his tail at the sight of Xander.

"How did it go?" Xander asked quietly, joining her.

She lifted her shoulders in a small, contented shrug. "We cried a bit, but we also laughed a lot. One step at a time, right?"

He eased himself onto the step next to her, their ankles

nearly touching. "One step at a time seems to be our thing."

She let out a slow breath, shoulders sagging in a mix of relief and exhaustion. "I am glad we are doing this. All of it."

He brushed his knuckles gently across her arm. "So am I."

They lingered there until dusk settled. The air cooled, but not by much, and the scent of rosemary drifted from a planter by the steps. Silas gave a soft huff and rested his muzzle on Xander's boot. After a moment, Emery spoke again in a voice just above a whisper.

"I think we can live here."

Her words sent a quiet thrill through him. He had dreamed of that phrase in various forms for what felt like forever. "You think we can be happy here?"

She did not hesitate. "I think we already are. Even when it is hard."

He nodded, a soft rush of gratitude filling his chest. Slowly, he turned and kissed her, letting the moment fill with warmth. The porch lights, which had switched on automatically, bathed them in a gentle glow. When he pulled back, he reached into his pocket and retrieved a small wooden carving. It was a simple figure of a porch swing, two miniature figures carved on the seat's edge. He pressed it into her hand.

She examined it closely, eyes drifting over the carved slats. "You made this? When?"

He shrugged, feeling a bit sheepish. "Night before last. It's the swing from the front porch, or at least my best approximation. I know it's rough, but..." He trailed off, uncertain how to explain the sentiment in words.

She looked up, her gaze full of understanding. "It's perfect."

He could see emotion dancing in her eyes. "You never really stopped waiting for me," she said softly.

His voice emerged a little rough. "I never wanted anyone else to walk through that door but you."

Her fingers curled around the carving as though it were precious, and she held it to her heart a moment before leaning in to rest her forehead against his. They breathed in tandem, letting the evening hush around them. Even Silas seemed to sense the intimacy, quietly settling his chin on his paws.

Eventually, they carried leftover sandwiches and iced tea out to the back steps for dinner. The sky was purple now, a curtain of twilight thickening over them. They talked about small things: how the newly planted lavender might fare in the summer heat, whether to repaint the reading lounge in seafoam green or keep it bright white, and what time they might try to visit David again in the hospital tomorrow. Each topic was light, yet behind every word lay the sense of building a shared life.

When they finished eating, Emery pressed herself against Xander's side, comfortable in the silence. Crickets chirped from the tall grass edging the driveway. He felt the steady rise and fall of her breath, and he reveled in the simple wonder of having her so close.

At last, they walked inside beneath the soft glow of the porch light. Emery insisted on washing the plates. Xander went upstairs to check if the windows in the main hallway were secure. A breeze had pushed one open earlier that day, and he wanted to make sure it was latched. Satisfied, he made his way to Emery's bedroom. The door stood ajar, warm lamplight stretching across the floorboards. He found her already curled under the sheets, her journal splayed open on her lap. But her eyes were closed, and the pen rested precariously between her fingers. She had fallen asleep mid-thought.

He approached quietly, taking in her peaceful expression. She rarely slept so readily. Careful not to wake her, he slid the pen from her hand and gently closed the journal. The corner of a page caught his eye. There was a line, scrawled in her distinct handwriting.

We didn't start over. We just started where we left off, with open eyes.

He swallowed the thickness in his throat. Setting the journal and pen on her bedside table, he gave her a final glance. Love, relief, and awe all mingled inside him. His heart felt fuller than it had in years. He turned off the lamp, then leaned to press a light kiss to her forehead, holding the moment like a fragile promise in his hands.

CHAPTER

THIRTY-ONE

EMERY

Travel Note: I left a part of myself in every city. But Charleston is where I came back to gather those pieces. Where I stopped running. Where I chose to become whole again.

—EW

Emery sat behind the steering wheel of her dusty sedan, staring at the tall, rectangular outline of Roper Hospital. The morning sun glimmered against the windows, casting scattered reflections across the parking lot. She tightened her fingers on the steering wheel for a moment, summoning the courage to climb out. Even through the car's closed doors, she could sense the bustle of the medical complex.

She finally opened the driver's door. A warm gust of air ruffled the hem of her linen skirt. Picking up her bag that held a notebook, some pens, and a half-read letter from Margot's

286

old stash, Emery made her way across the lot. Inside the building, the corridors glowed a pale yellow, humming with the subdued rhythms of gurneys and muffled footsteps. The antiseptic smell clung to everything, tiled floors, plastic chairs, the folds of the visitor badges. She pressed the elevator button for the seventh floor and tried to steady her breathing.

As she rode up, she thought of how often she had questioned whether coming home was a mistake. But each time, the house, the porch swing, and the renewed sense of belonging nudged her forward. When the elevator doors opened, she stepped into a quieter wing. A nurse at the station greeted her with a gentle smile, recognizing her from earlier visits. Emery gave a polite nod, heart pounding at the idea of finding her father in a worse state than the day before.

She pushed open the door to David's room slowly. The drawn curtains allowed a soft glow of mid-morning sunlight to pool by his bed. His eyes were closed, and the machine at his bedside whispered gentle beeps. For a second, Emery thought he might be asleep, but his lids fluttered open at the click of the door latch.

"Emmy," he said, voice low. He looked smaller than ever. His hair, once silver-gray, now seemed thinner against the pillow. But his eyes were alert, sharpened by awareness that time was shrinking around him.

Emery approached the chair by his bed, shrugging off her bag. "Hi, Dad." The words broke gently from her throat. "How are you feeling?"

His smile was faint but real. "Weaker, I suppose.

Doesn't matter much how I feel physically, as long as my mind is awake. Still writing?"

She nodded, reaching into her bag to retrieve her newest journal that always traveled with her through every emotional storm. "Every day," she whispered. She placed the journal on the thin blanket covering his legs. "I have a few paragraphs about Mom, about leaving Charleston, about all the mistakes I thought I'd never forgive myself for."

His gaze flickered over her face. "Then this," he said softly, patting the journal, "is what I've been waiting to hear."

She brushed a loose strand of hair from her temple and carefully opened the journal to a marked page. The sound of the turning paper filled the quiet room, underscoring how intimate this moment felt, how each word she was about to share had cost her years of grief and guilt.

She inhaled. "Okay, so this section is from what I've started calling my 'reclamation draft.' I'm weaving Mom's stories with my own travel reflections." She traced a finger over a line, then began:

I once believed that running was my only power. I wove my mother's unspoken warnings, my father's quiet love, and my own self-doubt into an excuse to board planes and never come back. But grief has a way of following you, it sits beneath every sunrise, every city skyline. There is no magic border to keep it away. I left because I was afraid Charleston would swallow me, the same way it seemed to swallow my mother. Now, returning, I see that fear was only half the truth. Love can swallow you too, but it can also hold you steady while you learn how to breathe again.

Emery paused, glancing over the rim of the journal to see her father's reaction. His expression was solemn, eyes closed, as though absorbing each word carefully. She cleared her throat and continued.

Maybe the reason I never wrote about Charleston in my published pieces was that it felt too close, too raw. But my mother deserved more than silence, and so did I. I have learned that no matter how many countries you circle, you still carry the weight of home inside you. The question is whether you are brave enough to face what that weight means.

She swallowed the lump in her throat and lifted her gaze. David remained still, his eyelids quivering slightly. The monitor's soft beep punctuated the silence. At last, he opened his eyes.

"That's real," he said, his voice trembling at the edges. "That's the kind of story that stays."

Emery forced back the tears threatening her composure. She wanted to hug him, to recite a thousand apologies for all the years she had been gone, but she knew he did not want regrets. That was never his style. He had always championed her independence, even when it confused or hurt him.

She set the journal aside. "I want to keep going and finish it. Maybe tie it together with the draft Mom left, the one about her own experiences in Charleston." She pulled a breath and reached for his hand. "Xander and I are talking about hosting a writing residency at the estate. A place for new stories to find a home."

His smile grew softer. "I heard about that from him," he said. "He's proud to take on such a big dream. And you, Emery, are the one who can make it alive with words."

His hand felt noticeably cooler than the last time she had visited. Every shallow line on his skin told a story of age and resilience. She gave his fingers a gentle squeeze, trying not to dwell on the changes that proved how little time they had.

"How's the house?" he asked.

"It's well, it's coming along. The porch swing is my new favorite place. We reinforced it. We even tested it with a few late night conversations."

David's eyes sparkled with something like pride. "I used to say that swing would outlast all of us." He paused, his breath trembling. "But it will be yours now, Emmy. All of it. Do what you will do best, make it beautiful again."

She exhaled. The weight of that inheritance, combined with the knowledge of everything the house had meant to Margot, threatened to overwhelm her. "I want to," she said softly. "I know it will not be easy, but I am ready."

They sat in companionable silence. Emery glanced at the bag near her chair, recalling the first time she flew back to Charleston, how uncertain she had been, how convinced that the city would greet her with bitterness. Instead, she had found acceptance, from Xander's hand on hers while she wept over old memories, from her cousin's persistent warmth, and from her father, who had never stopped believing she was worth welcoming home.

He squeezed her hand. "You didn't have to choose me, you know," she said, voice wavering. "You could have told me about who my real father was. You could have walked away from all the complications."

David shook his head slowly, eyes reflecting a sadness and a fierce love. "Of course I did. Every damn day."

Emery pressed her lips together, tears brimming. She leaned closer, laying her head gently against his shoulder. For a moment, she let herself be that little girl who once sat on his lap, listening to him read aloud passages from poetry books. In those days, she believed David was a fortress of certainty, unbreakable. Now, she realized that he was human, deeply flawed but overwhelmingly brave in how he chose to raise her as his own.

Eventually, anxiety crawled up her chest, reminding her that he needed rest. She rose from the chair, carefully placing the journal back in her bag. "Get some sleep," she whispered. "I'll come back soon."

His eyes moved toward the window, where sunlight cascaded across the sill. "Drive safe, Emmy."

"I will," she promised.

Her footsteps felt heavy as she left the room. Out in the hall, the nurse offered a sympathetic nod. Emery couldn't bring herself to speak, so she dipped her head in thanks and made her way to the elevators. Just as the doors slid shut behind her, she felt a hot tear slip down her cheek.

She remained quiet through the descent, letting the dull hum of the elevator motor fill the silence in her mind. Stepping outside, she was greeted by the mid-afternoon brightness that made her squint as she walked back to her car.

Driving through downtown Charleston, she let the traffic carry her thoughts. The market stalls near King Street were busy. A street performer tuned his guitar, and the crisp twang of strings momentarily carried through her open car window. That fleeting chord matched an ache in her chest.

At a red light, she gazed at the pastel facades of the old buildings, remembering how she used to see them as barriers, reminders of everything she couldn't wait to escape. Now, they felt more like protective walls, painted in cheerful colors to greet her sorrow without judgment. She gripped the steering wheel, tears slipping in quiet lines down her cheeks.

The light turned green. She drove on, following the broad oak-lined street that curved toward the outskirts where the Westbrook estate waited. Each block she passed felt like turning a page in the story she was still writing. She allowed herself one more soft sob before inhaling and pressing onward.

When she finally turned onto the long driveway leading to the estate, the sun was overhead, gilding the live oaks in a haze of gold. She parked by the porch steps. Silas ambled over with a sleepy wag of his tail. She looked at the broad porch, heart twisting when she spotted Xander leaning against the column. His expression caught the rawness in her face before she said anything. He set aside whatever he was holding, she thought it might have been a sketchpad for new balcony ideas and hurried down the steps.

Emery opened her car door and stood, shoulders slumping in exhaustion. She wanted to speak, but words jammed in her throat. The swirl of emotion from the hospital, from David's words, from the knowledge that time was slipping away, left her voiceless.

Xander didn't ask. He didn't need an explanation. He simply wrapped his arms around her, pulling her into a protective circle of warmth. She fell against his chest, pressing her forehead to the curve of his shoulder. His shirt smelled of wood polish and fresh air. The closeness unraveled the tension in her spine, and she allowed herself to release a trembling sigh.

Emery grounded herself in Xander's presence. Heat pulsed where his hands rested at her lower back. Each of his breaths underpinned how steady he tried to be, how he wanted to lend her that steadiness if she needed it.

After a minute, she drew back, glancing at him. "Sorry," she managed, voice raspy.

He brushed his hand across her cheek, shaking his head. "Don't ever apologize." The quiet reverence in his tone told her more than any words could. He took her hand and guided her gently up the porch, ushering her inside as Silas trotted behind. There was no demand for discussion. No push for her to smile. Just an understanding that she was home and that was enough for now.

They ended up in the dining room, sharing a simple lunch of leftover roasted vegetables and overly buttered bread. She could not recall tasting much of it, but the act of eating soothed her body. They talked in murmurs about small things, a squeaky floorboard in the library, a phone call Xander needed to return about reclaimed windows, and how the porch columns might need another coat of paint.

At last, she excused herself to the second-floor hallway, feeling heavy lidded but at the same time too restless to sleep. She knew what she needed to do, let the day's heartbreak settle into words. Quietly, she slipped into her bedroom, closed the door, and turned on the bedside lamp.

She pulled out her journal, flipping past old sketches of Istanbul market alleys and scribbled notes about the highlands of Scotland. The pages made her smile a little. It was peculiar to revisit the sense of wonder she had in those moments, traveling so far from home, certain she was finding her true identity. Yet here she was, writing what might be the most genuine sentences of her life in the very place she once dreaded returning to.

Lowering herself onto the bed, she set the journal in her lap and clicked her pen. The quiet of the house at night, broken only by the soft whir of the ceiling fan, offered an intimate refuge. She began writing a flood of impressions and memories from David's bedside visit. She wrote about reading the paragraphs to him, his reaction, the light in his tired eyes. She wrote about guilt, about how she used to blame Charleston for suffocating her, only to discover that she carried her restlessness within herself. She wrote about Margot's hidden truths, about the distrust that once wedged her and Xander apart. And through every sentence, she felt a renewed sense of purpose.

At times her hand cramped, but she pushed on. Pages filled with confessions and confusions, the lines scrawled unevenly. An hour might have passed; she paid no mind to the clock. Occasionally, she heard a door creak downstairs, presumably Xander stepping outside to let Silas roam for a final night patrol. He did not come up to interrupt her. Perhaps he sensed she needed this solitary communion with words.

Finally, when her thoughts steadied and the pen's ink threatened to run low, she read the last few sentences. Her heartbeat thumped in her ears. The flood of vulnerability had drained her, but in its wake, she recognized a new clarity, she was no longer shaped solely by what she had lost, but by what she was building.

She let the pen hover one last time.

Grief shaped me, but it no longer defines me.

CHAPTER

THIRTY-TWO

XANDER

Travel Note: In Reykjavik, the sun sets for only three hours in summer. In this house, the light feels just as stubborn. And for once, I am not afraid of how long it stays.
    —EW

Xander stood in the quiet corridor, a slight morning breeze drifting through the open window. His boots nudged an old rug that looked like it needed to be replaced. Sunlight spilled along the floorboards, drawing him forward. The study door stood halfway open, and he gently pushed it wider.

Inside, Emery sat on the rug among scattered papers, her mother's unfinished manuscript arranged to her right, and her own stack of handwritten notes fanned out to her left. Her hair was piled atop her head, secured by a pencil, and her cheeks were flushed with the focus that often overtook her when she wrote. She glanced up at him, blinking as if emerging from a dream.

"You've been busy," Xander said softly. He took in the sprawl of words, pages, and half-filled coffee mugs around her. Silas napped contentedly near the bookshelves.

Emery set down her pen. "I think I'm going to finish it," she said, voice hoarse but determined. "For her. But with my voice."

Xander's pulse quickened at the breakthrough in her eyes. He had grown accustomed to the sorrow that often lurked there, but today he saw an undercurrent of hope. He moved closer, lowering himself to sit next to her, careful not to scatter the pages. He lifted an old, typed sheet from Margot's draft and read a few lines in silence.

"She'd be proud," he said, sliding the page carefully back into place. As he spoke, he brushed his knuckles lightly against the side of Emery's hand. She leaned into his touch.

For a moment, neither spoke. Sunlight drifted across the ancient desk plastered with sticky notes. The overhead fan clicked as it turned. Margot's old words whispered across the paper like ghosts, and Emery's fresh notes promised new life, two voices melding into one story.

Eventually, Emery exhaled. "I need to see my dad. There's something I want to read to him." She stacked the pages neatly, pressing her palms on top as though trying to keep them safe.

He stood when she did, stepping aside to let her gather the manuscript and place it in a sturdy folder. She slipped her feet into sandals, then paused at the threshold of the study. Xander caught the scent of her shampoo, a comforting blend of chamomile and lemon. He squeezed her shoulder.

"Go," he said. "I'll be here."

She nodded, eyes reflecting gratitude, then slipped out of the room. He watched her retreating figure down the hall until she disappeared around the corner. The silence she left behind felt charged with purpose rather than sorrow.

He stretched his shoulders, noticing a tension there he had not felt earlier. There was work waiting on the porch, one final plank that needed replacing. He recalled how easy it was to sink hours into small tasks. With Emery here, every minute felt like an investment rather than an escape.

In the foyer, he grabbed a worn toolbox. Wooden boards leaned stacked against the wall, and he chose the plank he had prepared earlier, one he had measured three times to ensure it fit seamlessly.

Outside, the day was heating up, humidity rising from the marsh beyond the yard. He knelt by the porch steps. The plank he intended to replace showed a hairline crack from age and moisture. He pried it up with a crowbar, careful not to splinter the nearby boards. The weight of the plank in his hands felt like removing an old ache from the house. Dust motes caught the sunlight as he worked.

He fitted the new piece in place and tested its sturdiness with a small push of his palm. The sun pressed hot against his back, but he found satisfaction in the simple process. He hammered each nail with deliberate care, unwilling to rush. Small details, he had learned, carried the biggest truths.

Next, he retrieved a soft cloth and a tin of polish from the foyer. The front doorknob had tarnished over time, dulling the once-bright brass. He felt a kind of reverence as he ran the cloth across its surface. The squeak of the metal under his polishing effort seemed to speak of long histories, new beginnings, and the potential for what he and Emery were trying to create. When the handle gleamed under the rising sunlight, he stepped back. Refinishing that knob delivered a small sense of completion he had not realized he needed.

He wiped sweat from his brow and made his way across the yard to the carriage house. Once a neglected outbuilding, it now stood firm with fresh siding, its structure fortified by months of repairs. Inside, the air was stuffy, but the scent of pine and varnish made it feel welcoming to him. Tools hung neatly on the walls, and a newly built drafting table rested near the window, fashioned from reclaimed pine. He ran a hand over the polished surface, recalling the late nights spent carving those pieces, channeling his restless thoughts into shaping the wood.

On top of the table lay blueprints for the writing residency, a plan that once existed only as scattered notes in conversation with Emery. He gently unrolled them, smoothing out the corners until the designs lay flat. The sketches were a careful combination of open communal spaces and private reading nooks. He pictured eager writers sitting in the second-floor lounge, sipping coffee while the Charleston heat throbbed against the old windows. He pictured Emery leading workshops in the bright sunroom.

He thought of himself as a restless teenager, finding quiet corners in this very house to escape the noise in his own head. Now, he and Emery could build a place that offered that same sanctuary to others. It felt like coming full circle, transforming his own private refuge into a public offering of peace.

He made small marks along the edges of the blueprint, updating measurements for window frames and double checking the electrical plan. He wrote short notations on a separate notepad, scrawling possible improvements or sections that needed cost estimates. Each pen stroke stirred excitement in his stomach. This was no longer a half formed dream. It was becoming a legacy in motion, a chance for both him and Emery to do something mean-ingful with all the heartbreak they had survived.

A shift of light through the open carriage house door. He rolled up the plans and set them aside, carefully stacking them at the corner of the table. Then he heard a car engine in the driveway. Emery was home.

He left the carriage house and spotted her stepping from the sedan, folder clutched under one arm. When she looked up, he saw tears shining in her eyes, but a smile curved her lips. An indescribable relief crashed through him. He strode across the yard to meet her.

"He's tired," she said, voice trembling with emotion. "I think he's getting close to the end, and they mentioned hospice to me today. But he's at peace." She wiped her cheek with the back of her hand, trying to contain feelings that threatened to overflow.

Xander closed the distance and scooped her into an embrace. Her body felt small, pressed close as she exhaled shakily against his chest. He ran a hand gently up and down her back.

"Then he's resting easier," he murmured. "And you?"

She let out a trembling sigh, her breath warm against his shirt. "I read him a few pages I wrote. He smiled, you know? Said he was proud." She sniffed and drew back. "That's enough for me. For now."

He cupped her cheek, thumb brushing away the last tears. The humid air clung to them both, but all he focused on were her eyes. They spoke of sadness and acceptance, and a future that might not be weighed down by regret.

"Come on," he said, rubbing the tension in her shoulders. "Let's eat something. You haven't had dinner."

She nodded, and together they walked inside. The evening's calm wrapped around them in the foyer. He carried her bag to the table in the dining room where the overhead chandelier cast soft light. A fragile hush filled the space, as if the house was listening.

They prepared a simple meal side by side, slicing fresh tomatoes and laying out leftover pasta he warmed on the stove. Neither fussed with elaborate plating. Real conversation flowed in fragments, her father's condition, the letter she'd read to him, the small ways David had tried to comfort her before she left the hospital. He listened while cutting crusty bread and adding a butter pat to the skillet. Occasionally, she reached out and squeezed his arm or pressed her forehead against his shoulder. Each touch felt like a promise.

They ate in an unhurried quiet. The overhead fan stirred the air, and Silas dozed at their feet. As they finished, a hush settled even deeper, as if the house was waiting for them to decide their next step.

Not long afterward, they carried their plates back to the kitchen and turned off the lights. Xander took her hand without words. She followed him to the balcony, a space they had restored with care over the past weeks. Now, a woven blanket draped across the small outdoor couch. Soft, warm breezes moved through the screen, and lightning bugs glimmered over the lawn below like floating embers.

They settled together beneath the blanket, legs brushing. Emery's head found its place against his chest. He let his hand rest lightly at her waist and savored her warmth. Fireflies winked in the twilight. He could almost taste the salt from the nearby marsh, mingling with the lingering sweetness of the tomatoes they had eaten.

Her voice broke the stillness. "I don't know what happens next," she said, so quietly he almost felt the words more than heard them.

He brushed a kiss against her temple. "We live it," he replied, voice steady. The hush between them felt sacred.

She shifted closer, one hand splaying over his heart. He kissed her hair and breathed in the subtle citrus of her shampoo and the faint musk of Charleston's night air pressing in around them. Crickets sang in the bushes. Somewhere in the distance, a truck engine rumbled along the main road, but it was background to the quiet sanctuary they shared.

After a long while, they left the balcony and slipped back inside. She led him into the room that used to be hers alone, the bed draped with a simple quilt. A small lamp lit the desk near the window. On it, she had spread a notebook open to a fresh page. He watched as she sketched ideas for the upstairs suite, pencil moving with intent. She wanted to combine lodging for writers with an open reading space, plus a private corner dedicated to her mother's memory. Occasionally, she glanced at him over her shoulder, searching for reassurance.

He held her gaze. "You have good instincts on it," he said softly. He did not move closer yet. He respected the way she needed her own mental space. At the same time, he loved the curve of her back, the slope of her shoulders when she leaned over her notes. Every detail reminded him that she was here, and she was staying.

Eventually, she closed her notebook and turned, standing before him with a small, grateful smile. "Thank you for waiting," she whispered, voice barely above a breath.

A warmth squeezed his chest. He reached for her hand, drawing her closer until she stood between his arms. "Thank you for coming back."

They drifted toward each other like the final pieces of a

puzzle. He kissed her, softly at first, then deeper when he felt her sigh into his mouth. Emotion swelled in his chest, love and relief braided together in a sensation so fierce that it almost hurt. She ran her palms up his shoulders, and he closed his eyes, pressing his lips against her neck, tracing the line of her collarbone.

Their clothes fell away as they guided each other toward the bed. The gentle lamplight framed Emery's silhouette as he eased her onto the blankets. Everything felt hushed, as though the house itself honored this moment. He took his time, letting every sensation brand itself into his memory, the softness of her skin, the faint taste of salt on her throat, the sound of her breath catching when he whispered her name.

They made love in unhurried tenderness, bodies moving with certainty and longing. The tension of past years melted with every shared heartbeat. She tangled her fingers in his hair, and he caressed the arch of her back, steady in his devotion. Outside, a light breeze shook through the old oak tree. Inside, they found a new harmony that neither had dared imagine when their journeys first collided here again.

When they finished, they lay entwined in the deep hush of night. Her hair spilled across his forearm, and she stroked her hand along his jaw. He brushed a final kiss to her forehead, content to feel the warm press of her body, the way her breaths still came a little quickly.

A few minutes later, he caught her hand in his. Their fingers wove together, a quiet vow. In the lamplight, she smiled gently, eyes half-lidded with exhaustion and peace.

He could almost sense the house settling too, every floor-board quiet after years of waiting. They drifted into sleep still holding hands. Their fingers remained intertwined when the first glow of dawn broke across the horizon, chasing the darkness away.

CHAPTER

THIRTY-THREE

EMERY

Travel Note: In a tiny Scottish inn, a widower told me, "I keep her in my tea and in the silence she left behind." That is how I carry Margot now. Not in pain but in every word, I still have left to say.

—EW

Emery woke slowly to the sound of a soft breeze teasing the curtains. Morning light pooled across the hardwood floor, a gentle reminder that night had ended and a new promise began. She felt the warmth of Xander's hand draped over hers, his fingers only loosely curled against her palm. Her first breath carried an awareness that she had chosen this nearness, it was not a random gift from the universe. Her heart beat steadily beneath the thin sheet.

She turned her head. Xander was still asleep, his dark hair tousled against the pillow. For a moment, she closed her eyes again, letting the safety of the morning surround

306

her, letting the ghost of past doubts fade. She pictured her mother's face, no longer haunting her dreams but present in the calm of daybreak. Emery imagined Margot in that metaphor the old widower spoke of, resting in small rituals and quiet moments rather than in grief or regret.

Eventually, she slid out from under Xander's arm, pulled on her shorts and one of Xander's shirts and walked to the foyer. Her bare feet touched the cool floorboards, bringing memories of the estate's comforting creaks that once filled her with sadness. Now, those same creaks felt like an invitation to keep going. On the old console table near the front door, she noticed a large vase of white gardenias. The sight stirred her instantly. Laura was not one for long apologies, she preferred gestures to say what words rarely could. Emery's smile pressed against her lips as she lifted the card attached to the bouquet. It read, merely, Trying.

She found a pen in a kitchen drawer and wrote a quick reply on the back of the card. The kitchen smelled faintly of coffee grounds, a scent that seemed to cling to every morning in this house. In black ink, she wrote, "Me too. Brunch next week?" She set the note by the gardenias, trusting that Laura would see it soon. The white petals reminded Emery of fresh starts, rare, delicate moments that had to be nurtured. She did not want to let this one pass by.

After breakfast, simple scrambled eggs and sliced peaches, she took her time exploring each room of the estate, pausing at the threshold of the dining room, letting her gaze roam over the high ceiling and the windows that opened to the back porch. She remembered how cold it had felt when she first returned, the air weighed down by memory and regret. That chill seemed gone now. She pictured future laughter in these walls, the hum of new voices unafraid to share stories of heartbreak and hope. Instead of a mausoleum for old grief, the dining room would radiate a welcoming warmth for anyone brave enough to sit there. Maybe, she thought, a group of young writers would someday gather around the long table, passing around bowls of local produce and toasting with sweet tea and cheap wine.

From the dining room, she slipped into the hallway and traced her fingertips along the wallpaper's faded edges. She had thought about changing it but decided the existing pattern had its own scars worth keeping. Past the foyer, she stopped in the parlor. The battered coffee table still bore scratches from old celebrations, but now those marks felt earned, not lamented. She knelt to examine a chipped corner, imagining a group of residents sprawled around it, scribbling poetry or stacking manuscripts that captured both the heartbreak of the Lowcountry and each writer's yearning for home.

Upstairs, she meandered through the bedrooms that had once belonged to her mother and father. The door to Margot's old space stayed half-open, letting a sliver of light reach into its interior. Emery stood there, quiet in thought. She pictured crisp linen sheets and an inviting lamp on the nightstand, ready to make any guest, any writer, feel safe enough to put their deepest confessions onto paper. That was Margot's legacy, in a way. Each page

Emery wrote, each corner of this house she reimagined, she did with her mother's voice still echoing in her head.

Eventually, Emery headed downstairs toward the study. She found Xander waiting with two cups of fresh coffee. He wore a soft gray T-shirt and well-worn jeans, paint smudges along one knee. The desk in the study overflowed with grant applications, building sketches, and at least a dozen sticky notes in her loopy handwriting. A large map of the house's upstairs layout sprawled across the polished wood surface, each bedroom outlined in thin black marker. She set her mug down on a nearby shelf and sank into a chair, feeling relief in having him close.

They spent an hour or two reviewing the documents. Emery jotted small reminders in her notebook, cost estimates, deadlines, people she needed to contact about potential sponsorships. When she looked up, Xander was studying her face. She caught his eyes darting to the lines of tension in her brow.

"Are you sure about all of this?" he asked, his tone gentle.

She slid the stack of papers toward him. "I want it to feel like possibility," she said. "Like something her story, my story, made room for."

He reached across the desk and trailed his fingertips gently along the top page. "It does. These plans are yours now, Em, not just the house's. The difference is real."

She leaned over the desk, resting her chin on her folded arms. "Every time I think about leaving again, something about this place calls me back. I realize I'm done fighting it."

He exhaled softly. "Then maybe that's exactly what Margot wanted."

Emery gave him a quick, grateful smile, then gathered her car keys and purse. David's nurse had just called. He was resting peacefully, but Emery wanted to see him anyway. She excused herself, promising Xander she would be back soon. Outside, the sun shone bright across the front lawn. She inhaled deeply, tasting sea salt in the humid air. The marsh beyond the property shimmered with midday heat, a living painting she had once tried so hard to escape.

At the hospital, she found her father sleeping, as the nurse had said. His room felt warmer than usual, a soft glow from the overhead lights blending with a slice of sunshine from the half-drawn curtains. She pulled a chair beside the bed and set her bag on the floor. Gently, she reached for the battered folder that held her mother's manuscript. She opened it to a page she had yet to read to him, scanning the text quickly, reacquainting herself with Margot's words.

David stirred, his eyes blinking with effort. "You're here again," he said, voice raspy but laced with quiet warmth.

She placed a light kiss on the back of his hand. "Yes, Daddy. I brought some pages." She smoothed the corner of the manuscript. "I've been writing too. Adding pieces of my own, sort of weaving them into hers."

He closed his eyes, encouraging her to begin. She read Margot's reflections on the sorrow of certain Charleston summers, the spell of pluff mud at dawn, then paused to share a short section of her own, a page of raw honesty about leaving Charleston too soon and how the city had never truly left her, not in Morocco, not in Iceland, nor in any corner of the world where she tried to outrun old pain.

When she finished, David's eyelids fluttered open. He watched her with unwavering affection. She felt tears prick at her own eyes but kept her composure. "It's all in there," she whispered. "The truth. The cracks. The light."

He looked too tired to answer, but a faint smile curved his mouth. She squeezed his hand, letting the silence speak for them both. Then she stood, leaned over, and pressed a gentle kiss to his temple. "I love you, Daddy," she murmured.

She stayed a moment longer, anchoring herself in his presence as the nurse quietly checked the monitors. Emery's chest ached with gratitude and sorrow intertwined. She finally left, walking slowly down the corridor. Outside, the lingering heat settled over her shoulders, but she felt steadier than she had in a long time.

Back at the Westbrook estate, a quiet excitement took shape as Emery prepared for their first gathering this evening. Callie and Laura arrived first, each carrying dishes wrapped in foil. A pair of local friends followed, bearing bottles of wine. The newly remodeled dining room glowed under strands of soft string lights, the long table set with mismatched plates. Xander put the final touches on a chilled pitcher of sweet tea, while Silas wandered near everyone's ankles, hoping for titbits.

This was the first time so many voices had filled the house since before her mother's funeral. Emery marveled at the swirl of conversation. She heard Laura teasing Callie about mixing too many spices, and in turn, Callie jokingly threatened to ban Laura from her kitchen. One of Emery's new acquaintances from a local literary magazine chatted with Xander about the restoration process, clearly impressed by all the changes. It felt real, alive, not stifled by the tension of the past.

When the table was laden with food, Emery stood at one end, scanning the faces of her sister, her cousin, and family friends. She lifted her glass, and the clink of others followed, filling the space. She took a breath, bringing every half-broken piece of her heart to this moment.

"For stories we couldn't tell then but can tell now," she said, her voice carrying. "And for the people who stayed." She let her gaze land on Xander, and finally on Callie. "Thank you."

Their glasses rose in unison. Laura's expression softened as she tapped her glass to Callie's. There was a shared acceptance in that look, and of a wound closing. Xander offered Emery a small, proud smile from across the table, and Callie discreetly dabbed at her eyes, laughter hidden in her sniff.

The group broke into conversation and laughter. The plates passed from hand to hand, sweet tea and wine poured freely, and a lively debate about Charleston's best bakery ensued. Emery stayed quiet for a while, soaking in the sound of all these people forging new memories in a house once defined by sorrow. The walls that had absorbed years of grief now reflected a different kind of warmth. Even the beams up high seemed to sigh with relief, as though the estate too had waited for this night.

Before long, the dinner wound down. People wandered off in couples or small groups to admire the porch or to peek at the newly refurbished library. When the last guest departed, and Callie's car disappeared along the driveway, Emery found herself alone. The quiet that had once stung her now felt comforting. She wanted to walk the house one final time, to see it framed by this new nighttime glow.

She passed from the dining room to the foyer and paused at the base of the stairs, noticing the gentle lamplight flowing from the second-floor landing. The old floorboards creaked under her feet. There was no sense of emptiness, only a quiet reflection. She recalled the sliver of moonlight that used to show her to the door years ago when she felt desperate to leave. Now, that same moonlight guided her to stay.

At last, she stepped onto the porch. The breeze off the marsh carried the scent of jasmine and sea salt, a heady perfume that wrapped her. The porch swing waited. She ran her fingertips along the smooth wood of the backrest. The faint carvings of her and Xander's initials remained, a sign of all that had broken and been mended. Taking a seat, she drew a small journal from her pocket. She had scrawled an entry there earlier in the evening, and she checked the words under the porch lantern's soft glow:

I didn't return to the past. I reclaimed my place in the present. And in doing so, I remembered how to love the future.

She felt the weight of those words, the promise in them. Slowly closing the journal, she pressed her palm against the swing's armrest. The wood felt comforting beneath her hand, warm from the day's lingering heat. She breathed deeply, letting every trace of jasmine, sea salt, and legacy fill her senses.

CHAPTER

THIRTY-FOUR

EMERY

Travel Note: There's a proverb in Ghana: "A tree is known by its fruit." What we've planted here, this house, this love, it's bearing fruit. Imperfect. But ours.

—EW

Emery woke to the low rumble of a distant boat engine drifting in from the marsh. She blinked, registering the early morning light creeping through the sheer curtains. The breeze carried a faint saltiness that clung to her skin. A gentle weight pressed against her ribs, Xander's arm, warm and steady. She let her gaze settle on the ceiling fan above, its slow rotation making a soft clicking noise. She breathed in, realizing how different dawn felt when you were no longer anxious to leave. Moment by moment, she was learning how to stay.

She turned her head carefully so as not to rouse him. The curve of his face was relaxed in sleep, the worry that had once lined his face seemed eased. She wanted to

315

memorize this image of him, his tangled hair, the subtle scruff on his chin, that calm breath that rose and fell in a quiet rhythm against her. This was the life she had once believed was too fragile to hold. Yet here she was, holding it.

Her eyes moved to the bedside table. Her notebook lay there, its edges slightly frayed. It had become a companion for her dreams as she scribbled down bits of reflection before they had a chance to slip away. She shifted out from under Xander's arm and placed her feet on the floor. He murmured something indistinct but didn't stir. She paused and watched the morning light illuminate the shape of his shoulder. For a moment, she savored that he was truly here, not an illusion. She pulled on a lightweight robe and tiptoed from the room.

She made her way downstairs, the house's floorboards groaning softly as if greeting her in return. The air carried the scent of fresh wood polish from the night before. Every space felt open now, no longer weighed down by secrets. The front door was unlocked, she trusted it would be fine. She pushed open the screen and stepped onto the porch.

The marsh greeted her, its pale grasses shifting in the breeze. Sunlight cut across the horizon in gold and rust, silhouetting distant cranes. She inhaled deeply. This was a morning that whispered promise. For so long, she had dreaded mornings, each one reminding her of what she'd run from. Now she felt something new stirring, contentment.

She sank into a wicker chair and set her notebook on her lap. The porch swing, repaired and waiting, gave a small creak behind her as it stirred with the breeze. She opened a fresh page and wrote:

Sometimes healing looks like coffee in the quiet and a door you don't need to close behind you.

She read it twice and let the words settle. Then she placed the pen aside and gazed over the marsh. The air smelled of brine and wet grass. She recalled days in faraway places, cities that buzzed with color and movement. It struck her that none of those memories felt as close as this moment did now. A gentle hush surrounded her, inviting her to remain still rather than bolt elsewhere.

Eventually, the urge for coffee replaced her morning reverie. She entered the kitchen and started the drip pot. While it brewed, she watched the steam curl out the top, recalling the times she had found comfort in cups of foreign coffee, always alone. She no longer wanted to be alone if she could help it.

A shuffle of footsteps signaled Xander's presence. He appeared in the doorway with rumpled hair, wearing faded sweatpants and an old T-shirt. He offered her a sleepy smile.

"You're up early," he said, voice gravelly.

She smiled, pouring coffee into a mug. "Habit, I guess. I wrote something down." She gestured to her notebook resting nearby.

He nodded toward the pot for his own cup. "Mind if I join you on the porch?"

She gave a contented hum, feeling that familiar warmth in her chest even in the simplest exchange. "Of course."

They shared coffee under the rising sun. Together, they listened to the distant chatter of birds and the rustling of marsh reeds. No words were needed. After a time, he squeezed her hand gently and headed back inside to check on Silas, the golden retriever who had likely begun to wander the halls.

Before long, Emery found herself in the foyer, awaiting her sister's arrival. Laura had texted the night before, asking if she could come by to see the house's progress and to read a new piece of Emery's writing. Emery's chest fluttered with anticipation. Truth still knotted between them on occasion, threads of old tension that hadn't fully dissolved. But they were trying, and that effort felt more real than any resentment left behind.

Morning sunlight filled the entryway with a warm glow by the time Laura arrived, wearing a crisp blouse and carrying a small shoulder bag. She paused at the threshold, glancing around as though still expecting ghosts in every corner. Emery stepped forward.

"Hey," Emery greeted, trying to keep her tone light.

"Morning," Laura replied, matching the brightness in her voice with a rigid smile. "Place looks so different now."

Emery nodded. "No tapestries of gloom. The house is now happy."

Laura offered a small laugh. "The house and us both."

They wandered the halls side by side. Emery pointed out the newly finished trim in the library, the patch of clean wallpaper where Margot's old sampler once hung. Each detail spoke of care, no more chipped paint or peeling panels. At the same time, Emery couldn't help noticing how Laura's gaze darted around as if searching for pieces of the past. She wanted to reassure Laura that the past was still here, only no longer controlling them. On the upstairs landing, they stopped at a table where Emery kept her manuscript pages in a neat stack. Next to the pages, Laura saw that there was a folder with her name on it containing copies.

"You've made me a copy of the manuscript?" Laura smiled as she lifted a few sheets and scanned the typed words. She read silently for several minutes, her brows furrowing.

"You realize you're dramatizing a lot of our family's issues," Laura said dryly. A hint of teasing danced in her eyes.

Emery crossed her arms, smirking. "You know you're a bit dramatic, right?" She gestured to the page in her sister's hand. "But I wanted you to read it."

Laura exhaled, rolling her eyes with mock exasperation. "Oh, absolutely. I have to see if you made me the villain." She glanced at a paragraph. "I have to say, I come off only slightly villainous."

"Glad to hear it," Emery said, pressing her lips together to hide a grin.

They moved along after Laura scooped up the folder, holding it carefully against her chest. They eventually paused in front of Margot's portrait, which hung in the hallway overlooking the stairs. Margot's painted eyes stared outward with a serene expression that, in real life, had often been clouded by sorrow.

"She would've hated this much honesty," Laura

murmured, her voice hushed. "All those words you wrote about her struggles, about what really happened."

Emery followed her sister's line of sight. "She would've loved what it's becoming, though. It's not just about the pain, it's about what she gave us too."

Laura's eyes glistened for a second, and she quickly looked away. Emery didn't press the moment. They shared a familiar silence that spoke volumes, memories of Margot's final days and all the complexity wrapped up in their mother's name. Despite that heaviness, there was no longer anger here. It had softened into a nuanced understanding that both sisters carried in different ways.

They retreated downstairs with Laura still clutching the folder and promising to return the next day for the unveiling ceremony of the writer's retreat.

"I will be jetting off soon to my place in the Caribbean but wanted to stay to see this writer's retreat get off the ground. And you know, I will be your biggest donor, so you will need to really suck up to me from now on," Laura laughed as she headed toward the door.

Emery stopped and gasped. She took hold of Laura's shoulders and gave her a big hug. "How much exactly can I put you down for?"

"Whatever you need, sis. We are loaded."

"Well, that is a relief," Emery smiled.

"And remember, it is your turn to visit me next time, all right? And you will finally get to meet Henry, the love of my life," Laura said, putting on her sunglasses and opening her car door.

"That sounds like a good plan. I would love that as

soon as I get sick of this place," Emery smiled and waved goodbye. "See you tomorrow."

Emery stood alone for a minute, letting that odd sense of longing and relief settle over her. Everything had changed between them. Honesty did not necessarily come easily, but it came. That was enough. Today marked the official end of the estate's renovation. The main structure and every detail, from the porch banisters to the last piece of cedar in the attic, had passed inspection. The permits were final. The house was ready to welcome a new life, not just as a home, but as a place where Emery's dream of a writing residency would thrive.

She stepped outside and returned to the garden. She moved through the rows of rosemary and mint, checking the landscaping. The white shutters on the windows now gleamed in the sunlight, free of the chipping paint that had once made them look dreary. Gravel crunched underfoot as she surveyed the releveled drive. It was a simple detail, but it mattered. First impressions often started where a car door opened.

The front porch appeared inviting, with the swing, two rocking chairs, and a small table set up for tomorrow's event. A couple of planters brimming with bright begonias framed the entry, a subtle pop of color that Emery had insisted upon. She let herself smile at the memory of bickering with Xander over flower arrangements. It was a small fight, one that ended in laughter, like so many of their disagreements of late.

When she was satisfied, she went inside to help with the setup for the launch event. Boxes of linen napkins, a tray of glassware, and small stands for name tags awaited her in the foyer. The plan was to host local press, donors, writing professors and librarians as well as community members and friends who shared Emery's vision. The house, once overshadowed by secrets, would finally stand as a symbol of second chances.

She heard Xander in the parlor starting to set up folding chairs in the large living room. She walked in to see him aligning them near the windows. The afternoon light filtered through the glass at a flattering angle, illuminating the old hearth. She felt careful pride in each small arrangement. Something about physically placing the chairs for people to gather made it all real, no longer a dream pinned to blueprint paper.

Emery wore a pale-blue sundress that made her eyes seem deeper than ever. Xander paused as he noticed how natural she looked in the place she had once feared. She noticed his stare.

"Everything okay?" she asked, self-conscious while smoothing a hand over her skirt.

He nodded. "Better than okay. You look like you belong."

She ducked her head, her cheeks warming. "Thank you."

He stepped closer. "You ready for this?"

She exhaled, glancing at the empty chairs. "I think so. There was a time I couldn't have imagined wanting anyone to see this house again, let alone celebrate it with us."

With the setup done, she moved out to the porch and

Xander followed. He balanced two glasses of sweet tea, and an old quilt draped over his arm. He settled beside her in the wicker chairs and handed over one glass. His expression showed curiosity. "You're writing again. That a new project?"

She smiled. "My next chapter."

He pretended an air of wounded pride. "Am I in it?"

She set her notebook aside, leaning her head gently against his shoulder. "You're the whole story." Her pulse quickened at the intimacy of that admission. For a moment, she recalled the day she returned with doubts about him and about them. Now, she could hardly picture a day without him anchoring her. Staying no longer felt foreign. It felt like something she had chosen with full certainty.

Night settled around them, the garden soft with shadow. Fireflies moved across the yard, winking like tiny beacons. A chorus of frogs croaked from the marsh. The windows of the estate glowed in gentle lamplight, making the interior look warm and inviting instead of haunted. Emery sipped her tea, tasting sugar and relief.

Xander adjusted the quilt over her knees. She closed her eyes momentarily, listening to the soft hush of wind rustling the leaves. Then she opened her eyes to the courtyard of low-lit flowers and bugs, a scene that felt alive with possibility.

"I'm here," she said quietly, nearly under her breath. She wasn't sure if she spoke to Xander, to herself, or to the memory of the house that had once let her go and welcomed her back.

His voice rumbled low, "Yes. You are."

And she was. Fully, without apology. The words tasted final, an acceptance of the journey she had walked. No more wandering, no more locked doors. She was in the place she belonged.

She closed her notebook, letting the pen rest on the faded cushion beside her. The scent of jasmine curled through the air, mingling with earth and salt. Past heartbreaks moved through her mind, but they no longer held power over her. She had grown beyond them, shaped by love and candor.

She looked at the house, saw its tall windows and gently painted columns. Every patch of reworked floor, every corner newly stripped of secrecy, confirmed that this estate, her estate, was prepared for the stories yet to come. She inhaled one more time, letting the sweet perfume of night-blooming flowers fill her lungs.

"I'm here," she said again, this time louder, as if addressing the entire marshland. Xander's hand slipped into hers, their fingers intertwining. She leaned her head softly against his shoulder. And for the first time, the words didn't feel like a declaration. They felt like truth.

CHAPTER

THIRTY-FIVE

XANDER

Travel Note: In New Orleans, I danced through grief. In Charleston, I stood still through it. And in this house, I let it go without forgetting what it gave me in return.
—EW.

Xander rose before the first streaks of sunrise could draw color across the sky. He ran his fingers through his hair, quietly stepped into his jeans, and reached for the folded T-shirt on the nearby chair. Outside the bedroom, the hallway felt cool against his bare feet. He walked downstairs and out onto the front porch, gently pushing open the screen door so it would not squeak and wake her. A light breeze rustled across his arms, lifting the faint scent of marsh grass and brine. He went back into the house and down the hall into the kitchen to start the coffee. Moments later, he was back out on the porch and set his mug on the wide wooden rail, then inhaled the morning as if it were a gift. Birds sang their dawn

325

welcomes, an uncertain chorus that always reminded him how time continued, no matter who stayed or who left.

Silas padded out from behind him, nails clicking against the porch planks. Xander knelt to scratch behind the dog's pale ears. Silas closed his eyes with a low groan of pleasure. The dog was older now, each day showed a bit greyer around his muzzle. But his devotion was steadfast. In a way, Silas reflected this house's heartbeat, patient, forgiving, quietly waiting for those who needed shelter.

Xander straightened and looked out over the yard. The porch swing, where he had shared countless moments with Emery these past months, stirred in the breeze. He curled a hand around the wooden arm of it and sat. The wood felt smooth against his palm, almost warm to the touch even in the cool air. He remembered when that swing was broken, squeaking with every shift of weight. Now it was steady and safe, like so many pieces of this life they had rebuilt.

He sipped his coffee as the sky began to lighten. Over the marsh, a stripe of pale gold signaled dawn's approach. This moment, settled, easy, was one he had rarely known in the years since Emery left the first time. He was always waiting back then, thinking she might return, thinking the house deserved her footsteps and laughter again. Now that she was here, he realized how different it felt not to wait, but simply to be.

Silas nudged his calf. Xander smiled at the dog, then set his mug aside. He crossed the porch to the steps and surveyed the property. He wanted to check every detail before the official dedication ceremony later in the day.

They had turned the estate into a writing residency wing, something that started as a spark of an idea and grew into a purpose for both of them. He still could not believe it was real.

Starting from the porch, he walked the gravel path that cut through the lawn. The early light crept through the tall oaks, casting long shadows on the grass. Every corner he examined made him proud. The fresh paint on the shutters had dried to a crisp, clean finish. The garden brimming with rosemary near the carriage house gave the yard a gentle fragrance. The newly laid gravel in the drive glinted with scattered shells, making the approach to the estate feel welcoming. Each improvement was a physical sign of hours of sweat and intention.

He returned to the porch and slipped inside quietly. When he shut the door, he could hear voices down the corridor. Emery's soft laugh rose, then a warm greeting to someone else. He followed the sound to the foyer, where she was gently arranging name tags and a stack of small notebooks on a table. Two local high school students who had been recommended by their writing teachers milled around, glancing at her for direction. Xander observed from the threshold.

Emery wore a summer dress that brushed just above her knees. The gentle movement of the fabric as she walked gave her an air of calm confidence. She looked so different from the guarded woman who had first stepped beneath this roof months ago. The interns, one with a short pixie haircut and the other wearing large round glasses, peppered her with questions about table arrangement and seat placement. Emery answered them with a patient laugh, gesturing to the main hall where they planned to host the dedication.

Seeing her like this, Xander felt his heart tug in recognition. She was radiant in a way that went beyond her features. She was alive with hope. She tossed a grin toward him when she caught him standing in the doorway. He did not grin back. He offered a small nod, an unspoken understanding that they had created something new here together.

He heard a car coming into the drive, and he walked back out on the porch and down the steps. It was Laura. He walked out on the drive, and she pulled up next to him. Emery came out onto the porch to greet her sister. After a brief hug, Laura held up a piece of folded paper. Xander instantly recognized David's crisp handwriting on the outside. "I think Dad would want you to have this before everything starts," Laura said, offering the letter to Emery. Emery took it, her expression a mixture of reverence and sorrow, and slipped it into her dress pocket before leading her sister inside.

Callie arrived minutes later and was soon standing in the foyer, handing out name tags with a bright smile. As the morning advanced, more people arrived, local writers, professors of literature from The Citadel and the College of Charleston, several librarians from the county branches, a couple of journalists from a small local paper, family friends and neighbors, and a group of donors Emery had already started courting. The main hall was filled with low chatter and the faint scuff of shoes against polished floors.

Xander drifted among them, exchanging handshakes, ensuring everything ran smoothly. He noticed Emery's new student interns, checking out the library and exclaiming about the architectural details. Every so often, Xander felt he might burst with pride.

He took a moment to remember Emery's father. David had quietly passed in his sleep shortly after he had been moved to hospice care weeks before. On the day of his death, his last request was to have both his girls with him. Emery and Laura arrived minutes after they got the call. They stood on either side of the bed and held his hand, each one whispering their goodbyes as he slipped from this world. It was a bittersweet moment as they shared their grief together. Now, a framed photo of him rested on a side table, next to a short note he had written giving the estate his blessing. Finally, Emery gathered everyone in the parlor where the chairs had been set up, calling them together with a polite, "If I could have your attention, please." All eyes turned to her. She glanced at Laura, who gave her an encouraging nod. In her hands, she clutched David's letter, still folded. She pressed it to her heart for a moment, inhaling a calming breath.

Emery's fingers trembled slightly as she unfolded the creased paper. She cleared her throat gently. "Before we share the news we came here to give, my sister and I wanted to read something our father wrote not long before he passed. Some of you may know that in his final days, he took great comfort in reflecting, in writing, quiet moments of memory and meaning. This was one of the last things he put down on paper. We believe it speaks for him better than we ever could."

She glanced once at Laura, who gave her the faintest nod, then looked down at her father's words and began to read:

"This house has known silence. It has known sorrow, the kind that lingers in corners, which settles into the floorboards and waits for someone brave enough to let the light back in. For a long time, I thought it would stay that way. But I was wrong. Because today, this house knows something different. Today, it knows story.

"It knows laughter echoing down the hallways again. It knows footsteps that don't sound like ghosts but like life returning. It knows sisters whispering in the kitchen. It knows music, and forgiveness, and the scent of bread baking. It knows the crackle of old fires rekindled.

"That's what my daughters have given it. That's what love restored. Not the kind of love that demands perfection, but the kind that stays. The kind that heals. The kind that dares to come home, even after everything.

"If walls can remember, then let these ones remember this, that silence isn't the end of the story. That loss can live beside joy. And that sometimes, the most sacred kind of redemption comes not from starting over but from finally choosing to stay."

Emery's voice broke slightly at the last word. She folded the page slowly, her fingers brushing the ink one last time. All around them, the silence held, not heavy but reverent. And when she finally looked up, there wasn't a dry eye in sight.

Laura stepped forward as Emery folded the page, her throat working as she tried to swallow the knot forming there. She had always been the steady one, the one who filled out the forms, kept things moving, didn't cry unless the door was closed and the lights were off. But now, something shifted.

Her hand reached for Emery's, fingers intertwining tightly. She looked out at the faces before them, some old friends of their father's, some barely more than strangers who had found a place in their orbit. All of them silent. Waiting.

"My dad was the easy one in the house filled with stubborn and creative females," Laura said, her voice quiet but clear. "He always said the right things. He was proud, stubborn, private. He loved this place. He loved us. In the way he left the porch light on. In the way he made pancakes with too much syrup. In the way he hired Xander to make this house what it is today, even when he was falling apart inside and out." She paused, her chin trembling as she looked at Emery, then back to the crowd. "I think these were the words he'd been trying to say our whole lives. Now that they're finally here, it feels like he gave us a way to begin again."

"So, thank you," she added softly, voice catching. "For being here. For remembering him with us. For helping this house keep its story."

A moment passed. Then someone in the back exhaled, a small, reverent sound, and others began to nod. A murmur of love and memory moved through the room like a prayer.

Emery smiled through her tears, her hand still tightly held in Laura's.

Laura squeezed her hand, leaning in to whisper so only Emery could hear, "He would have been so proud of you, Em, of us." The word us hung in the air, a bridge built over years of silence.

Emery squeezed back, her own voice thick with emotion. "We did it, Laura."

It was not about the house anymore. It was about reclaiming their story together. The look that passed between them was one of shared history, finally unburdened.

"There is one more thing we wanted to share," Emery said, her voice steadier now. "Something my dad knew about before he passed, something he gave us his blessing for."

"We are reopening the house," she said. "Not for us alone but for the community, for artists, writers, healers, for anyone who needs a space to rest or to rediscover what home feels like."

"It'll be called *The Westbrook House for Story and Sanctuary*," Emery added. "Part retreat, part residency, part remembrance. A place where voices can rise where silence once lived. Where people can come not because they're perfect, but because they're searching."

There was a pause, and then a wave of warm, startled laughter and clapping as people realized what she'd just said. Emery leaned in and kissed her sister's temple, her eyes wet again, but this time with joy.

"He would've loved that," someone whispered from the crowd.

Emery nodded, her voice catching. "That's what we wanted. To honor what came before and build what comes next. One chapter at a time."

When the clapping subsided, Emery offered a closing note of thanks and directed everyone to explore the newly dedicated spaces upstairs. People dispersed, praising the restoration, asking about future workshops, commenting on how the floors gleamed like new.

In time, the bustle wound down. Guests trickled out with murmurs of congratulations and promises to coordinate upcoming seminars. The students helped tidy the foyer, then left their excitement as well a tangible hum that lingered even after they were gone. By late afternoon, the estate was quiet again. Sunlight streamed in through the tall windows of the side yard, and the house itself was taking a grateful bow.

Xander found Emery outside, lying on a blanket beneath the magnolia tree near the old garden gate. She had her elbows propped behind her on the grass, leaning back so she could gaze up at the white blossoms overhead. When she spotted him, she patted a spot beside her. He lay next to her, letting the lawn's warmth seep through his jeans. He could see the day's emotional weight settling on her, but it wasn't the crushing burden of grief he remembered. This was different. It was the good kind of tired. In the soft glow of the sun, he looked at her, a wave of quiet awe washing over him.

"The woman who was once afraid to even step on the

porch just dedicated that same porch to storytellers," he murmured, the words feeling inadequate to capture the magnitude of her transformation.

She turned in his arms, her eyes glistening. "I wouldn't be standing here without the man who rebuilt it for her."

Her words, a simple, profound acknowledgment, sent a warmth through him that had nothing to do with the lingering summer heat. It was validation. It was partnership. He knew words weren't enough for a moment like this. "Margot and David would have loved today," he whispered against her hair, the tribute feeling necessary.

He felt her rest her head against his chest, a gesture of complete surrender and trust that made his heart ache with a fierce, protective love. He held her, breathing in the scent of her hair, feeling the steady beat of her heart against his. All the ghosts, all the secrets, they felt a million miles away.

She raised her chin to look at him. "This was your dream as much as mine. Do you feel it came out the way you hoped?"

He considered her question, reflecting on the months of sanding, painting, nights spent wrestling with old foundations, and days spent patching emotional wounds. "It came out better," he said. "Because we didn't just fix the house. We built something new. There's a difference."

A breeze whispered through the magnolia leaves, scattering a few petals at their feet. She glanced at the pale shapes on the grass, then reached for his hand. "What now?" she asked.

He laced his fingers through hers. The question

sparked anticipation in him, but it did not carry the old fear. "We keep building," he answered. "And when we don't know what to do, we swing on the porch."

She laughed, a sound like water dancing over rocks. "I love this house," she said, releasing his hand so she could pluck a fallen bloom from the grass. "Not just the wood and paint, but everything it came to represent. It's strange that I spent so long avoiding it."

He watched her twirl a fallen flower and noted the quiet resolve in her eyes. "I love what it became," he said softly, "because you came back to it. You came home." He kissed her.

They stayed there, letting time slip gently over them. After a while, she rose, brushed grass from her dress, and murmured something about trying to salvage a quick dinner from the leftovers. He teased her that the students probably devoured most of it, but she grinned and went inside anyway. Xander lingered under the magnolia tree a moment longer, grounded in the knowledge that the day had been everything they had hoped for.

Night settled in soon after. The scent of salt air thickened as darkness draped the property. Crickets and frogs started their familiar symphony in the shadows near the marsh. Inside, the estate glowed with the warm light of a few scattered lamps. Xander prowled quietly from room to room, ensuring windows were closed and the day's clutter was put away. He glimpsed Emery at one point, her shoulder against the frame of a door, flipping through the planning document for the center. She smiled at herself, lost in thought.

Eventually, she disappeared into the second floor. He assumed she was winding down for the night in the bedroom. Left alone in the hallway, he felt the perfect quiet surround him again. He let out a breath he had been holding without realizing, then headed to the study, where Emery's writing desk stood near the large window.

Her journal lay open, a pen balancing across the pages. A small lamp cast a delicate glow across the pages. He remembered how, once upon a time, she guarded that journal with her life. Now she left it open, trusting him not to betray her words. He slid his hand along the edge of the desk, recalling how he had repaired a crack in the wood not long ago.

He eased himself into the chair and set the pen aside for a moment, studying her handwriting. He recognized lines about the dedication ceremony and a list of future goals she wanted for the residency. Every word spoke of a woman who had chosen to stay.

He had spent years restoring the bones of this house, patching cracks and replacing rotted wood, all while hoping she would return. But watching her fill these pages, he realized his work had shifted. He was not just fixing what was broken anymore, he was building a life with her.

Her words, her plans, her presence, they were the true foundation. And a foundation this strong deserved more than an unspoken hope. It deserved a promise. This was not a question anymore. It was a cornerstone.

He gently turned to a blank page.

He exhaled, heart lightly pounding, and thought about

how to put what he felt into words. He was not a writer, not the way Emery was. But he had spent so long caring for her and for this house that he realized pen and paper might be his best chance to mark a new threshold.

He picked up the pen. He was not sure if the words would come easily. Slowly, he sketched the outline of the porch swing, the two silhouettes leaning toward each other, a silent promise that they would never again endure heartbreak alone. A swirl of lines hinted at their hands clasped. He shaded the background just enough to show the shape of the porch, though he kept it simple. The real focus was them.

He stared at his drawing for a long moment. Then he added a short inscription beneath the sketch. The tip of the pen glided over the page, his breath tightening with every letter. He needed her to see this, to understand it was not a question but a hope. The house had been broken, he had been broken and so had she. They had come together to rebuild something stronger.

He wrote:

Some things break so they can be rebuilt stronger. Marry me.

ROBIN'S NOTES

I started writing *The Truth Between Us* not to escape my past, but to explore the kind of life I used to imagine when I was a girl growing up on Lantana Drive, in the West Ashley section of Charleston, South Carolina. I went to Stono Park Elementary and graduated from St. Andrews High School—now long gone—perched close to the marshes of the Ashley River. I spent humid afternoons catching crabs, watching the tide roll in, and occasionally spotting a stray alligator.

From ages seven to thirteen, I lived at Connie Maxwell Children's Home in Greenwood, South Carolina. That's where my love of books began—when I helped my third-grade teacher, Mrs. Timmerman, shelve and organize the campus library. I read every book I could get my hands on. Stories became my refuge and my compass, helping me imagine worlds far beyond the boundaries of my own.

I've built a lifelong career in the book industry—working with university presses, helping launch

Amazon/CreateSpace (now Kindle Direct Publishing), and creating IngramSpark, both platforms that continue to empower indie authors across the world. Today, I serve as President of LMBPN Worldwide Publishing, one of the fastest growing publishers in the US today. Even now, I think often of that little library at Connie Maxwell, and how the right story at the right time can change everything.

The Truth Between Us let me explore a life I never lived, but often wondered about. Through Emery and Xander, I wrote about longing, guilt, grief—and the hard-won hope of second chances. Though I now live far from Charleston, in the Sandia Mountains of New Mexico along the winding Turquoise Trail, the Lowcountry still lives in me. It shaped my voice, my values, and my belief that stories —like people—are worth saving.

Thank you for reading. If you've ever felt like an outsider looking in, or wondered whether it's too late to be truly known, I hope this book finds you at the perfect moment.

—Robin Cutler

THE STORY CONTINUES

The story continues in book two, *The Woman I Was Before,*
coming soon to Amazon

OTHER FLORID ROMANCE BOOKS

To be notified of new releases and special promotions from Florid Romance, please join our email list:

https://floridromance.lmbpn.com/about/sign-up-for-our-newsletter/

For a complete list of books published by Florid Romance please visit our website:

https://floridromance.lmbpn.com/

BOOKS BY MICHAEL ANDERLE

Sign up for the LMBPN email list to be notified of new releases and special deals!

https://lmbpn.com/email/

For a complete list of books by Michael Anderle, please visit:

www.lmbpn.com/ma-books/

CONNECT WITH MICHAEL ANDERLE

Website: http://lmbpn.com

Email List: https://michael.beehiiv.com/

https://www.facebook.com/LMBPNPublishing

https://twitter.com/MichaelAnderle

https://www.instagram.com/lmbpn_publishing/

https://www.bookbub.com/authors/michael-anderle